Sorry Siracusa
Original/e

AF238504

Sorry Press ®

Sorry Siracusa ist die erste Station einer nomadischen Writers Residency. An jedem Halt entsteht eine Sammelband, der Kurzgeschichten von einheimischen Autoren und Residents bündelt. Durch die Augen der Literatur vermitteln sie einen facettenreichen Blick auf den Ort und im Laufe der Zeit soll so eine Bibliothek literarischer Reiseführer und ein kontinuierlicher kultureller Austausch entstehen.

Sorry Siracusa è la prima tappa di una residenza nomade per scrittori. A ogni tappa verrà realizzata un'antologia che raccoglie i racconti di autori locali e residenti. Attraverso gli occhi della letteratura, ognuno trasmette una visione sfaccettata del luogo e, nel tempo, si creerà una biblioteca di guide di viaggio letterarie e uno scambio culturale continuo.

Sorry Siracusa
© Sorry Press®, Munich 2024
Editor: Lukas Kubina
Proofreading: Sofia Kouropatov
Design: Wiegand von Hartmann
Printing: Benedict Press

Printed in Germany
ISBN 978-3-910265-21-9

Villette was first published in *La Sicilia è un'isola per modo di dire*
by Mario Fillioley (Minimum Fax; 2018). Sorry Press® has reproduced
it with kind permission of the publisher and the author.

The English translations are by Shane Anderson (Kubina, Sack),
Caroline Schmidt (Bonelli, Hirsch, Suffrin),
and Jamie Small (Fiderio, Fillioley, Moschella).

Special thanks to Niccolò Benetton, Giovanni Fiderio, Maria Vittoria
Trovato, and the Accademia di Belli Arti Siracusa / MADE Program
for hosting the Sorry residents. Grazie mille!

Index
Original/e

Index
English

Giovanni Fiderio
Il Vecchio n.1

Il Vecchio entra in libreria con l'indice della mano sinistra curvato in direzione del bancone della cassa dove sta seduto chi lavora. Così quando ti giri per guardare chi sta entrando, il dito sta già puntando dritto verso di te. Una volta che ha superato l'uscio, ti accorgi che anche il suo capo pende lievemente verso sinistra: è il suo modo di annunciare che la domanda che sta per farti era già pronta prima che uscisse da casa e lui l'ha tenuta sulla punta del dito fino alla consegna.

Tutto il resto del suo corpo è rilassato in un'andatura morbida a falcate ampie come possono permettersi le persone abbastanza alte di statura.

Segue un «Eeeeeee, mi ordini per cortesia questo libro, perchè sicuramente non ce l'avete in libreria» smorfie «Figuriamoci! In questa città non lo conosce nessuno un libro così» ride compiaciuto delle occhiatacce ricevute «Questi libri non li legge nessuno qui e d'altra parte perchè dovrebbero, mica qualcuno qui pensa.»

«Di che libro si tratta?»

Mi consegna un foglietto scritto a mano col titolo del libro e l'autore, facendo roteare la mano che lo tiene.

«Ah si, questo libro ce l'abbiamo!» esclamo io dopo aver controllato sul computer «Giro fortunato.»

«Non è vero, stai sbagliando» risponde lui mezzo indispettito.

«No davvero, è proprio il libro che c'è scritto qui, vado a prenderglielo.»

«Non è possibile. Perchè ce lo avete?»

«Lo abbiamo ordinato per l'uscita.»

«Perchè, mi vuoi dire che qualcuno legge questa roba qui?»

«Può capitare.»

«Fammi vedere» sfoglia il libro «Ma cose da pazzi! E chi è che a Siracusa leggerebbe un libro del genere? Voglio conoscerlo.»

Ovviamente a volte non abbiamo il libro richiesto in pronta consegna e in quel caso lo ordiniamo. Quando il libro arriva è raro che Il Vecchio lo compri subito e lo porti a casa per leggerlo, questo accade raramente, solo con alcuni libri.

Solitamente invece, quando viene a ritirare il libro, lo tiene in mano, lo sfoglia e lo commenta in diretta: «Mmm, addirittura» oppure «Ah! Ma quindi questo è proprio un cialtrone, qui ci sono scritte solo fesserie.»

Altre volte dopo averlo sfogliato si rende conto che il libro non era come lo aveva immaginato o che gli è utile solo per alcune parti e quindi chiede se può farsi delle fotocopie delle poche pagine che gli interessano. Noi lo guardiamo basiti e divertiti dal suo continuo oltraggio alla normalità e gli facciamo noi stessi le fotocopie che gli servono.

E' un trattamento speciale e devo ammettere che non sempre abbiamo chiaro il perchè facciamo delle eccezioni per lui. Credo sia dovuto al fatto che è un tipo schietto e onesto, ma soprattutto assetato di libri belli. E' uno studioso appassionato dall'animo punk e non è facile trovare persone così a ottant'anni suonati. Alcune volte invece il libro va bene e lui ci assicura che lo acquisterà presto, non appena vincerà al gratta e vinci o al lotto. E lo fa, sia chiaro, devo ammettere pure che vince relativamente spesso. Nell'attesa della vincita ci prega di tenere il libro in vetrina o comunque ben esposto, come un'esca, giusto per vedere se qualcuno lo nota, se qualcuno lo sfoglia o addirittura lo compra. Dev'essere il suo modo per cercare persone affini e gioire del fatto che là fuori qualcuno apprezza un libro suggerito da lui.

Adriano Sack
Eine nahezu furchtlose Frau

Als Domenico Corsini nach einer halben Stunde nicht erschienen war, seufzte Anette Schwalbinger und bestellte sich einen weiteren Coco Chanel. Sie genoss den Geschmack des Hollunderblütensirups. Selbst wenn ihr alter Freund noch auftauchen sollte, wäre ein kleiner Schwips kein Problem. Sie hatten schon ganz andere Räusche miteinander überstanden.

Die Bar lag hinter den Ruinen des Apollotempels in Siracusa. Schwalbinger war die Älteste im Raum, am Fenster nippten nur zwei junge amerikanische Touristen an ihren Drinks. Sie blickte auf die ausgewaschenen Planken ihres aus Treibholz gebastelten Tischs. Mit dem Alleinsein hatte sie kein Problem. Sie liebte es, vor sich hin zu starren und nachzudenken. Und es bereitete ihr Vergnügen, dass sie Andere damit verunsicherte. Der Kellner hatte sie erst ignoriert, dann mit übertriebenem Respekt auf Englisch angesprochen. Da hörte für sie der Spaß auf, denn auf ihr Italienisch war sie stolz. Sie hatte vier Semester in Florenz studiert, dort sechs Kilo zugenommen und erwachte noch Jahrzehnte später manchmal mit dem Geschmack von frischen, gebratenen Steinpilzen auf der Zunge. Die leichte Schleimigkeit und die untergründige Frische, wie hatte sie diese Stadt nur verlassen können? Sie hatte dort dreizehn Liebhaber gehabt, was ihr damals eine magere Ausbeute erschien, aber für eine Studentin der Religionswissenschaften beachtlich war. Mit einem der Männer, nämlich mit Domenico Corsini, hatte sie 40 Jahre später noch sporadischen Kontakt. Möglicherweise, weil er der Einzige gewesen war, der nicht nur sich selbst beim

Reden zuhörte. Dann allerdings hatte er entdeckt, dass er Männer noch ein bisschen lieber mochte als die deutsche Kommilitonin. Wie beides zusammenhing, darüber machte sich die Schwalbinger, wie sie sich gern nennen ließ, weil es sie vage an Tschechow erinnerte, schon lange keine Gedanken mehr. Der schwule Domenico war der hübscheste und begabteste Student ihres Jahrgangs. Und wie seine Professoren später wohl sagen würden: die größte Enttäuschung.

Die beiden waren nächtelang durch das schummrige Florenz spaziert, leicht angetrunken und berauscht von der Strenge und Intelligenz, die diese Stadt noch immer ausstrahlte. Er war dann zurück nach Sizilien geflohen, weil sein Herz von einem Deutschen gebrochen worden und seine Mutter krank geworden war. Er setzte sein Studium halbherzig in Messina fort, seine Nachrichten wurden seltener und seltsamer. Sie hatte ihn erst schrecklich vermisst, dann über den Bußprediger Savonarola und seinen Einfluss auf totalitäre Ideologien des 20. Jahrhunderts promoviert. Als sie wieder im grauen Stuttgart saß und ihre Jobchancen abwägte, war ihr die Religionswissenschaft abhandengekommen, und sie hatte mithilfe ihres Nebenfachs Psychologie Karriere gemacht.

Anette Schwalbinger war eine stämmige Frau mit der Durchsetzungskraft eines Aufsitzrasenmähers. Sie hatte die grauen Augen einer Möwe und trug ihre weißen Haare so straff zurückgebunden, dass sie bei gutem Licht wirkten wie ein Heiligenschein. Diese zwei Sätze hätte sie aus jedem Manuskript gestrichen, sie mochte keine Umwege, verließ sich nur in

Notfällen auf Humoristisches, und sie lehnte es ab, nach Äußerlichkeiten beurteilt zu werden. Nach ihrem Studium war sie auf Wegen, die in dieser Geschichte nur angedeutet werden, in der Personalabteilung eines großen deutschen Autoherstellers gelandet. Dort war sie schnell unverzichtbar und eroberte schließlich den Posten Chief Officer Human Ressources, was knapp unter dem Vorstand war und in den Wirtschaftsteilen der Zeitungen, die es damals noch gab, vorschnell als Zeitenwende gedeutet wurde. Der Widerstand im Unternehmen war allerdings enorm. Bei der Markteinführung eines kleinformatigen SUVs war sie mal auf eine johlende Gesprächsgruppe zugelaufen, in deren Mitte ihre junge Mitarbeiterin Jude Klingendorf, die mit dem Stecker in der Nase, stand und kreischend lachte. Sobald ihre Chefin in Hörweite war, waren alle hastig verstummt, und Klingendorf eilte zum «Top-Ups» holen.

Schwalbinger musterte die alkoholgeröteten, teilweise noch pickligen Gesichter ihrer männlichen Kollegen, von denen keiner seine Hilfe beim Drink-Holen angeboten hatte. Diese schauten betont irgendwo hin – auf ihre hochpreisigen Sneakers, auf die Getränke der Mittäter, auf andere Markteinführungsteilnehmer, die vielleicht zur Hilfe kommen und die lähmende Stille unterbrechen könnten. Da wusste sie, dass sie in diesem Laden ziemlich allein war.

Später hatte Anette Schwalbinger ihre Mitarbeiterin mit sanftem Druck dazu gebracht, ihr den Inhalt des Gesprächs zu nennen, in dessen Zentrum eben jener Spitzname stand, der die anderen zum Feixen gebracht hatte. Nervös mit der Nase zuckend flüsterte Jude Klingendorf das Wort Hodenklemme, Anette Schwalbinger aber zuckte nur mit den Schultern. Natürlich war sie ein Störfaktor. Weil sie eine Frau war, vor allem aber, und das wog viel schwerer, weil sie eine Frau war, die Männern nicht gefallen wollte. Das war schlimmer als gleicher Lohn oder die Frauenquote, Schwalbinger war insofern an allem schuld, was ihre Automännerwelt aufrüttelte. Das war objektiv betrachtet keine Rolle, mit der sich irgendein Mensch wohlfühlen kann, doch sie war damit einverstanden. «Weil ich es kann», hatte sie sich selbst gesagt. Davon war sie noch immer überzeugt.

In Siracusa war sie, weil ihr Unternehmen für die «mittlere Führungsebene» diese Reise verordnet hatte. Es sollte um Team Building gehen – und um Themen, die in dem Ablaufplan wolkig als «Amp Up Corporate Culture!!!» bezeichnet wurden. «Wieder so eine Doppel-Anglizisme, die für alles und nichts steht. Und dann diese blöden drei Ausrufezeichen!!!», hatte sie zu Jude Klingendorf gesagt und in den vegetarischen Burger gebissen, den es neuerdings in der Kantine gab. Anstatt zu antworten hatte sich diese mit den Gurkenscheiben beschäftigt, die ihr aus dem Brötchen gerutscht waren.

Schwalbinger war am Vortag angereist, um sich nach vielen Jahren der Funkstille (mit einer gewissen Beharrlichkeit dachte sie in so altmodischen Begriffen) mit Domenico über die frühchristliche Sekte der Esterianerinnen zu diskutieren. Diese waren ein Mythos im Religionswissenschaftler:innenmilieu. Im

Freundeskreis von Jesus, darüber war sich die progressive Forschung seit langem einig, hatte es nicht nur Männer gegeben. Dass sein «Lieblingsjünger» Johannes in Wahrheit weiblich oder nonbinär gewesen sein musste, war offensichtlich. Auch sein Evangelium war stilistisch anders und wenn man ehrlich war: besser geschrieben. Dass es neben Maria Magdalena noch weitere Frauen gegeben haben musste, die von den Männern zügig und gründlich aus der Geschichtsschreibung und Mythologie getilgt worden waren, schien ebenso klar. Eine dieser Frauen sollte Ester geheißen haben, eine Witwe mit vier Kindern und einer florierenden Ziegenzucht. Als sich nach der Kreuzigung die Gemeinschaft um Jesus zerstreute, hinterließ sie den Hof ihrer ältesten Tochter, was zu Streit unter den Kindern führte. Ester aber bestieg ein Schiff, dass sie von Palästina nach Sizilien brachte. Die Stadt Siracusa war nur ein Abglanz ihrer einstigen Größe, aber noch immer eine Metropole. Ester begann dort zu predigen, wurde mehrfach verhaftet und nur deshalb wieder entlassen, weil eine Frau in Fragen der Gotteslästerung nicht ernst zu nehmen war. Sie gründete eine der ersten christlichen Gemeinden im Mittelmeerraum. Angeblich sollte es noch eine Höhle geben, unweit der Katakomben von Siracusa, in denen diese Pioniere ihre Rituale feierten.

Schwalbinger war Rationalistin. Sie war sich nicht sicher, ob es diese Person wirklich gegeben hatte, oder ob es eine Wunschfantasie feministischer Geschichtsschreibung war. Domenico Corsini aber hatte einen schwärmerischen Artikel über sie geschrieben. Sein

Aufsatz war in einer Zeitschrift erschienen, die als so unwichtig galt, dass ihn seine Exkollegen zwar wahrgenommen hatten, aber ihr Weltbild unerschüttert blieb. Sie hielten ihn spätestens seit diesem Aufsatz für einen Provinzspinner ohne akademische Perspektive. Er verdiente sein Geld mit Italienischunterricht und in dem er für die notorisch faulen Studenten der Universität in Catania die Hausarbeiten schrieb – denn die Fleißigen setzen sich nach Bologna oder Urbino ab.

Schwalbinger hatte vor vielen Jahren mit Religionsgeschichte abgeschlossen, aber ihre Neugier nicht verloren. Vielleicht hatte der Mann ja wider Erwarten was Interessantes entdeckt. Außerdem freute sie sich, ihn wiederzusehen.

Ganz schön drall, war ihr erster Gedanke. Dicke Arme, runder Bauch in engem T-Shirt, der Nagel des kleinen Fingers fast obszön lang und gepflegt, weil das für Wohlstand stand. Oder für beiläufigen Kokaingenuss, wie Anette Schwalbinger sehr wohl wusste. Sein schwankender Gang konnte von Muskelkater oder Daydrinking herrühren, da war sie gerade nicht sicher. «Schöner denn je», sagte er mit einem Lächeln. Und da war es wieder, dieses Flirren im Kopf. Sie war nicht mehr in ihn verliebt, vielleicht war sie das nie gewesen, aber ihr fiel in diesem Moment wieder ein, wie es sich anfühlte, wenn ein Mann, es konnte auch eine Frau sein, es zu allererst und vielleicht nur darauf abgesehen hatte, dass sie sich wohlfühlte. Vielleicht waren es doch nicht nur die Steinpilze gewesen, die sie vermisst hatte.

«Ich habe mit dem Direktor vom Paolo Orsi telefoniert. Der hörte einfach nicht mehr auf zu quatschen. Wir können da morgen ganz früh hingehen, ich will Dir was zeigen.», erklärte Corsini seine Verspätung. Und damit war ihr Fachgespräch auch beendet. Es wurde ein Abend unter zwei Menschen, die eine Wirrwarr an Gefühlen füreinander empfunden hatten und beide ihren Frieden damit gemacht hatten. Sie lachten etwas zu laut und tranken fatalerweise einen Coco Chanel nach dem anderen. Als aber der Barkeeper in der inzwischen leeren Bar ein kleines Briefchen auf den Tisch legte, stand Anette Schwalbinger auf, verlief sich auf dem Weg zu ihrem Hotel nur einmal und legte sich in ihr viel zu weiches Bett.

Corsinis Augen waren so rot wie auf dem berühmten Dornenkronen-Porträt von Fra Angelico, und sein Schweiß roch bitter. Doch er stand pünktlich um sieben Uhr morgens vor dem Archäologischen Museum von Siracusa. Trotz seines Zustands gelang es ihm, den Direktor abzuschütteln, nachdem dieser Schwalbinger fünfmal als hochverehrteste Professorin betitelt hatte. Corsini führte sie durch den leicht angeschimmelten Bau, der aus Sextaedern bestand, und blieb vor einer Vitrine mit antiken Münzen stehen. Manche davon bis ins feinste Detail ausgearbeitet und gut erhalten, andere so ausgewaschen von Wasser und Zeit, dass gerade noch das Profil eines Menschen erkennbar war. Auch die vergilbte Liste mit den Namen der Exponate war kaum noch leserlich und die jeweiligen Namen waren nicht zuzuordnen. Wahrscheinlich waren die Münzen in den letzten Jahrzehnten umarrangiert worden, die Liste aber nicht. Das Chaos des Museums machte Frau Schwalbinger nervös, zumal sie hier keine Möglichkeit hatte, mit ein paar resoluten Griffen für Ordnung zu sorgen. Doch Corsini scharrte vor Aufregung mit dem linken Fuß – vielleicht waren es auch die Amphetamine in seinem Blut. «Das ist Appolonia, die Ehefrau eines hohen römischen Beamten. Sie war eine der ersten Esterianerinnen», sagte er und tippte so energisch gegen die Vitrinenscheibe, dass Schwalbinger fast eingegriffen hätte: «Und das hier ist Fürst Adriano. Er hatte den schönsten Arsch von Siracusa in der hochrömischen Phase. Er wurde gepfählt und verbrannt, weil er vor dem Apollotempel über die Barbarengötter der Griechen und Römer gespottet hatte.» Schwalbinger fragte sich, ob hochrömisch ein Fachbegriff war, sie kannte ihn jedenfalls nicht. Außerdem machte ihr Magen unerfreuliche Geräusche. Sie hätte nicht ohne Frühstück in das Museum gehen sollen. Auch der säuerlich-faulige Atem ihres alten Freundes erschöpfte sie: «Wirklich faszinierend. Aber vor Deiner nächsten Veröffentlichung sollten wir unbedingt telefonieren. Vielleicht kann man das besser platzieren…». Sie stieg ins Taxi und versuchte gar nicht erst sich anzuschnallen, denn sie traute den italienischen Gurten nicht. Corsini winkte ihr mit seiner brennenden Zigarette hinterher.

Die Auto-Delegation war in einem Luxushotel untergebracht, das auf einem riesigen Parkplatz in der Nähe des Fischmarktes lag. Ausufernde Begrüßung, sizilienfeindliche Witze und das übliche Sich-selbst-auf-die-Schulter-Klopfen: Schwalbinger hatte ihr Gehirn so programmiert, dass sie bei solchen Veranstaltungen weghören konnte und trotzdem alles mitbekam, sodass sie nicht von einer plötzlichen Frage überrascht werden konnte. Der Vormittag plätscherte ereignisarm vor sich hin, schon nach 20 Minuten hatte sie im Stillen ausgerechnet, was die ganze Reise gekostet haben musste. Eigentlich ein Skandal. Aber der neue SUV hatte wieder Verkaufsrekorde gebrochen, und das Geschäft im Nahen Osten hatte sich auch wieder erholt. Dann ergriff Mark Feist das Wort. Er war die vielleicht rätselhafteste Figur in der Firma. Ein ehemaliger Zehnkämpfer, der sich beim Stabhochsprung den linken Knöchel gebrochen hatte, was seine Sportlerkarriere beendet hatte. Seine stets knapp geschnittenen Hemden verrieten, dass er noch immer in Wettkampfform war, er trainierte viermal in der Woche mit dem CEO in dessen Privatgym. Seine Rolle im Autokonzern war ebenso dubios wie angsteinflößend. Offiziell lautete sein Titel Agent of Innovation, und man wusste nie, ob er die Meinung des obersten Chefs nachplapperte – oder improvisierte. Am liebsten zitierte er Peter Thiel und Udo Jürgens.

«Wir haben uns hier an diesem historischen Ort getroffen, wo einst das Schicksal Athens besiegelt wurde», fing er mit übertriebenem Pathos und leicht faktenwidrig an: «Athen war damals die Nummer eins im Mittelmeerraum. Man lernt nirgendwo so viel wie aus den eigenen Fehlern, hat ein großer Sänger aus Österreich mal gesagt. Ich glaube aber, wenn wir genau hinschauen, dann können wir aus den Fehlern der anderen noch mehr lernen. Auch wir sind die

Nummer eins. Nicht nach Umsatz, nicht nach Stück-zahlen, aber was Innovation und Image betrifft, macht uns keiner was vor. Float like a butterfly, sting like a bee. Das können wir besser als die Zauberkünstler aus dem Silicon Valley, die bis heute keinen anstän-digen Verbrenner auf die Straße gestellt haben. Und selbst als die Trickdiebe aus Fernost, die mit unseren Erfindungen Blechkisten zu Dumpingpreisen basteln – auch wenn ich das bei einem Meeting in Guangzhou vielleicht anders formulieren würde…».

Schwalbinger war gerade dabei, wieder in ihren Weghörmodus umzuschalten, da wechselte Feist überraschend das Thema. «Um die Nummer eins zu bleiben, dürfen wir nicht träge werden. Wir müssen outside the box denken, disruptive mit uns selbst sein, heilige Kühe schlachten. Oder zumindest auf die Gnadenweide führen.» Der Stilmix von Feist war bemerkenswert, Schwalbinger fragte sich, ob sie sich die Highlights aufschreiben sollte. Insgesamt war der Vormittag amüsanter, als sie zu hoffen gewagt hatte.

«Und eine dieser heiligen Kühe ist die Abteilung HR. Sie wird von einer meiner Lieblingskolleginnen geleitet, die großartigerweise mit uns nach Siracu-sa gekommen ist. Auch wenn sie wie üblich etwas früher als wir aufgestanden ist.» Feist deutete eine Verbeugung in Richtung von Anette Schwalbinger an: «Aber wenn wir ehrlich sind, ist die Abteilung HR eine Gemischtwarenhandlung, wo mit der glei-chen Sorgfalt Überstundenregelungen, Elterngeld und Diversität gehandelt werden. Das ist historisch gewachsen, hatte auch seine Berechtigung. Aber es ist, bei aller Liebe, nicht mehr state of the art.» Feist hatte sich warm geredet, was man an seinen regelmäßig zuckenden Brustmuskeln erkannte. Er ließ den Blick über die ergeben lauschenden Zuhörer schweifen, blieb einen Tick zu lang bei Jude Klingendorf hängen. Anette Schwalbinger war unterdessen vor Wut äußerlich ganz ruhig geworden. Aber sie spürte, wie ihre Hände sich verkrampften. «Was ich vorschlage, klingt vielleicht wie ein Schock, doch wir haben eine ganze Reihe von Best-Case-Studien aus Südkorea und Kanada, wo die interessantesten Unternehmen genau dieses Model schon implementiert haben. Die Stichworte sind Dezentralisation und radikaler Fokus auf Corporate Culture. Kündigungen, Arbeitsverträge, Überstundenregelungen, das ganze Gedöns, wird jetzt von kleinen Einheiten in den jeweiligen Units erledigt. Dafür brauchen wir keine aufgeblasene HR Abteilung und ihre endlosen Sitzungen mit dem Betriebsrat. Die entscheidenden Fragen, die Fragen, die darüber entscheiden, ob wir in 30 Jahren immer noch on top of the world sind, sind Diversität, Work-Life-Balance, innovation acceleration, flexibility shift. «No company HAS a culture, every company IS a culture», wie Peter Thiel in seinem Bestseller «From Zero to Hero» schreibt. Dafür richten wir eine kompakte neue Abteilung ein. Die Corporate Culture Cell. Double C».

Das musste doch korrekterweise Triple C heißen, dachte Anette Schwalbinger, die Schlampigkeit nur schwer ertrug. Aber sie wusste, dass das nichts zur Sache tat. Hier ging es um ihren Kopf. Es war eine öffentliche Hinrichtung. Und das reichte offenbar

23

noch nicht. «Und für diese Aufgabe, da waren Marius und ich uns einig», redete Feist weiter (Marius war natürlich der Vorname seines Gym-Buddy, dem CEO): …ist niemand besser geeignet als unsere Kollegin Jude Klingendorf. Sie soll unsere Corporate Culture Superagentin werden.» In den Applaus hinein bat Feist sie auf die Bühne.

Jude Klingendorf stand auf, deutete eine ironische Verbeugung an und hielt beide Hände flach aneinander, eine Geste der Bescheidenheit und Selbstgratulation, die man von Pharrell Williams kennt. Ihr weißes Kleid saß perfekt, und über der linken Schulter hing an einer länglichen, goldenen Kette eine Handtasche mit Doppel-C. Schwalbinger fragte sich, ob es eine Fälschung war, denn sie kannte das bisherige Gehalt ihrer Mitarbeiterin. Über deren treulose Machtergreifung war sie verblüfft. Klingendorf hatte sie jahrelang derart angehimmelt, dass ihr kurzfristig der Gedanke kam, die junge Frau könnte in sie verliebt sein. «Danke für Euer Vertrauen.», sagte Klingendorf, obwohl keiner der Anwesenden ihr bisher irgendetwas anvertraut hatte: «Ich will hier nichts verkünden, ich will in den nächsten Tagen und Wochen vor allem zuhören. Und ich will mich bei meiner Kollegin, Mentorin und ich hoffe sagen zu dürfen: Freundin bedanken. Von ihr habe ich alles gelernt, ohne sie stünde ich heute nicht hier. Here's to you, Anette Schwalbinger!»

«Wusstest Du davon?», fragte der Kollege aus der Kleinwagenabteilung beim Mittagessen. Schwalbinger schaute auf den Olivenölfleck auf seinem kurzärmeligen Hemd und sagte: «Klar. Genau genommen war das meine Idee». Das war so offenkundig gelogen, dass es das Gespräch beendete, und das war auch ihre Absicht gewesen. Später machte die Gruppe einen Bootsausflug um die Insel Ortigia. Trotz des herrlichen Maiwetters war das Meer unruhig und das Boot knallte immer wieder gegen die Wellen, so dass die vorderen Passagiere von der hochspritzenden Gischt durchnässt wurden. Jude Klingendorfs Kleid war so nass, dass man ihre schönen Brüste deutlich erkennen konnte. Ihr perlendes Lachen sorgte, sicherlich völlig unbeabsichtigt, für zusätzliche Aufmerksamkeit, bis ihr Mark Feist sein leichtes Sommerjackett aus Kaschmir-Seiden-Gemisch anbot. Sie lächelte und lehnte lässig ab. Dann beugte sie sich über den Bootsrand und übergab sich mit einer Ausgiebigkeit, die maßlos und unanständig wirkte. Für Anette Schwalbinger war es der schönste Moment in einem bis dahin bemerkenswert missglückten Tag.

Vor dem Aperitivo stand ein Besuch der Katakomben auf dem Programm. Optional und mit Triggerwarnung versehen, schließlich hatte man erst kürzlich ein paar echte Skelette in einer bis dahin verschlossenen Kammer entdeckt. Anette Schwalbinger konnte an diesem Spätnachmittag das schlechte Englisch des Tourguides und den schlurfenden Gang ihrer Kollegen nicht ertragen und bog an einer Kreuzung der unterirdischen Wege ab, um ihre Ruhe zu haben. Bald hörte sie das wiehernde Lachen des Kollegen aus der Kleinwagenabteilung nur noch aus der Ferne. Wie seltsam diese Straßen waren, gesäumt von den Grabfächern, die in den Sandstein gehauen waren, ungefähr so groß wie die Pritschen in einem Liegewagen der Bahn. Nur kürzer natürlich. Wann hatte es noch mal begonnen, dieses Wachstum der Menschheit? Mit der industriellen Revolution? Wie jeder Mensch, der sich noch nicht vollständig aufs Internet verlässt, ärgerte sich Schwalbinger über Details, die sie mal gewusst hatte und nicht sofort aus ihrem Gedächtnis abrufen konnte. Sie bog um eine weitere Ecke und blieb an der Kreuzung zweier Gänge stehen. Jetzt hörte sie gar nichts mehr. Wo die anderen wohl waren? Jedenfalls ein Segen, diese Ruhe in den kühlen, feuchten Räumen. Dann ging das Licht aus.

Es war tatsächlich stockdunkel. Noch nicht einmal Notleuchten waren zu sehen. Vielleicht gab es auch keine. Anette Schwalbinger seufzte. Sie kannte das wacklige italienische Stromnetz noch von damals und erwartete, dass die Katakombenbirnen in wenigen Sekunden wieder flackernd anspringen würden. Im Schein der Taschenlampe ihres Handies tastete sie sich ein paar Schritte vor. Sie müsste nur die Hauptachse der unterirdischen Wege finden und dann rechts gehen. Dann würde sie sich wieder in Richtung des Ausgangs bewegen. Ganz so einfach war es dann doch nicht, aber sie war keineswegs beunruhigt. Auch dann nicht, als sie sah, dass der Ladestand ihres Telefons bei drei Prozent lag. Schließlich fand sie die schwere Metalltür am Ausgang. Diese bewegte sich keinen Millimeter, Anette Schwalbingers Klopfen klang leise und stumpf. Sie setzte sich auf die Schwelle und stellte ihr Telefon wieder aus. Hier unten hatte sie ohnehin kein Netz, und sie wollte Strom sparen.

Nun wartete sie. Und wunderte sich. Die Kollegen mussten ihr Fehlen bemerkt haben. Bestimmt würden sie gleich zurückkehren. Aber warum dauerte das so lange? Oder der Strom würde wieder anspringen. Oder, ja was eigentlich?

Und ohne dass sie es bemerkt hatte, war auf einmal die Angst da. Bei ihren unzähligen Gesprächen und Treffen mit Mitarbeitern und Bewerbern hatte sie stets unauffällig auf zwei Fragen gezielt: Was war seine/ihre größte Hoffnung? Und was die größte Angst? Schwalbinger wusste, dass Menschen nicht nur von dem gesteuert werden, was sie erreichen wollen. Sondern auch von dem, was sie um jeden Preis vermeiden wollen, was Panik in ihnen weckte. Für erstaunlich viele waren es Prüfungen. Für andere Menschenmengen. Oder ein Alptraum, ein Monster, die riesige Ratte im Käfig aus «1984», die nur darauf lauert, freigelassen zu werden und sich ins Gesicht reinfressen zu können. Jeder Mensch, so glaubte George Orwell, hatte diese eine Urangst, mit deren Hilfe man ihm das Menschsein entreißen konnte. Diese Urangst wollte Anette Schwalbinger finden. Das mag krude klingen für die Personalchefin eines Autoherstellers, aber es war nur ein Gedankenspiel, und Anette Schwalbinger hatte keinerlei sadistische Neigung. Kleinen Kindern lächelte sie stets zu, auch wenn sie ihre Entscheidung, keine Kinder zu haben, nie bereut hatte. Selbst Wespen, die sich in ihre Wohnung verirrten, fing sie wieder ein und ließ sie draußen fliegen. Sie hatte keine Freude am Quälen, aber das Interesse, den Dingen auf den Grund zu gehen. Deswegen war sie, ohne

27

jede akademische Expertise, eine Expertin in Phobien. Interessanterweise hatte sie sich selbst dabei ausgelassen. Spinnen, Flugzeuge, bellende Hunde, Menschenmengen. Nichts davon flößte ihr Angst ein. Mangelnde Furcht sei ein Zeichen von Fantasielosigkeit, hatte Martin Suter mal geschrieben. Typisch Schweizer, typisch Mann, fand Anette Schwalbinger. Denn Furcht kannte sie nicht. Nur die eine, aber mit der hatte sie ihren Frieden gemacht.

Bis zu diesem Abend in Siracusa, als sie allein in der Dunkelheit vor den kalten, leeren Grabfächern kauerte und langsam begriff, dass sie bis zum Morgen hier warten müsste. Der Schwellenstein an der Tür war feucht, wie sie leider zu spät gemerkt hatte, als ihre Hose schon klamm war und an Hintern und Oberschenkeln klebte. Sie trat auf der Stelle, um sich aufzuwärmen und den Stoff durch die Reibung zu trocknen. Dann tappte sie durch die Dunkelheit, aber wohin und warum? Vorhin waren ihr die Katakomben grabesstill erschienen, jetzt hörte sie die Geräusche der Finsternis. Links hinter ihr ein flinkes Scharren, nicht weit vor ihr Trippelschritte, irgendwo tropfte es. Sie lehnte sich an eine Wand. So stand sie nicht ungeschützt in der Dunkelheit, dachte sie, und dieser Gedanke verstärkte ihre Angst. Dann spürte sie ihre Beine müde werden. Die linke Wade krampfte bereits. Sie kannte das schon. Es würde nun mit jeder Minute schlimmer werden.

Und weil sie eine Realistin war, tat sie das Naheliegende: Sie leuchtete mit ihren letzten Prozenten Handylicht in die Grabnischen, bis sie eine in Hüfthöhe fand, die trocken und sauber wirkte. Anette Schwalbinger kroch in die Nische aus Stein, in der vor Jahrtausenden eine Tochter des großen, mächtigen Siracusa vergeblich aufs Jenseits gewartet hatte. Dort lag sie jetzt und hoffte auf den Morgen. Bequem war es nicht, und viel Platz war auch nicht über ihr. Als sie sich auf die Seite drehte, berührte sie fast die steinerne Decke. Aber wenn sie schon mal hier war, dachte sie mit einem Anflug von Ironie, dann konnte sie sich auch eine Strategie überlegen, wie sie diese Natter Klingendorf und den dümmlichen Zehnkämpfer austricksen konnte. Die beiden hatten viele Startvorteile: Sie war jung, sah aus wie Meghan Markle und beherrschte die Klaviatur des modernen Machtkampfs. Er wiederum kannte den nackten Penis des CEO und wusste, wie viel Kilo er bei der Beinpresse schaffte. Classified information also. Und was war sie? Eine wütende, ältere Frau mit schweren Beinen und tausendseitigen Michelangelo-Biografien im Bücherregal. Ein Auslaufmodell. Dieser Gedanke allerdings machte Anette Schwalbinger gute Laune. Sie kicherte leise. Weil ihre momentane Situation so absurd war, die Intrige gegen sie so kindisch. Vor allem aber kicherte sie, weil diese Grabkammer so unheimlich war. Da war es wieder dieses Scharren. Und diesmal klang es, als seien mehr als nur vier Füßchen unterwegs. Würden sie den Weg in ihre Kammer finden? Und was dann?

Sie musste eingeschlafen sein. Ihr Nacken schmerzte, sie zitterte, in der Höhe ihrer Nieren spürte sie einen Stein. War der vorhin auch schon dort gewesen? Schwalbinger tastete nach dem Stein, um ihn aus ihrem Grabfach zu werfen. Seltsam, wie leicht der war! Noch leicht benommen von ihrem Schlaf betastete sie ihn. Er war vielleicht so groß wie ein Apfel, hatte zwei Vertiefungen und kleine, regelmäßige Rillen in einer Reihe. Und mit dem langsam erwachenden Bewusstsein, wurde ihr klar, was sie in der Hand hielt. Es war ein Menschenschädel. So klein, dass er von einem Kind stammen musste. Andere hätten ihn vielleicht erschrocken weggeschleudert, doch Anette Schwalbinger hielt den Schädel sanft und fest in ihren Händen. Wie man den Kopf eines Kindes halten würde, wenn es Trost braucht. Sie hatte vor langer Zeit beschlossen, dass Beten für sie keinen Sinn ergab; das Formelhafte daran gefiel ihr nicht. Aber die einzige Angst, die sie bei sich hatte finden können, war die Ahnung, dass sie ganz allein auf der Welt sein könnte. Und hier hatte ihr der undogmatische Überrest Religion geholfen, der ihr geblieben war und sie sicher durchs Leben begleitet hatte: Irgendetwas gab ihr die Sicherheit, dass sie es nicht war. Sie hielt also den Schädel, in dem einmal ein Gehirn und eine Seele gewohnt hatten, und sagte leise: Danke.

Als sie wieder aufwachte, sah sie fahles Licht und hörte zwei Männer durch die Gänge streifen und plaudern. Sie diskutierten über den Fußballer Riccardo Calafiori. «Der sitzt im Rock im Mannschaftsbus. Und diese Haare. Ich sag Dir, der ist schwul!», sagte der eine. «Na, und: An den Trikots hat der FC Bologna Millionen verdient. Der kann doch ficken, wen er will. Solange er meinen Sohn nicht angrabscht.» Diese

Diskussion kannte Schwalbinger auswendig. Und sie wollte die beiden Katakombenwächter lieber vermeiden. Sie glitt aus ihrer Schlafnische und stahl sich nach draußen. Dort blinzelte sie in die krasse sizilianische Morgensonne. Ihre Philipp-Bree-Tasche beulte sich etwas, denn den Schädel hatte sie mitgenommen.

«Wo waren Sie denn gestern Abend? Wir haben sie vermisst.», sagte Mark Feist, als Schwalbinger den Frühstückssaal betrat. Vor Sorgen runzelte er die glatte Stirn und spannte den Bizeps an, der aus dem engen, weißen T-Shirt quoll. «Alles gut, Anette? Können wir mal sprechen?», fragte Jude Klingendorf, ohne ihre Sonnenbrille abzusetzen. «Ich brauchte gestern Abend einen Moment für mich. Aber tutto a posto», sagte Schwalbinger im Vorbeigehen und suchte sich einen freien Tisch. Auf dem Weg durch den Saal hörte sie unterdrücktes Kichern. Und weil Anette Schwalbinger trotz ihres genauen Blicks für Menschen, doch immer das Beste annahm, kam ihr erst jetzt ein Verdacht. Vielleicht war es kein Versehen gewesen, dass man sie in den Katakomben eingeschlossen und vergessen hatte. Sondern ein gehässiger Streich.

Anette Schwalbinger setzte sich an den leeren Tisch, nahm den Kinderschädel aus ihrer geräumigen Tasche und stellte ihn rechts neben ihr Gedeck. Dann ging sie zum Frühstücksbuffet. Sie betrachtete die getrockneten, eingelegten Pflaumen. Wer hatte sich die eigentlich ausgedacht? Schwalbinger kannte nur einen Menschen, der sie regelmäßig verzehrte, und das war ein Kollege mit trägem Darm. Dann entdeckte sie einen flachen Kuchen mit einem handgeschriebenen Schildchen, auf dem «Hausgemacht» stand. Es waren nur noch zwei Stücke vorhanden, und Anette Schwalbinger nahm sich beide. Weil sie jedoch eine nette, mitfühlende Frau war, fühlte sie sich sofort schlecht wegen ihrer Gier und Rücksichtslosigkeit.

Es war unbehaglich still geworden im Frühstückssaal des Luxushotels. Die anderen Gäste starrten auf den Kinderschädel, manche bemühten sich, ein Gespräch am Laufen zu halten. Mark Feist ließ seinen Stuhl über den Steinboden kreischen, stand auf und schritt energisch zu den Wärmewannen der Eierspeisen. Links gebratener Speck, rechts gestocktes Flüssigei, in das das Schwitzwasser der Aluminiumdeckel getropft war. Feist schaufelte und schaufelte, bis auf seinem Teller ein Berg aus Ei, Speck und Würsten war. Er ließ den Deckel etwas zu laut fallen und ging in Richtung seines Tisches. Auf dem Boden vor ihm lag eine große Schreibe gebratenen Specks in einer Lache flüssigen Bratfetts. Feist sah sie nicht, weil sein Blick wie meist in die Ferne und die Zukunft gerichtet war. Für einen kurzen Moment dachte Schwalbinger, dass das Leben eben doch ein Slapstick war. Sie sah, wie ihr Widersacher auf dem Speck ausrutschte, wie er seinen Teller noch zu retten versuchte, wie der Riesenhaufen gestocktes Ei auf seinem weißen T-Shirt und seinem Pectoralis Major landete.

Das aber geschah nicht. Mark Feist, der Agent of Innovation, trat einfach nur auf die Speckscheibe. Und diese verursachte keinen grotesken Unfall, sondern gab lediglich ein widerwilliges, ziehendes, schmatzendes Geräusch von sich. Feist schreckte auf. Er hätte irgendwohin schauen können. Auf seinen Eierberg mit dem draufgestreuten Pfefferstaub, auf die widerspenstige Speckscheibe, auf den riesigen Parkplatz mit den kaputten Ticket-Automaten. Vielleicht sogar zu seinem Tisch, wo die Kollegen versuchten, die gespenstische Szenerie zu ignorieren. Er aber schaute zu Anette Schwalbinger. Nur einen Augenblick, aber einen Augenblick zu lang. Und in seinen hin- und weghuschenden Augen stand Schuld geschrieben. Als hätte der schmatzende Speck sein Geheimnis verraten.

Schwalbinger aß sorgfältig, fast pedantisch – und jetzt zum Glück ohne Reue – ihren Mandel-Zitronen-Kuchen. Sie genoss jeden Bissen und beschloss, bei ihrem nächsten Sizilienbesuch die Barockstädte im Südosten zu besuchen. Seit Jahren war sie nicht mehr im Caffè Sicilia gewesen, und die Cassatina sollte immer noch großartig sein. Langsam wickelte sie den Kinderschädel in eine Serviette, steckte ihn in ihre geräumige Tasche und erhob sich. Sie musste sich noch die Zwischenräume mit Zahnseide säubern und die Zunge bürsten, so wie sie es immer vor langen Meetings tat. Jetzt wusste sie, was zu tun war.

Lucia Moschella
Costa

«Oppure potremmo andare alle Saline».

«Serve il biglietto ormai».

«E la Costa Nera?».

«Chiusa pure quella. È franato un pezzo»

«Quindi non c'è più nessuna spiaggia libera?».

«Kind of».

«Andiamo alla riserva».

«L'hanno bruciata».

«Ma perché, aveva tutto questo giro?».

«Dopo l'articolo del New York Times, sì». spiegò. «Dài, *amuni*».

Partimmo in motorino senza meta apparente, come al liceo. Io non tornavo nella mia città da un po'. Qui, per i miei studi e il mio lavoro di biologa marina, mancavano canali e sbocchi (la maggior parte di biologhe marine che conoscevo: istruttrici in centri di snorkelling). Me n'ero andata a diciotto anni. Per diverse ragioni – nessuna delle quali era antipatia ostentata per questo posto, come molti miei conoscenti – tornavo di rado e nei periodi comandati: Natale, Pasqua, Estate. Non senza che la cosa mi provocasse un discreto fastidio.

Quando Alice mi passò il casco e mi invitò a sedere sulla sella del suo Scarabeo, mancavo da così tanto che potevo misurarlo con ipermercati demoliti, ricostruiti e finiti, riserve incendiate e spiagge mangiate, dal mare e dalla gente. Questo tratto era franato, quell'altro incenerito; quasi tutto era stato dato in pasto a privati che ne avevano

La giornata era rovente. Avevo sentito che le temperature alte erano sempre più invasive da queste parti e ora lo constatavo sulle mie cosce, dove il sole batteva dritto e la pelle riluceva e scottava, appena lenita da un alito di vento manco troppo fresco. Ogni tanto dovevo passarmi i palmi della mano per neutralizzare il calore.

Sullo Scarabeo di Alice non si parlava, come al liceo. Ricordavo la sua regola: in moto lei non apriva bocca, perché se lo faceva finiva per mangiarsi i capelli, su cui poi sentiva l'odore di saliva che li aveva impastati e la cosa le faceva «sette schifi». E in ogni caso, a parlare in moto non si capiva niente.

Non sapevo perché al supermercato mi avesse invitato a farmi sentire, ma io (e il perché lo sapevo: non avevo più amici, qui) le avevo scritto sul serio. Cambiamenti di cui ero certa: era ritornata al suo storico profumo Narciso by Narciso Rodriguez, che aveva indossato per prima al Liceo Classico, per poi abbandonarlo quando la metà della popolazione femminile dell'istituto aveva iniziato a farne uso; vestiva molto meno sportiva di un tempo, via le Vans dentro le Tod's; aveva aggiunto al suo parlato alcuni intercalari inglesi, che io non usavo neanche quando tornavo in Italia dai miei periodi di ricerca all'estero.

Uscite dalla città il vento mi schiaffeggiò coi nostri odori – zagara, mirto, asfalto bollente, seccume, benzina. Ai lati della strada la natura era quella di sempre ma ora ogni spazio mi pareva segreto, invalicabile dietro insegne in inglese, promettenti e ben studiate. Sembravano rebus, o collage di parole casuali da quotidiani stranieri.

PITÌTTU – BIODYNAMIC TASTING
MAD – MYSTICAL AGRICULTURE & DESIGN
CAPO BEACH – FASHION SAND RELAIS

Sotto le insegne trionfavano ingressi serrati. Intravedevi: brecciolini pregiati, colonnati di ulivi, siepi geometriche, fontane d'acqua. Alice imboccò una stradina sterrata e malmessa, fece slalom tra le buche e inchiodò davanti un grande cancello semiaperto.

«Qua, di solito, è fattibile» promise.

Attraversammo un edificio abbandonato. Una specie di ex ristorante, ex teatro, ex spazio per i sabato sera estivi. Ravanavo nella mia memoria per individuare immagini di vita trascorse là dentro. La pizzata con una vecchia comitiva dei miei. Qualche saggio di danza moderna di una delle mie cugine. L'esibizione della cover band di quell'emaciato con cui l'estate del 2009 *mi facevo gli sgami.* Quel posto mi ricordava e non mi ricordava: ero sicura che qualcosa lì dentro fosse successo, nella mia vita, ma non ero certa di cosa; erano episodi appena accennati, vaghi. Le memorie di una città natale abbandonata sono questo: sogni lucidi che non sai se e come si sono ripetuti.

Dal ventre del cemento affacciammo su un unico scoglio a picco sul mare. L'acqua era blu oltremare ma in mezzo al brillare delle onde galleggiava sghembo un velo opaco e parecchie pagliuzze di plastica. Sugli scogli c'erano già due coppie: non ci si entrava.

«Sediamoci qua e aspettiamo che qualcuno si alzi» disse indicando un gradone di cemento.

«Ma che era, 'sto posto?».

«Boh. *Ask* Alajmo!» rispose lei.

Ridemmo. Alice mi aveva raccontato poco prima che Alajmo, il nostro ex professore d'arte del liceo, si era reinventato contestatore della città «turistificata». Durante il festival di musica chiamava la polizia perché misurasse i PBM a cui veniva sottoposto il Castello; quando un nuovo chiosco sul mare inaugurava, lui verificava eventuali abusivismi; era spesso l'unico contestatore in Comune se il sindaco affittava Piazza Duomo per la sfilata della collezione Spring Summer a case di moda milanesi brandizzate MADE IN SICILY. Alajmo mi pareva, da solo, la «buona» e giusta vecchia guardia.

«Uno *scassaminchia* di prima categoria!» aveva detto Alice. «Io coi festival, con le sfilate, ci lavoro. Se non venissero turisti nel mio b&b, che lavoro farei qua? Me ne dovrei andare, come te» aveva detto con una smorfia. «Ha questo blog, La memoria inventata, dove segnala tutte le storie false che girano per la città. Una volta se la prende con le Ape Car turistiche, per le concessioni o perché raccontano cazzate ai turisti, un'altra dice che quel miracolo non è successo o quella brochure è sbagliata, ma che palle! Tie', beviti questo» mi disse passandomi una bottiglietta di plastica con un liquido arancione dentro. «Niente di *freak*» mi rassicurò. «Sali minerali, carnidina, magnesio. Altrimenti svieni, con questo caldo» disse.

Mi passai una mano sulla fronte. Grondavo.

«Dico che le persone vogliono solo storielle da riferire agli amici a tavola una volta rientrati in Connecticut. *Chettefrega* se sono vere o no» disse facendo un sorso pure lei. «Con la Madonnina, poi, è impazzito!».

Il liquido lasciava in bocca un gusto acido e salato, con un aroma di arancia tipico dei farmaci.

«Che Madonnina» chiesi asciugandomi la bocca.

«La Madonnina appesa al muro, quella di Alfredo Romano».

«Sì, so qual è» rivendicai.

«Dice che le Ape Car raccontano che è spuntata una notte, come un miracolo».

Sorrisi. «Io c'ero quando l'hanno piantata» dissi. «Però, in effetti, se è una *minchiata,* perché devono raccontarla».

«Ascolta, una volta dei miei turisti texani mi hanno scritto un feedback privato, 'Ciao Alice, solo per segnalarti che crediamo che nella stanza comune ci sia un fantasma che arriva tra le due e le tre di notte e mette a soqquadro tutto, in caso tu voglia chiamare qualche medium.' Credono ai fantasmi, capito?».

No, non capivo, ignoravo il suo ragionamento e anche la sua etica. Ignoravo chi fossero «i suoi» turisti e perché si dovesse o non si dovesse credere ai fantasmi o alla Madonna o alla carnitina. Sapevo che la turistificazione – l'*overturism,* avrebbe detto lei – era un problema ma non volevo battibeccare: sarei dovuta tornare a casa sulla sua moto e, se Alice era rimasta come al liceo, sarebbe stata capace di piantarmi là in mezzo al nulla.

«Certo che questi non schiodano» lamentai indicando gli scogli.

«Te l'ho detto, è per questo che di solito me ne sto a casa in piscina. *Te* non sei voluta venire».

Chettefrega, te: perché, oltre che in inglese, Alice parlava romano? Ad ogni modo la gente era tanta, tantissima, diceva lei, i turisti nel suo b&b arrivavano a ruota, per fortuna stranieri, mica tirchi come gli italiani – che pretendevano lo sconto, si lamentavano di tutto, ti distruggevano casa e ti facevano pure la recensione negativa. Doveva dire che da quando le persone la recensivano anche come host, quindi come persona, aveva paura di tutto.

Perché le recensioni non erano sulla loro casa ma anche su di lei, capivo? Tutto il mondo recensiva ogni cosa: i b&b, le Adidas usate, i biglietti dei concerti. E spesso non recensivano la cosa che scambiavi. Recensivano te. La persona. Esistere era essere passibile di voto. Comunque lei, doveva dire, aveva tutte 5 stelle. Ma aveva solo stranieri. Gli italiani… Gliel'avevano detto tutti, quando aveva cominciato, e lei pensava fosse uno stereotipo. Poi aveva constatato lei stessa, al cento per cento. Non c'è altro di dire: gli italiani ti chiedono lo sconto, si lamentano di tutto, ti distruggono la casa e ti fanno pure la recensione negativa.

Nessuno si alzò dallo scoglio nella parentesi della nostra chiacchierata e Alice sarebbe dovuta rientrare per un check-in. Si passava la mano sul nuovo tatuaggio, il contorno dell'isola, su una pelle bianchissima. Sì, lo sapeva, era pallida, ma non aveva tempo per andare a mare, e se anche ne avesse avuto, avevo visto, no? Non c'era dove andare, e faceva troppo caldo. E poi il sole era *impruvulazzato,* come se gli fosse passato sopra un velo di polvere. L'avevo notato? Non era più come quando eravamo piccole noi – disse così: piccole. Aveva sempre una patina grigiastra sopra, anche quando era pieno.

«È Scirocco».

«Mh» fece lei. «È Scirocco da sei mesi ormai. L'ultima giornata di sole pieno che ho visto, io e te traducevamo dal greco. Boh, non lo so. C'è un'atmosfera pesante. È come se la *muddura* fosse entrata nelle ossa delle persone. E poi i crolli. Hai sentito?».

Mi guardai intorno come se ci fosse qualche segnale da cogliere o mi fossi persa qualcuno che avrebbe dovuto aggiornarmi.

«La costa crolla» spiegò.

«Ah, sì, ho letto. Eh, l'erosione».

«Sì» sembrò dubitare lei. «Succede di continuo, ormai».

Il Faro Rosso era crollato una notte di gennaio, svenendo in mare in mezzo a un banco di buio freddo. I giorni successivi l'equipe di esperti – tutti provenienti dal Nord, per essere considerati tali – aveva ispezionato i fondali e confermato le cause naturali.

Cose che avrei scoperto dopo:

1) non si era sentito alcun boato

2) durante il crollo, il cielo si era completamente oscurato

3) ricognizioni subacquee avevano trovato solo una sottile coperta di cristalli rossi: di fatto, il Faro si era smaterializzato.

Ai crolli costieri eravamo abituati, ma quello del Faro ci aveva spezzato il cuore – la nostalgia di serate di Tennent's coi nostri e le nostre cotte dei licei, il videoclip di due cantanti locali girato con la luna piena, la vana lotta sociale dei cittadini che non aveva comunque evitato che il Faro diventasse l'ennesima exclusive experience della città. E poi, il collasso.

«Vabbè» sorvolò Alice di punto in bianco. «*Amunì*».

Alice mi riaccompagnò. La ringraziai (riaffiorò solo a quel punto la stranezza del nostro incontro a distanza di così tanta assenza). Le restituii il casco.

«Senti» mi disse poi lei. «Quando poi sei partita, io e Matteo, per un periodo, ci siamo effettivamente visti».

La fissai.

«Matteo Campo» precisò lei, come se non sapessi il cognome del mio primo ragazzo. Cadde il silenzio.

«Ho pensato di dirtelo tante volte» disse. «Anche quando me l'hai chiesto. Ma boh, ero piccola, non ci riuscivo. Non mi usciva proprio di bocca».

Mi sistemai la gonna.

«Non che ora conti qualcosa» aggiunse. «Tu vivi fuori, lui ha i due figli con quella tizia».

«Scusa, è che ho sempre voluto dirtelo e ultimamente di più. Poi ti ho incontrata al supermercato, ho detto: è un segno».

Non aveva importanza, ora che erano passati quindici anni, dirle che il motivo per cui avevo lasciato Matteo era una gelosia incontrollabile nei confronti di nessuno se non di lei, guarita in molti anni di analisi – altrimenti non avrei saputo ascoltarla per ore stra parlare dei suoi inutili problemi col suo b&b. Che me facevo, ora, di quella confessione?

«*'Sti cazzi*» dissi a parole sue e le poggiai una mano sulla spalla. Sfrecciarono alle nostre spalle due ragazzini in moto – pelle imbrunita dal sole, tatuaggi, no casco. Tirarono su la saliva con la bocca in senso di «apprezzamento» nei nostri confronti.

Di una o di tutte e due?, mi venne da pensare.

«Farai qualcosa queste sere?» mi chiese Alice.

«Ho visto di questa *dinner night* a casa di quella chef americana, Dawn. Me ne ha parlato un'amica californiana» dissi.

«Sì, la conosco» si precipitò a rispondere. Poi fece il gesto che conoscevo a lei e alle persone di questo posto, labbroni in giù, sopracciglia all'insù, per dire: *c'ha ffari.*

«Ci vuoi andare?».

«Mi piacerebbe» insistetti.

«Sai quanto costa?».

«No, quanto costa?».

«Quelle cene partono da 100 euro, fino a 200» disse mentre sbatteva energicamente il bauletto. «Non so quanto guadagni tu, ma per me è *off limits.* Sono cose per turisti. Ti posano sulla tovaglia di lino un tappeto ostriche dell'Atlantico, due alici del supermercato con un po' di battuto di erbe e un ramo di finocchietto pisciato dal gatto, ti danno un vino macerato e ti taggano sui social scrivendo *Livin' the Sicilian dream.* Se vai, dimmi com'è» tagliò corto.

«Ma da che parte stai?» mi irritai io, anche se la cena non c'entrava affatto. «Le leggende false sì, e le cene a 200 euro no?».

«Le storie sono una cosa. I soldi della gente, un'altra».

A casa cercai La memoria inventata. Era un blog sgraziato, la grafica dei tempi delle connessioni a 56K: su una foto sgranata della città, un Calibri senza grassetti o corsivi criticava l'eccessiva turistificazione del centro storico e sfilacciava i punti critici del discorso turistico, riportando le complessità appiattite dagli slogan. Si poteva essere d'accordo con lo stigma della colonizzazione e della brandizzazione di una terra, sì. Ma dove la mettevi Alice che se non avesse lavorato col turismo avrebbe dovuto andarsene – smorfia – come me?

Dopo la sezione sulla numismatica ellenica e quella sull'Area Marina Protetta, in grande e a parte trionfava la sezione «GIGIÀNTI». Il bottone apriva un pop-up di avvertimento:

ATTENZIONE: I FATTI DI QUESTA SEZIONE POTREBBERO URTARE LA VOSTRA SENSIBILITÀ

Alajmo raccontava di creature mitologiche che da sempre abitavano la stratosfera. Secondo la leggenda di un'antica civiltà scomparsa (come si rintraccia una leggenda di una civiltà scomparsa? mi chiedevo) – secondo la leggenda, quindi, i *gigiànti* avevano abitato la terra sin dal Pleistocene, ma non erano affatto andati via, diceva Alajmo: invece erano rimasti a gravitare intorno alla terra senza farsi vedere, per controllare cosa combinassimo noi umani. Si vendicavano con gli umani che toglievano troppo alla natura ed elargivano premi a chi invece la onorava. Secondo Alajmo, così erano state costruite le piramidi e le zigurrat: un premio dei *gigianti* per gli studi astronomici.

Poi Alajmo usciva definitivamente pazzo: diceva, solo per darci «contezza» delle dimensioni di queste creature, che i *gigiànti* avrebbero potuto usare le palme come cotton fioc, e appioppava il terremoto del 1990, in cui il Santuario della Madonna delle Lacrime, appena costruito, era rimasto intatto, a un tentativo di pulizia dentale di uno dei gigianti: «Ha tentato di usare il Santuario come noi uno stuzzicadenti Samurai».

Stavo scoppiando a ridere quando sentii un'Ape Car fermarsi sotto la via della mia stanza: raccontava ai suoi passeggeri, in un inglese-italiano urlato e mimato, la storia della Fonte Aretusa.

«Alfeo, Greek man very old, come to Siracusa because here the femminine too beautiful! Very, very beautiful. Blue eye, black hair. E Alfeo from Greek says Nooo, noooo, I go, too beautiful, I go, I go, I go! E so Alfeo find Aretusa, blue eye black hair».

Ahhh, mmmmh, nice, sentivo masticare ai turisti galvanizzati.

«Ok? Want to take pictures?» chiese l'autista.

Sapevo che la leggenda de Le Metamorfosi voleva tutto il contrario: Aretusa, predata da Alfeo, aveva implorato Zeus di trovare un modo per sfuggirgli al punto che il dio aveva acconsentito a trasformare la giovane in acqua dolce. Alfeo, testardo stupratore, ritrasformatosi nuovamente in acqua salata, l'aveva seguita fino a poter penetrare Fonte Aretusa attraverso un piccolo foro sul fondo della pozza d'acqua, ancora oggi visibile.

Infine, sapevo la verità: che la Fonte era solo uno dei tanti sfoghi della falda freatica della città. Per strana che fosse una fonte d'acqua dolce vicino al mare, era comunque meno stravagante di una fonte generata da un turismo sessuale mitico o peggio da un tentativo di stupro romanticizzato.

Stavo quasi per parlare quando mi ricordai cosa mi aveva detto Alice quel pomeriggio: che i tizi delle Ape Car era meglio non *inquietarli,* non dar loro fastidio. Chiusi con forza la portafinestra del balcone: l'Ape Car, in moto, scorreggiava in aria un puzzo di benzina insopportabile.

«Thank you for coming. Enjoy our best life!» disse Anne, la chef americana.

Valicato il portone, la tavola mi aveva imbambolato come le lampare un banco di sarde: mezza illuminata da candelabri d'epoca, era acchittàta in maniera cerimoniosa e decadente. Da un tovagliato di pizzo bianco uomini e donne con abiti ampi di lino spizzicavano duroni lucidi e mandorle sparse con uno studio casuale. I commensali sganciavano i piccioli dei duroni tirandoli tra i denti. Masticavano, ciucciavano i noccioli. Qualcuno cercava dove gettarli, altri li sputavano direttamente a terra. Nella mano libera tenevano (tutti alla radice dello stelo del calice) piccole quantità di vini d'un giallo sporco o rosso scarico. Era un normale cortile tipico dell'isola, di quelli dove la gente come me ci avrebbe parcheggiato la berlina, la moto, quasi mai la bici elettrica. Lei ci aveva organizzato una cena. Mi piaceva questo cambio di prospettiva inedito.

«Che piacere conoscere qualcuno della città» aveva detto Anne.

«Grazie» avevo detto come se fosse merito mio. «Bello, qui».

«Sì, *un* meraviglia» aveva risposto in italiano. «A parte qualcosa» continuò indicando i cestini della spazzatura per la differenziata. Mi indicò gli altri commensali:

- un produttore musicale che viveva a Berlino
- un giovane artista portoghese col suo agente
- due amiche fashion blogger bielorusse
- una coppia gay che aveva una galleria d'arte nelle Marche
- Anne
- io.

Capii le regole essenziali: le sigarette si spegnevano dentro le valve d'ostrica sparse sul tavolo; era possibile parlare con chiunque senza presentarsi prima – la sola circostanza di trovarci lì doveva garantire per noi; se ti offrivi di andare a rabboccare l'acqua nella brocca, Anne si alzava subito e andava al posto tuo, quindi era meglio tirare su la brocca guardando in direzione di Anne e lei senza troppi indugi sarebbe corsa al piano di sopra, dove c'era la cucina.

La cena iniziò con un gran plateau d'ostriche (ostriche di dove? mi chiesi facendo eco alla domanda di Alice di quella mattina) e proseguì con una tartare di tonno con guacamole di avocado di un produttore locale (lo sanno quanta acqua ci vuole? mi chiesi pensando al Lago di Pergusa che si era appena ridotto a una pozza d'acqua) e una pasta alla siracusana scotta («I don't like chewy chewy pasta», spiegò Anne a tutti, «I prefer pasta like this», e s'innalzò per lei un gran mormorio d'approvazione).

Avevo girato un bel po' di mondo ma i contesti artistici continuavano a farmi sentire fuori luogo; setacciavo

47

sempre la mia conoscenza per dire qualcosa di intelligente, qualcosa che potesse dare a me, donna di scienza, una parvenza creativa o quantomeno interessante. Chi fa arte ha sempre un fare dell'arte, anche quando infilza coi rebbi una patata sbollentata.

Qualche bottiglia più tardi i discorsi si fecero più ampi, la musica, le arti, le direzioni dei nostri tempi. Mi sembrò di respirare un po' di cose del mondo – di sentirmi qui, a casa mia, ma con la «gente giusta». Mi affascinò il caleidoscopio di esperienze dei miei interlocutori e interlocutrici e mi sorprese di avere tanta vita in comune, di poter sostenere così tanti temi di discussione: il microdosing di LSD, l'ennesima band di Thom Yorke, lo specchio Unghia di Castiglioni, le pentole Creuset. Non diverso da certe cene che ho fatto all'estero, mi tradii a pensare.

Era tutto un grande impasto, il mondo? Ma no. E non era manco come diceva Alice; con cui, mi sorprendevo a scoprire ora, avevo meno argomenti di cui parlare che con queste persone, che invece parevano sincere, dirette. Era questa la gente come me. Con Alice non sapevo mai che dire e il mio pomeriggio mi appariva ora per quello che era sempre stato: il suo monologo.

Quando il tema della tavola passò alle migliori spiagge di casa mia tentai più volte di inserirmi ma parlavano di lidi dove non ero mai stata, che avevo solo visto dal retro della sella di Alice, su Instagram o che al limite avevo sentito nominare. Erano troppo cari, e anche quando fossero stati della fascia più economica sarebbero sempre costati troppo per noi, cresciuti col mare gratis.

Sentii poi Anne suggerire alle fashion blogger di andare all'Area Marina Protetta e immaginai subito il tipo di uso che loro ne avrebbero fatto sui social: foto dei loro cappelli di crochet colorati sopra topless turgidi, video del loro stato «naturale» a mangiare una pesca con le mani sbrodolandosi sull'ombelico, riprese a ragazzi abbronzatissimi che si tuffavano a capriola da uno scoglio.

Liquidarono le spiagge in poco, quando un argomento più succoso si affacciò a tavola: i peggiori ristoranti della città (le *tourists' traps*) per poi spostarsi sul *longterm problem* dei «local» e la spazzatura. Nessuno mi interpellava, io non interpellavo loro. Anzi mi interessava proprio ascoltare. D'altra parte, la vita «local» che conoscevo io era solo per sentito dire. Non mi sentivo più local di loro.

«Fanno così» disse Anne indicando teatralmente i cesti per la raccolta differenziata. «Questa merda, al centro del tempio!» aggiunse.

Tacqui. Non capivo se avessero ragione i miei compaesani che usavano i cortili bui e *accupùsi,* senza aria e senza un pezzo di vista solo per stipare la spazzatura, o se erano giusti loro, che apparecchiavano una tavola imperiale a un metro dagli scarafaggi.

Arrivati alla decima bottiglia – Anne stava biasciando in bocca al produttore berlinese – salii in cucina a rimboccare l'acqua dentro la brocca. Non cercai il lavabo: da che ero nata, nella mia città l'acqua non era mai stata potabile e qualcuno non la dava neppure ai cani. Arrivata al piano di sopra mi fermai. Ero stordita io o quel posto era stato rivoltato. La cucina era la spesa

49

vomitata: impasti di pane e burro montato, gambi di coriandolo del supermercato («È del giardino del mio vicino», aveva detto), coltelli sporchi di sangue di tonno, bucce di aglio, piatti rotti a terra e stoviglie della colazione nel lavabo. C'erano confezioni di ogni cosa dappertutto e plastica a ogni passo. La pasta, di una marca economica, era per metà a terra, cotta e appiccicata alle cementine. Un forno era stato stipato con violenza all'angolo della stanza. Ancora dentro la busta del supermercato, due confezioni vuote di mandorle.

«Che casino» commentò l'artista, che era appena uscito dal bagno e si faceva largo calciando la roba a terra per uscire. Lo vidi poi affiancarsi sul tavolo incuriosito, come a scansionarlo.

«Ci verrebbe bene, un quadro» dissi.

Lui sorrise.

Poi si soffermò su una delle confezioni per leggere le informazioni di prodotto. «Ah, mandorle local!» disse ridendo, e uscì dalla porta. «Non so come fate» disse, e uscì dalla porta.

Stavo per rincorrerlo fuori quando mi avvicinai – infastidita di non averci pensato per prima – e lessi l'etichetta.

ORIGINE: CALIFORNIA

Riaffacciandomi dalla scalinata li trovai tutti col naso all'insù. Guardavano nel cielo pesto una macchia luminosa, tondeggiante e irregolare, che si accendeva e si spegneva nascosta da una nebulosa più chiara. Aveva una forma composta: un tondo sopra e una specie di cestello sotto, come la stilizzazione di un teschio. Sarà lo Starlink di Musk, li sentivo dire, Secondo me è una lanterna di quelle che volano, Forse sono gli alieni, faceva eco qualcuno. Era bello godersi quelle illusioni e interpretazioni del paranormale che, pensavo, per secoli dovevano essere state le forme di sopravvivenza minima di intere comunità. La verità è un privilegio dell'età moderna.

Ipotizzai anche una forma di allucinazione collettiva, come credevo di certi episodi di cui avevo sentito parlare: l'isoletta dove gli abitanti erano convinti di aver visto delle sirene in carne e ossa, i miracoli dei santi e delle statue. Scesi le scale con la brocca d'acqua, la posai sul tavolo e mi sistemai al mio posto senza dire nulla.

«Dov'eri?» mi chiese Anne.

«Ho preso l'acqua in cucina».

«L'hai visto?».

«Mh-mh» annuii.

«Era strano, no?».

«Beh» dissi. «Più o meno».

Anne mi guardò interrogativa e con lei il produttore.

«Sòfia, sai qualcosa? Dicci!» disse l'artista con un sorriso.

«Ok» mi incoraggiai col suo sguardo. «Avrete di certo sentito» esordii «dei *gigiànti*» abbassai il tono di voce per assicurarmi di avere l'attenzione di tutti. Solo a quel punto continuai. «È una storia a cui crediamo noi del posto» dissi. «Se volete ve la racconto».

Lukas Kubina
Workation

Gabi ist mit den Fotos nicht zufrieden. Sie taucht mit geschlossenen Augen unter Wasser und behutsam wieder auf, dabei legt sie ihren Kopf in den Nacken. Ihre schwarzen Haare liegen frisch schimmernd über den akzentuierten Schlüsselbeinen und fließen ihr in einem glatten Strom den Rücken hinunter. Sie zieht das nasse Feinrippunterhemd fest nach unten und strafft es wie eine zweite Haut. Dieses Mal achtet sie sorgfältig darauf, dabei nicht die Sicht auf ihren Po in dem schwarzen Bikinihöschen zu verdecken. Jetzt noch einen Träger verschieben, um die Tanline freizulegen. Nach einem prüfenden Blick auf ihre Brüste beginnt sie, der Kameralinse verschiedene Posen anzubieten.

Mike bewundert, wie sie die Außenwelt ausblenden kann. Es ist zwar noch früh morgens, aber auf dem Badegerüst am Diana Felsen ist schon reger Betrieb. Golden Ager absolvieren ihre Morgenroutine und schwimmen in kräftigen Zügen dem Horizont entgegen. Ein muskulöses Männchen mit Glatze macht Gymnastik. Er strotzt seinem Alter und bewegt sich wie ein junger Turner. Ein dünner Spargel campiert neben drei Grazien. Er macht einen Annäherungsversuch und platziert seine Gitarre in ihrem Hoheitsgebiet. Dabei wirkt er so sexy wie ein evangelischer Religionslehrer, der fest daran glaubt, die Herzen beim Singen zu gewinnen.

Danke für diesen guten Morgen. Danke für diesen schönen Tag. Mike summt ein Lied aus der Schulzeit, wie ein Schatten springt der Text von der Wand seines Unterbewusstseins und tanzt durch seinen Kopf.

Danke für diesen guten Morgen. Danke für diesen schönen Tag. Im Rhythmus der Melodie spannt er Trizeps und Bauchmuskulatur an. Während er Gabi fotografiert, kneift er die Arschbacken zusammen, um bei den jungen Italienerinnen einen günstigen Eindruck zu machen.

Unter die Einheimischen mischen sich die Frühaufsteher aus Hotels, Fremdenzimmern und privaten Unterkünften. Er hört Französisch, Deutsch, Spanisch und Russisch. Die Russen hatte er vorhin schon mit bösen Blicken bestraft. Seit der Invasion in die Ukraine stehen sie bei ihm automatisch unter Generalverdacht. Auf der Treppe zum Wasser entwickelt sich ein Stau. Hinter Gabis Hinterteil reihen sich Badende auf, die unterschiedlich zufrieden in den schwachen Wogen treiben, sich an Gottes Natur erfreuen und geduldig darauf warten, dass sie, also Gabi, die Badeleiter freigibt. Einige Herrschaften scheinen zu hoffen, dass der Augenblick verweilt, Mike wird es latent unangenehm. So ungesittet am Strand, das fühlt sich nicht richtig an. In Spanien und Frankreich sind die Frauen oben ohne. In Albanien sind die Strände menschenleer. In Italien ist das wieder anders. Wieso eigentlich? Der Papst? Die Kirche? Die Sexualmoral? An den alten Griechen oder an den Römern kann es nicht liegen, die haben es bunt getrieben. Sei's drum. Andere Länder, andere Sitten. Andere Titten, hatte Ludwig immer gesagt, «Andere Länder, andere Titten». Mike will Gabis Nippelshow beenden und legt sich demonstrativ ins Zeug, Gabi mit einer Bilderflut aus verschiedenen Einstellungen zu befriedigen.

It's a wrap. Er liegt auf dem Rücken und denkt an das römische Reich. Das Wort Solarium lässt ihn träumen. Solche Begriffe leben in Italien einfach fort. Solarium. Er denkt an die Römer, die hier die griechische Kolonie eroberten. An den römischen Legionär, der Archimedes erschlug. »Störe meine Kreise nicht» waren seine letzten Worte. Zu Schulzeiten hat Mike es geliebt, das Zitat auf dem Pausenhof auszupacken. «Störe meine Kreise nicht, Ludwig!» klingt so viel besser als «Geh scheißn, Wiggerl». Seine Gedanken schlingern. Er bräunt sich gerne. Vitamin D. Außerdem steht es ihm einfach besser. Er ist halt ein südländischer Typ. Bleich geht gar nicht, da sieht er aus wie eine Leiche. Im Winter geht er daher ins Solarium nordischer Art, mit künstlicher Bestrahlung, Augenschutz, Lendenschurz und 10 Minuten Taktung. Unter der Sonne Siziliens gefällt es ihm natürlich viel besser. Er denkt an seine Freunde in Wien, die sich gerade durch herbstliches Sauwetter quälen. Er freut sich tierisch. Da hat es ihn besser getroffen. Wer hätte das damals gedacht, nach der Matura? Seine Kameraden sind grau geworden. Je besser der Notenschnitt, desto schwerer hat es sie erwischt. Sie quälen sich durch ihre Berufe in Kanzleien, Grossraumbüros und Kreativstudios. Sie haben Kinder, Autos, Häuser und keinen aufregenden Sex mehr. Sie sind alt geworden. Er ist jung geblieben. Sein Undercut ist frisch rasiert, seine ironischen Tattoos vermehren sich, seine Haut ist gut geölt und vergilbt nicht.

Neben ihm wird Gabi unruhig. Sie fängt an, ihre Sachen zusammenzulegen und in ihrem Strandbeutel zu verstauen. Mike würde lieber ausgiebig schwimmen gehen, aber er weiss, dass da nichts zu machen ist. Er dreht ihr noch eine Zigarette an, um sich ein bisschen Zeit zu erkaufen. Aber nur die eine, sagt sie. Mit angezogenen Beinen kaut sie Kaugummi und raucht gleichzeitig. Schwermütig blickt er auf das Meer. Die steigende Sonne lässt es glitzern. Er spürt eine Verbindung mit den Zeiten. So schön die Pausen auch sein mögen, Gabi hat ja recht. Sie sind hier zum Arbeiten. *Workation.*

In der Mittagspause gehen sie zum Markt. Schnell treiben sie in einem Touristenstrom, der aus dem Nichts entspringt und sie mitreißt. Gerade waren sie noch am Apollon Tempel und haben sich die alten Steine angeschaut, jetzt sind sie Teil einer Herde, die sich selbst durch den Markt schleust. Nicht jeder Stand in der Ladenzeile ist offen, aber drei Marktschreier genügen, um sagenhaften Lärm und Betriebsamkeit zu entfachen. Weil Gabi und Mike einen produktiven Vormittag verbracht haben, lassen sie sich Zeit. Sie halten bei einem Händler, der seine nordatlantischen Austern mit Diego Maradona bewirbt und für jede Bestellung einen Plastikbecher Hauswein verspricht. Gabi und Mike sind sich einig: *Work hard, play hard.* Nach zwei Runden Austern erwähnt Gabi, dass sie heute sonst noch nichts gegessen hatte. Mit dem Wein wird es Mike zunehmend egal, dass er keine italienische Grammatik beherrscht, dass er im Grunde genommen keine zwanzig Worte Italienisch kann. Auf Italo-Spanisch redet er fröhlich auf den Händler und seinen Standnachbarn ein, einen Zwerg, der mit Heilkräutern handelt und einen Dialekt spricht, den außerhalb seines Bergdorfs sowieso niemand versteht. Gabi entschuldigt sich und übergibt sich ein paar Schritte weiter in einer schmalen Seitengasse. Sie wischt sich den Mund mit einer Serviette ab, nimmt einen Schluck Wasser aus der Plastikflasche und kehrt zu den neuen Freunden zurück, als Mike eine dritte Runde Wein mit einer symbolischen Auster bestellen will. Gerade rechtzeitig berichtet sie ihm, was ihr gerade passiert ist und dass sie jetzt gerne den Aperitivo abschließen würde, es sei jetzt an der Zeit, im Lokal eine schöne Flasche Weisswein zu bestellen. Aufreizend flüstert sie: Einen Grillo. Eiskalt. Mike findet den Vorschlag ganz großartig. Gabi mag zwar eine zierliche Mädchenfrau sein, aber hart im Nehmen ist sie. Das gefällt ihm. Sie lassen sich auf einer Terrasse auf der Marktgasse nieder. Zum Grillo bestellen sie ein Fritto Misto und eine Carbonara di Mare. Interessiert beobachten sie das Treiben: «C'est très touristique», sagen Franzosen, «Do you have fish?» fragen Amerikaner den Kellner, der zwischen Fischauslage und Frutti di Mare Dekoration steht. Untereinander unterhalten sie sich ausufernd über ihre «Gelato» Erfahrung. Die Deutschen schweigen, um nicht als Touristen aufzufallen. Sie spielen Italiener, die Rolle ihres Lebens, und glauben dabei, sie fallen nicht auf.

Dann teilt sich das Meer und ein Kreuzfahrtschiffkapitän tritt auf die Bühne. «Capitano Schettino auf Freigang», scherzt Mike. Der Herr der Meere stolziert in seiner schneeweißen Galauniform umher und versucht den Mädchen schöne Augen zu machen. Auch Gabi steuert er an, die seine Blicke nicht nur erwidert, sie fixiert ihn geradezu, leckt mit ihrer Zungenspitze über ihre Oberlippe und überschlägt die Beine so langsam, dass er ihr Höschen mehrere Semester studieren könnte. Nervös dreht Schettino ab. Mike und Gabi lachen herzlich und bestellen sich jeweils noch ein Glas 0,2l. Weil es halt so schön ist.

Das Bourbonische Gefängnis liegt verlassen neben dem Markt am Rande von Graziela, dem ehemaligen Fischerviertel, wo die Kleinkriminellen in Ruhestand gegangen sind und Leute aus dem Norden ein Häuschen erworben haben und nun ihrerseits im Rentenalter den Süden gentrifizieren. Die Lage und die Dimensionen des freistehenden Objekts sind spektakulär. Der Grundriss ist ein Rechteck mit einer Seitenlänge von vierzig mal fünfundvierzig Metern. Die dreistöckige Ruine erreicht eine Höhe von fünfundzwanzig Metern. Es wurde 1854 fertiggestellt und war zeitweise eines der modernsten und fortschrittlichsten Gefängnisse in Europa, bis es das Erdbeben Santa Lucia 1990 aus dem Dienst beförderte. Die Einheimischen nennen es Casa cu n'occhiu («Haus mit einem Auge»), da es nach den Prinzipien des britischen Philosophen Jeremy Benthams geplant wurde. Eine polygonale Struktur mit einem Wachturm in der Mitte ermöglichte dem Aufseher ständige Kontrolle, ohne dass die Insassen bemerkten, dass sie beobachtet wurden.

Mike braucht keine Fantasie, um das Potential zu erkennen. Weißwein zum Mittagessen und ein geschulter Blick in die unmittelbare Nachbarschaft genügen: Es sind nur wenige Meter vom Markt. Die Yachten der Gäste könnten gleich dahinter im Hafen anlegen. In der Ferne reihen sich die Basilica Santuario Madonna delle Lacrime und der Etna am Horizont vor der Bucht auf. Den makellosen Meerblick stört nur die Parkgarage, mit einer Begrünung könnte man das Problem aber ästhetisch lösen und sich zudem ein ökologisches Image verschaffen. Vielleicht sogar eine Sehenswürdigkeit schaffen und einen Kakteenpark platzieren, der die Anlagen auf Ischia oder Lanzarote alt aussehen lässt? Mit den richtigen Mitteln sollte es auch möglich sein, einen Beach Club am Dock zu installieren. Dort könnten die Gäste direkt mit ihren Beibooten ankommen. Und durch einen Tunnel in das Hotel gelangen, abgeschirmt von der Außenwelt. Hollywood will nicht gesehen werden. Hotel Pannottico. A Luxury Resort. Mikes Begeisterung kennt keine Grenzen.

Erst als sie durch ein Loch im rostigen Stahlzaun klettern, bemerken Mike und Gabi die beiden französischen Geschäftsmänner, die sich auch Zutritt zu dem Areal verschafft haben und sich angeregt, von Geldströmen und Reichtümern halluzinierend, unterhalten. Sie sind sicher nicht die ersten Immobilienentwickler, die die Beute wittern und hier herum delirieren. In ihren gut betuchten Anzügen und den schön gescheitelten, geföhnten Frisuren wirken sie wie Boten aus einer anderen Welt.

Grußlos und entschlossen geht Mike an den beiden Haifischen vorbei zum Haupttor. Gabi wiegt kurz ihre Hüften für die Frenchies, dann beginnt sie vorsichtig über Scherben und Schutt zu tippeln und Mike zu folgen. Er ist ungewöhnlich unruhig. Eigentlich mag er Lost Places und den speziellen Nervenkitzel, der sich dort einstellt. Der Location Check im leerstehenden Gefängnis lässt ihn schaudern. Was für Verbrechen die Insassen wohl begangen haben? Was diese Wände eingesperrt haben, um die Gesellschaft zu schützen? Wer sonst geht durch das Tor, ein und aus, seitdem es ausgehängt ist und offen steht? Mit tiefen Atemzügen kann er die Ohnmacht überwinden und zwängt sich durch den offenen Türspalt ins Innere. Im gedämpften Licht tappt er einige Meter in das Gebäude, bevor er an einer Stelle stehen bleibt, von der Durchbrüche in Räume führen, die wiederum in andere Räume führen, die in andere Räume führen. Er macht seine Telefontaschenlampe an und mustert die unübersichtliche Lage. Vor ihm führt der Flur wahrscheinlich zum Treppenhaus. Links fühlt sich besser an. Wegen des direkten Tageslichteinfalls wirkt es weniger unheimlich. Er klettert über Müll und Geröll in den ersten Raum. Am Boden sind Spuren eines Lagerfeuers. Leere Konserven und Bierflaschen sind in einer Ecke verteilt. An der Wand entdeckt er ein Graffito: «SEMBRA CHE HO IL CA**O LUNGO 1m». Daneben illustriert ein Riesenschwanz den Spruch. Mike muss schmunzeln. Für diesen Hinweis reicht sein Italienisch.

Geräusche lassen ihn aufschrecken. Hinter ihm ist jemand. Ruckhaft fährt er um sich und sieht, wie

Gabi sich in den Raum tastet. Erleichtert atmet er auf. Ach, du bist es. Für Location-Checks solltest Du vielleicht besser keine Stöckelschuhe tragen. Schau Dir das Graffito an, da steht «Es scheint, dass ich einen meterlangen Schwanz habe.» Auch das Tageslicht ist super hier. Er lacht. Da könnte man schon was machen, oder? Gabi nickt passiv. Sie teilt seine Leidenschaft für Ruinen Begehungen nicht, folgt ihm aber, schließlich sind sie ein Team und der Erfolg spricht für sich. Dort, wo er hofft, etwas zu entdecken, fürchtet sie sich aber insgeheim davor, etwas zu entdecken.

Und dann hören sie Geräusche. Woher sie kommen, können sie nicht feststellen. Verstört schauen sie in alle Richtungen. Dabei sehen sie aus wie zwei Rehe im Scheinwerferlicht eines Autos, das sie im nächsten Augenblick überfahren wird. Fallen im 1. Stock Katzen fauchend übereinander her, sind es Seufzer aus der Vergangenheit, oder ist es nur die Meeresbrise, die die Ruine klappern lässt? Will man die Ursache überhaupt kennen? Raus hier, flüstert Gabi. Ja genug, wir sind fertig hier, lass uns Kaffee trinken gehen. Mike versucht lässig zu bleiben, dabei hat er Angst vor seinem eigenen Schatten.

After Work. Mike und Gabi machen einen Bootsexkursion. Ihre Kollegin Rosa hat empfohlen, mit einem umgerüsteten Fischerboot einen Ausflug an die Küste der Isola di Siracusa zu machen. Sie treffen sich am Hafen. Rosa sieht großartig aus, ihre dicken, braunen Locken springen in Spiralen in alle Himmelsrichtungen, in der Mitte ihr fröhliches Gesicht mit den smaragdgrünen Augen. Ihr Badeanzug hat einen tiefen Rückenausschnitt und legt ein schönes Muster Muttermale frei, darüber trägt sie eine knappe Jeansshort. Mike kann ihr partout nicht zustimmen, nein, ihre Zwillinge haben diesen Körper nicht zerstört. Gemeinsam gehen sie an Bord. Rosa hat sie auf die Gästeliste gesetzt, also können sie ohne Fahrschein passieren. Sie steigen mit einer Leiter auf Deck und suchen sich einen Platz. Gabi legt sich in eine Hängematte, die parallel zur Reling gespannt ist. Rosa und Mike sitzen auf bunten Campingstühlen. Gemeinsam bilden sie einen geschlossenen Kreis. Das Boot legt ab.

Im Seegang baumelt Gabi metronomisch in der Hängematte. Die Sonnenbrille steht ihr schief im Gesicht und sie wirkt etwas zerzaust. Sie erklärt Rosa, dass sich das ja schon beinahe wie die Black Mamba anfühlt, ein Fahrgeschäft auf dem Prater, und schlägt vor, besser eine Flasche Weisswein zu bestellen, so sei das ja nicht auszuhalten. Mike geht unter Deck, um den Wein, drei Plastikgläser und einen Kühler zu holen. Auf dem Weg mustert er die restlichen Passagiere. Zwei Familien haben ein größeres Camp errichtet. Die beiden Buben daddeln am Smartphone. Die Eltern unterhalten sich laut und leider auf Deutsch. In Berlin sind Herbstferien. Investment Talk. Um das zu unterstreichen, trägt eine Frau sogar ein BITCOIN T-Shirt. Starkes Statement, denkt sich Mike. Und fragt sich, ob wohl ihre Kinder ihren Körper auf dem Gewissen haben oder sie schon immer ein Nilpferd war? Bodyshaming. Mike schämt sich. Manche

Dinge erträgt er einfach nicht und fährt aus seiner Haut. Nicht okay. Kinderlärm ist so ein Trigger. Oder Unordnung. Offene Schranktüren, der falsche Tisch im richtigen Restaurant oder dieses lässige Genie der BITCOIN Bros. Die Kryptokumpels spüren seine Feindseligkeit nicht und rufen sich ungehemmt weitere Buzzwords zu während sie Flaschenbier trinken.

Neben ihnen schläft ein Typ in einer Hängematte. Mike beneidet seine Gelassenheit und nimmt sich vor, sich eine Scheibe abzuschneiden. Während er den Wein einschenkt, kommt er aus seinen Gedanken zurück und versucht sich aus den Bruchstücken ihres Gesprächs einen Reim zu machen. Rosa erklärt: Wer laufen konnte, hat Sizilien verlassen. Zurück bleiben nur die, die nicht fliehen konnten. Oder die in die Unterwelt fliehen. Selbst die Nymphe Arethusa hat dort, durch ihren unterirdischen Flussverlauf, weitreichende Verbindungen. Gabi lacht etwas zu laut. Mike merkt, dass sie auch keinen Schimmer hat, was das mit Nymphen zu tun hat. Rosa fährt fort, dass leider auch nur diejenigen hinzukommen und sich hier ansiedeln, die aus guten Gründen vor ihrer Heimat fliehen und den brain drain mit ihren zweifelhaften Biographien schwer auffangen können. Sobald sie also laufen kann, sobald ihre zwölfjährigen Zwillinge volljährig sind, wird auch sie weg sein. Das hat sie sich geschworen. Sie würde am liebsten nach New York. Aber auch Wien interessiert sie, ob es denn stimmt, dass dort die Lebensqualität so hoch sei, jedes Jahr wieder liest sie in der Zeitung diese Liste der lebenswertesten Städte und fragt sich, was das bedeuten mag.

Mike verteilt die Gläser. Erst jetzt bemerkt Rosa ihn, unter der kubistischen Sonnenbrille erröten ihre Wangen. Sie besinnt sich darauf, Berufliches von Privatem zu trennen und lenkt das Gespräch zum Immobilienmarkt und seinen lokalen Eigenheiten. Dafür zeigt sie auf die Küstenlinie von Isola, an der sie, weniger als vierhundert Metern entfernt, entlang schippern. Seht her, genau genommen ist es ein Naturschutzgebiet. Bebaut ist es ja offensichtlich trotzdem. Wie man gut sehen kann. Aus der Vogelperspektive, vom Land und vom Wasser. Noch besser: Ohne Auflagen! Keine Einschränkungen. Illegal, scheiß egal. Ihr solltet Euch die verlassene Ferienanlage am Punta della Mola ansehen. Diese Ruinen warten auf eine Inszenierung. Sie zwinkert den beiden zu. Seht ihr den Pool da? Mike und Gabi folgen ihrem Zeigefinger mit den Augen: An einer Klippe hängt das Kopfende eines Schwimmbeckens. Die Kante ist unter der Last eingeknickt, ein Teil des Pools ist mit ihr abgebrochen und abgestürzt. Hinter dem ausgetrockneten, zerbrochenen Becken krallt sich die Villa auf dem Felsen fest und verteidigt Träume mit Meerblick. So sieht ein *Infinity Pool* aus, wenn man den richtigen Fixer kennt. Das sollte das Symbol Siziliens sein, das auf die Flagge gehört. Nicht diese dreibeinige Gestalt, aus deren Vagina ein Kopf rausschaut.

Sie ankern vor der Küste und hängen die Badeleiter ins Wasser. Als Mike auf die Planke geht, hat er noch immer das Wort Vagina in seinen Ohren, genau so wie es Rosa mit ihrem breiten, italienischen

Akzent auf Englisch über die Lippen kam. Vagina. Er federt im Seegang auf und ab. Vagina. Am höchsten Punkt springt er ab und setzt einen makellosen Köpfer an. Splash. Vagina. Wieder an Deck holt er die zweite Flasche Wein. Auf Deck legt ein DJ Italo-Disco und Ibiza-House auf. Die BITCOIN Bros und Schwestern tanzen losgelöst. Als Donatella Milani's Ci Stai angespielt wird, zieht Rosa Mike aus der Hängematte, um Gabi und ihr zu folgen. Barfuß und in nassen Badesachen kreisen sie tanzend um sich. Rosa erwischt Mike, wie er sie beobachtet, mit softer Begier. Sie lächelt ihn an, dann dreht sie sich weiter und schreit den Refrain über das ionische Meer in den Nahen Osten. Der DJ liest die Signale. Als nächstes erklingt eine Rihanna Hymne, Rosa und Gabi explodieren gleichzeitig. Sie liegen sich in den Armen und schmettern: *'Cause I didn't mean to hurt him / Coulda been somebody's son / And I took his heart when I pulled out that gun / Rum-pum-pum-pum / Rum-pum-pum-pum / Rum-pum-pum-pum / Man down*

Mikes Seele ist in Schwingung. Damit angefangen hat sie, als sie in der Abenddämmerung nach Ortigia zurückgekehrt sind. Vor der Hafeneinfahrt lag ein Boot der zivilen Seerettung mit spanischer Flagge. Unweit von zwei italienische Fregatten. Im Westen ging die rote Sonne über Isola unter, im Osten flog ein Schwarm Stare fantastische Formationen über der Arethusa Quelle. An der Promenade standen Paare. Ineinander verschlungen blickten sie auf den Sonnenuntergang oder fotografierten sich gegenseitig.

Wenig später liegt das Boot im Hafen vertäut. Rosa hat sich mit einem flüchtigen Kuss auf die Wangen von Gabi und Mike verabschiedet und ist mit ihrem Scooter losgeknattert. In dem Tempo wird sie eine Weile brauchen, um über die Landstrasse nach Agusta zu gelangen, um bei ihren Eltern das Abendessen und Ratschläge fürs Leben zu bekommen, die Zwillinge mit nach Hause zu nehmen und ins Bett zu stecken. Mike und Gabi sitzen vor einer Bar an der Arethusa Quelle und glotzen in das Lichtspiel, das die rote Sonne in der Abenddämmerung hinterließ. Wieder ein Tag weniger auf der Erde. Gerade hatte er die Nachricht erhalten, dass sein bester Freund Vater wurde. Baby geht's gut. Frau geht's gut. Alles gut. Schon wieder verpasst Mike etwas Monumentales, weil er auf Dienstreise ist. Ein afrikanischer Straßenhändler spürt sein plötzliches Unglück und macht das, was ihm das Leben gelehrt hat, er macht das Beste draus und macht geschäftliche Avancen: Diese Powerbank porta fortuna! Echt, die Powerbank bringt Glück? Aber ja, doch! Lachend gibt Mike ihm einen Euro. Der Afrikaner grinst ihn breit an und zieht weiter..

Vor ihnen hält eine zur Rikscha umgerüstete Ape. Auf der Rückbank sitzen zwei amerikanische Senioren in amerikanischen Seniorenuniformen: Er trägt dieses Granddaddy Nike Modell, Bermudas und ein weites Polohemd. Sie eine kurze Legging, ON Turnschuhe, ein Trägershirt und eine Schirmmütze, die ihren Fahrer wie einen Golf Caddy aussehen lassen würde, wenn er nicht so vor Sprezzatura strotzen würde. Mit der Sonnenbrille in den zurückgegelten

Haaren beugt er sich über sein Telefon und spricht lange Italienisch darauf ein. Als er fertig ist, dreht er sich zu seinen Passagieren auf der Rückbank und lässt die englische Übersetzung abspielen: *Arethusa war einst eine wunderschöne Nymphe, die sich gerne der Jagd und dem Sport hingab. An einem heißen, sonnigen Tag stieg sie in den Fluss Alpheios, um darin zu baden. Dabei wurde sie vom gleichnamigen Flussgott überrascht und bedrängt. Auf ihrer Flucht konnte Arethusa die Göttin Artemis um Hilfe bitten. Artemis verwandelte die verzweifelte Nymphe in eine Quelle, deren Bächlein unter der Peloponnes und unter dem Meer hindurchfloss und auf der Halbinsel Ortygia, einem Teil von Syrakus, wieder austrat.* Die weibliche Maschinenstimme wurde von einem Anruf unterbrochen, den der Fremdenführer auf Lautsprecher entgegen nimmt. «Pronto!» Er dreht das Zündschloss und tuckert, einhändig lenkend, einhändig telefonierend, mit seinen Touristen ab. Auf dem Heck der Ape ist eine Werbetafel montiert: Ortigia Ape Experience. Touren in allen Sprachen!

Gabi war müde und ist schon allein ins Apartment gewankt. Nach dem Saufen in der Sonne hat sie der Campari Soda paniert und sie bekam die Bootsfahrt nicht mehr aus den Beinen. Anders Mike, der jetzt voll in Fahrt ist, wie in einer Schiffschaukel überschlägt sich seine Freude. Niemand kann diese Kräfte bremsen, sie müssen sich auspendeln oder abstürzen. Seine Prozession führt ihn zu einem Lebensmittelladen bei der Cala Rossa, der am Lungomare drei Tische aufgestellt hat und dort abends kaltes Bier in Flaschen verkauft. Der Sohn der Besitzerin grüßt den hungrigen Wolf wie einen alten Freund und stellt ihm eine große Flasche Moretti hin. Mopeds und Fußgänger machen den Corso, wirklich jeder Einheimische grüßt den Händler, er antwortet mit Handzeichen, es ist ihm sichtlich unangenehm. Dorfdepp? Maskottchen? Mit mildem Blick und Achselzucken scheint er Mike's Gedanken zu kommentieren. Das Bier ist eine herrliche Erfrischung, Mike nimmt zwei tiefe Schlücke und ist wiederhergestellt.

Neben ihm sitzt ein Spanier von der Seerettung. Der Print auf der Brust seines Achselshirts stellt klar, dass es sich um einen echten Antifaschisten handelt. Ein antifaschistischer Matrose also, der gerade versucht, bei zwei jungen Amerikanerinnen einen Stich zu machen, indem er ihnen erklärt, wie man den Nahostkonflikt lösen kann. Um mit einem Ohr zu lauschen, muss Mike nur leise trinken. Was er da zu hören bekommt, überrascht ihn wenig: Postkolonialer Freiheitskampf. Israelischer Genozid. Westliche Unterdrückung. Palästinensische Opfer. Unterkomplexe Zusammenhänge und inkohärente Argumentation. Na ja, denkt sich Mike, dieser Manolo ist halt nicht die hellste Leuchte. Komisch, eigentlich verträgt er keine dummdreisten, antisemitischen Aktivisten. Erst neulich musste er in Wien seine Dealerin canceln, weil sie auf Instagram ständig würdelose Lügen und kränke Hetze verbreitet hat. Schweren Herzens, das schon, aber Anstand und Moral waren ihm wichtiger als Kokain und Ecstasy. Mit Manolo verhält es sich anders: Mike ist ein wenig eifersüchtig. Menschen vor dem Ertrinken retten. Humanismus gegen globale Ungerechtigkeit. Das macht Sinn. Manolos Leben hat einen Zweck. Sein Beruf ist seine Berufung. Manolo muss keinen Ablass betreiben, keine Spenden tätigen, keine Almosen verteilen. Manolo schläft auch so gut.

Mike hat enorme Kopfschmerzen. Sein Schädel steht unter Hochdruck. Er braucht einen Augenblick, das Zimmer zu erkennen, in dem er gerade aufwacht und sich bemüht, die Augen offen zu halten. Wie kam er nach Hause? Warum liegt er in einem nassen Bett? Sein Körper brennt. Er entdeckt Schürfwunden am rechten Unterarm, einen blauen Fleck am Oberschenkel und angeschwollene Kratzer am Knöchel. Seine Haut ist salzig. Mit diesen Indizien kommen die Erinnerungsfetzen zögerlich an die Oberfläche. Er war im Mondlicht schwimmen. Er war eins mit dem Meer. Es drang in ihn ein. Sein Rauschen drang in ihn ein. Schwerelos. Sorgenfrei. Mit jedem Tauchgang wollte er länger unter Wasser bleiben. Er drang in das Meer ein. Sein Rausch drang in das Meer ein. Als er am Ende aus dem Wasser steigen wollte, warf ihn der Seegang gegen die Wellenbrecher. Oder der Rausch. Er hatte den Aufprall kaum gespürt.

Nachricht von Gabi: *Wo bleibst du, Hase? Heute letzter Tag. Raus aus dem Bett!* Mike schlurft in die Küche. Er macht Kaffee und schluckt eine 800mg Ibuprofen mit einem Glas heißen, abgekochten Wasser. Gestern war geil, heute fühlt sich Mike wie in einer leeren Badewanne, aus der gerade das Wasser abgeflossen ist. Unbehagen. Er startet seine Morgenroutine:

Frühstück – Proteinshake für den Body – Liegestützen und Sit-Ups – Typ Käfigkämpfer – und dann packt er die Badesachen ein, um zur Plattform am Felsen aufzubrechen. Blitzartig erinnert er sich an die Spanier. Er packt seine Badesachen, um im Meer zu schwimmen, in dem Menschen ertrinken. Was für Spaßbremsen. Er wirft die Badetasche über die Schulter und öffnet die Tür. Eine diffuse Ahnung hält ihn zurück und lässt ihn kehrtmachen. Mike klappt hastig seinen Laptop auf. Wo sind die Dateien? Schlagartig friert es ihn. Das erste Mal in Sizilien. WO sind die Dateien? Der Ordner ist leer. Okay. Mike versucht, nicht panisch zu werden. Er holt die Speicherkarte und stochert sie in den Eingang. Kalter Schweiß auf der Stirn. Shit, auch der Speicher ist leer. Natürlich ist er leer, er hat ihn gestern selbst gelöscht. Als er aufspringt, um seinen Kopf gegen die Wand zu schlagen, rutscht ihm die Badetasche vom Arm. Er knallt seinen Kopf frontal gegen die Fliesen. Einmal. Zweimal. Dreimal. FUCK. Obwohl der Schmerz ihm Linderung bringt, hört er auf, bevor seine Stirn aufplatzt. Stattdessen schmeißt er einen Stuhl durch die Wohnung und räumt die Plastikdecke in einem Zug vom Tisch ab. Der Laptop fliegt auf den Boden. Unbeirrt reißt er ein kleines Ölgemälde (ein naives Stillleben) von der Wand, um es an die Wand gegenüber zu schleudern.

FUCK. Was für ein Fiasko. Die Arbeit von fünf Tagen: Verloren. Volle fünf Tage Produktion: Futsch. 10.000 Euro: Pulverisiert. FUCK FUCK FUCK. Bebend holt er sich einen Beutel Eis aus dem Eisfach, um seine Stirn zu kühlen. Mühsam beruhigt er sich. Er zwingt sich, vorwärts zu denken. Was bleibt ihm auch anderes übrig. Er muss den Flug umbuchen und das Airbnb verlängern. Sofern es nicht schon vermietet ist. Und er muss wieder ran: 8 Stunden Sex mindestens. Ob Rosa überhaupt Zeit hat, nochmal den Dreier zu drehen? Sie muss sich doch unter der Woche um ihre Zwillinge kümmern. Ok, zur Not kann sie sie mitbringen und sie sollen im Nebenzimmer spielen. Wichtiger ist, dass sie ihnen eine Rabatt gibt oder es am Besten umsonst macht. Das Budget reicht nicht mehr. Niemals. Cazzo. Sein Schwanz hat sich gerade erholt. Schon beim Gedanken zu ficken, zieht es ihm die Hoden zusammen. Unbezahlte Überstunden tun weh.

Giovanni Fiderio
Il Vecchio n.2

Il Vecchio entra in libreria con l'indice puntato verso gli espositori di cartoline.

«C'è un monolite simile a questo qui dell'Argimusco e si trova a Monte Lauro» mi dice prendendo e scrutando una delle nostre cartoline «Si tratta di una roccia che risale a molto tempo prima rispetto alla formazione dell'Etna.»

«Interessante» rispondo.

«Milioni di anni prima. E' questo il punto interessante, capisci?»

«Credo di si»

«Noi non siamo in grado di immaginare una dimensione di tempo così grande, non siamo abituati a concepire una cosa del genere.»

«Ok.»

«Fra l'altro sull'Argimusco ci sono diverse formazioni di quel tipo mentre a Monte Lauro ce n'è soltanto una.»

«Non lo sapevo.»

«Figuriamoci, non lo sa nessuno. Per questo sono venuto. Credo che quel luogo sia interessante da vedere per la fotografa.»

«Certo, dobbiamo andare a scovarlo.»

«Allora mi fai il favore di dirglielo, riportale il mio messaggio.»

«Non mancherò di farlo. Lei invece ricordi che la fotografa vorrebbe farle un ritratto.»

«Ma neanche per sogno. Gliel'ho già detto che non voglio essere fotografato. E poi, perchè? Non c'è alcun motivo per cui io debba essere fotografato. A cosa servirebbe?»

«Chi può dirlo, non ho mai capito come o perchè decide di fotografare qualcuno. Suppongo ci sia qualcosa che la affascina.» accenna un sorriso «E poi, insomma, sembra che lei abbia vissuto alla grande, tutte queste storie che racconta ci aprono scenari della memoria e dei luoghi.» «Infatti prima o poi bisogna che mi paghiate per tutte queste informazioni.»

Ci lanciamo reciprocamente un'occhiata scherzosa, poi cambio discorso:

«Dov'è stato ultimamente? Era da un pezzo che non veniva a trovarci, ha forse fatto un viaggio»?

«No. Mia moglie è stata male. Anche io sono stato male. Ma adesso è passato tutto.»

«Mi dispiace.»

Rimaniamo un attimo in silenzio sull'uscio della libreria a guardare le auto in fila su corso Umberto I. Penso non sia il caso di approfondire l'argomento, lui non parla mai volentieri dei suoi acciacchi.

Decido di deviare ironicamente sulla politica:

«Siete stati male per via delle elezioni, non è vero? Anche noi non l'abbiamo presa bene.»

«Ma che dici? Si sapeva che sarebbe andata così già mesi prima dell'inizio della campagna elettorale. Potevo mettertelo per iscritto che sarebbe finita in quel modo.»

«Veggente! Sapeva anche che la destra avrebbe vinto nel resto d'Italia?»

«Certamente! E ti dico pure che va bene così, in fin dei conti sì, hanno vinto» fa roteare la mano con sufficienza «ma di quanto hanno vinto? Di centinaia, forse migliaia di voti. Non milioni.»

«Ma non va bene comunque.»

«Invece si, devono governare, devono amministrare, devono spendere tutti i soldi proprio come hanno promesso. Va bene perchè questo è l'inizio della loro fine.»

Annabelle Hirsch
Die Tränen

Es begann mit einem vorsichtigen Fiepen. Wie das eines Hund, den man ausgesperrt hat. Ein langes Quietschen, angehaltene Luft, ruckelnde Seufzer, ein vorsichtig rausgedrückter Ton. Ich saß in meiner Wohnung, in der kleinen Kammer, die auf unseren winzigen Innenhof zeigte und versuchte zu schreiben. Über die weinende Madonna von Syrakus. Das Tränen vergießende Marienbild, das die Stadt im Sommer 1953 für einige Wochen zum Zentrum des Glaubens gemacht hatte.

Es war der 29. August jenes Jahres, Antonina Iannuso erwachte an diesem Morgen aus einer entsetzlichen Nacht. Ihre ohnehin schwer verlaufende Schwangerschaft hatte sie gegen drei Uhr morgens erblinden lassen, als sie die Augen nun wieder öffnete, stellte sie mit Freude fest, dass sie wieder sah. Nur war das, was sie sah ungewöhnlich: Die Gipsmadonna über ihrem Bett weinte. Ihre Tränen tropften kontinuierlich auf das Bett herunter, das Kopfkissen war schon ganz feucht. In Syrakus, in den Straßen rund um den Hafen, den Apollo-Tempel, am Markt, unter den Schiffsbauern und Fischern, sprach sich die Sache schnell herum. Binnen weniger Stunden versammelten sich hunderte Menschen vor dem Haus der Via Degli Orti, in den folgenden Tagen reisten Kranke und Leidende aus ganz Italien an. Sie beteten zur weinenden Madonna, streckten Taschentücher in ihre Richtung, um sie mit ihren Tränen zu befeuchten, hofften, diese könnten Schmerz lindern und harte Schicksalsschläge verjagen. Irgendwann mischte sich die Kirche ein. Dann auch die Wissenschaft. Man schickte eine Probe der Tränen ins Labor, verglich sie mit der eines Menschen und stellte mit Erstaunen fest: Sie waren identisch. Es war, so sagte man, ein Wunder.

Eine französische Zeitschrift hat mich beauftragt, dieser Geschichte zu ihrem siebzigjährigen Jubiläum noch einmal nachzugehen. Ich sollte Leute treffen, die damals dort gewesen waren. Seit zehn Tagen streifte ich auf der Suche nach Zeitzeugen gemeinsam mit Lucio, meinem Fotografen, durch die verwinkelten Gassen des ehemaligen Fischerviertels Graziella und die Strassen rund um das Sanctuario della Madonna delle Lacrime, unweit des ursprünglichen Geschehens. Wir haben mit dem Priester gesprochen, der diese gigantische Träne aus Beton, die man Ende der Sechziger Jahre über einem ehemaligen Demeter Tempel zu Ehren der Madonna erbaut hatte, haben ältere Damen und ältere Herren besucht, die dem «Wunder» als Kinder beigewohnt hatten. Wir haben in dunklen Küchen gesessen und in Innenhöfen in denen Kinder und Katzen um die Wette jaulten, waren mit vielen Espressi versorgt, mit Mandel-Keksen und dem ein oder anderen Arancino gefüttert worden und haben fast immer die selben Worte gehört: «Die Madonna hat vier Tage lang geweint. Ihre Tränen waren echt. Es waren Tränen des Mitleids. Tränen der Liebe.» Einige erzählten, sie hätten selbst geweint und sich dafür geschämt, andere fühlten sich von dem Erlebnis bis heute beseelt. Wieder andere, wie Niccolo, ein alter Herr, den wir am Vortag in seinem Zeitungskiosk aufgesucht hatten, fand das ganze schlicht unheimlich. Er war zehn, als die Madonna anfing zu weinen, seine

Mutter hatte ihn zu dem Spektakel mitgeschleppt. In seiner Erinnerung blieben zwei Gefühle stark: Angst und Verwirrung. Ich war gerade dabei, die Notizen zu unserem Treffen zu transkribieren, tippte «mi ha fatto paura, mi fa sempre paura» in meinen Laptop als das Winseln im Haus erklang.

Anfangs habe ich mich nicht gewundert. Ich kannte die meisten meiner Nachbarn nur als Geruch oder als Klang und war es dadurch gewohnt, sie auf eine intimere Weise zu erleben, als es in einer frontalen Begegnung je möglich wäre. Dass gegenüber von mir jemand lebte, ahnte ich zum Beispiel nur, weil immer Morgens, ganz früh, eine Zigarillo-Schwade zu mir rüber weht. Ansonsten sah die Wohnung zu jeder Tages- und Nachtzeit aus, wie so viele auf der Via Nizza, verstaubt und verlassen. Von der Familie im Erdgeschoss wiederum wusste ich durch die Nelken, Kardamom und Kümmel Wolke, die gegen ein Uhr morgens aufstieg, dass sie späte Arbeitszeiten und ein Faible für orientalische Eintöpfe hatten, die Leute über mir erlebte ich meist nur als Sound. Den einen, weil er seiner Tochter jeden zweiten Tag aufs Neue erklären musste, er könne wirklich nicht Zuhause bleiben, er müsse in die Akademie, unterrichten, den anderen wegen seines Schnarchens. Es war ein Schnarchen, so laut, dass das gesamte Haus bebte und die Wände wackelten, die Eruption des Etna, sie fand täglich über unseren Köpfen statt. Die einzige Person, deren Gesicht und Namen ich kannte war Benedetta. Ihre Wohnung lag im Erdgeschoss, direkt unter meiner. Sie war eine freundliche aber wenig gesprächige Dame. Wenn ich Morgens zu meinem Schwimmtreffen mit Lucio, unserem Termin am Felsen, immer um Punkt acht, aufbrach oder Nachmittags von Interviews nach Hause kam, sah ich sie oft in ihrer Küche sitzen und rauchen. Wir grüßten uns, «Buongiorno», «Buonasera», manchmal, wenn es wieder einmal regnete, raunten wir ein «che brutto tempo» und zuckten mit den Schultern wie um zu sagen, was soll's. Ansonsten wusste ich nichts über sie, nichts über ihr Leben. Bis jetzt. Nun wusste ich, dass sie Kummer hat. Das Weinen kam eindeutig von ihr.

Wäre es dabei geblieben, hätte ich mich nicht eingemischt. Jeder soll ungestört weinen dürfen, laut oder leise, Zuhause, im Cafe, im Bus oder auf der Parkbank. Ich halte ungestörtes Weinen für ein wichtiges Grundrecht, nur schwoll der Ton mit jeder Minute weiter an. Was sich erst vom vorsichtigem Fiepen, zu einem expressiven Schluchzen, mit viel Rotz und Tränen, entwickelt hatte, wurde nun zu einer Art Urschmerz. Einem Leid, das so tief zu sitzen und sich mit einer solchen Wucht durch die Eingeweide meiner Nachbarin nach oben zu drücken schien, dass es klang, als müsse diese gewaltvolle Bewegung ihren Körper entzwei spalten. Als würde sich ihr Inneres nach Außen stülpen und bald mit einem lauten Klatsch vor ihren Füßen landen, wie Erbrochenes. Benedetta schrie, jaulte, hämmerte. Sie stieß dumpfe und schrille Laute aus, würgte, gurgelte, schrie erneut. Ich entschied mich, meinem Diskretionsprinzip zum Trotz, nachzusehen. Ich lief die Treppe ins Erdgeschoss hinunter, wunderte mich, dass es sonst niemand tat, und klopfte. Einmal, zweimal, dreimal. Beim vierten Mal öffnete sie die Tür.

Si? Ja? Sie sah mich an, als gebe es keine Erklärung für mein unaufgefordertes Erscheinen. Sie war irritiert, ich war es auch. Entgegen dem, was ich erwartet hatte, ein nasses Gesicht, schwarze Schliere des Mascara unter den Augen, angespannte, gequälte Züge, verstärkte Falten, eine kurzzeitige Verhärtung des Gesamtbildes durch Schmerz, so wie ich es von mir und anderen kannte, sah Benedetta aus wie immer. Ruhig, mittelalt, gelangweilt. Ihr blondiertes Haar leuchtete unter dem Neonlicht ihrer Küche gelblich wie ein Getreidefeld, sie trug einen fliederfarbenen Sportanzug aus Frottee, darüber eine Schürze. Tutto a posto? Alles in Ordnung? Si si, tutto a posto. Ich lugte diskret, so diskret ich konnte, in ihre Wohnung. Auf dem Herd stand ein Metalltopf mit brodelndem Wasser, auf dem Tisch Zeitungsseiten, darüber ausgepuhlte Fava-Bohnen und die Kadaver frischer Erbsen. Im Hintergrund lief der Fernseher. Sie war am Kochen. Sicher, dass alles okay ist? Jaja. Da ich etwas ratlos da stand, unsicher, was ich tun sollte, drückte sie die Plastiktür ihrer Wohnung langsam wieder zu. Ihre Augen waren konzentriert auf mich gerichtet, so als sei die Verrückte hier nicht sie, sondern ich. Ich entschuldigte mich für mein Eindringen und ging verwirrt zurück nach oben.

Ich machte mir einen Tee und setzte mich wieder an meinen Schreibtisch. Zurück zu der gruselig weinenden Madonna. Der Mann in meinem Ohr, Niccolo, beschrieb gerade die ungewöhnlich rosigen

Backen der sonst so bleichen Madonnen-Figur, ich notierte «aveva le guance rosse», als das Schluchzen erneut erklang. Wieder spulte Benedetta die komplette Skala des Leidens ab. Vom erstickten Fiepen, hin zum lauten Heulen und schließlich dem Schreien der schieren Verzweiflung. Als sie zur vierten Runde ansetzte, immer wilder wurde, immer lauter, immer heftiger gegen den Tisch schlug und klang, als würde sie bald alles um sich herum demolieren, wurde mir die Sache unheimlich. Ich packte meinen Laptop ein, hielt unten vor ihrer Tür noch einmal kurz inne, dann verließ ich das Haus. Draußen war es entsetzlich warm. Die Sonne zerdrückte die Luft zu einer kompakten Masse, einer Mischung aus Salz und Staub, das Atmen fiel mir schwer. Ich lief vor zum Felsen, dem Scoglio, dem Fixpunkt der Halbinsel. Oben an der Balustrade standen wie immer ein paar Herren und blickten auf die glitzernden Punkte des Wassers und die Wellen, die sich wütend gegen die Steinwand warfen, als habe sie ihnen etwas getan. Unten versuchten junge Männer auf dem Felsen lesende oder sich sonnende Frauen anzuflirten: Che leggi? Di dove sei? Hai l'ora? Ein Fischer zog gerade einen Pulpo an seiner Angelschnur nach oben, das Tier tanzte mit seinen Armen in der Luft, wie die Schlangen auf dem Kopf der Medusa, im Hintergrund leuchtete die Stadt hellbeige, fast weiss. Der Castello Maniace, die bröckelnden Fassaden, die Kuppeln, die wie kleine Brüste in den Himmel ragen, sahen unwirklich aus, so real und doch nie ganz zu greifen. Wie eine Fata Morgana, eine Illusion. War es möglich, dass ich all das fantasiert habe? Habe ich mir das Weinen, die Schreie, das Hämmern nur eingebildet? Stieg mir meine Recherche zu Kopf oder wünschte auch ich mir schlicht jemanden, der an meiner Stelle trauerte, der für die erdrückende Stille des Schmerzes einen Ausdruck fand?

Vielleicht muss ich an dieser Stelle erwähnen, dass auch mich zu dieser Zeit ein Kummer plagte. Monate zuvor war eine Frau, die ich geliebt hatte oder geglaubt hatte zu lieben, unvermittelt aus meinem Leben verschwunden. Eines Tages war sie einfach fort. Ohne eine Nachricht. Ohne ein Wort. In der ersten Zeit verkraftete ich ihre Abwesenheit überraschend gut, ich war gelassen, fast fröhlich. Ich wunderte mich schon, dachte, ich hätte mich wieder einmal getäuscht, wieder einmal eine Liebelei mit Liebe verwechselt, bis mein inneres Boot eines Tages kippte und mich ohne Vorwarnung und ohne Schwimmweste ins kalte Meer warf. Auf einmal fühlte ich mich, als würde ich ertrinken. Ich paddelte hilflos durch die endlose Weite, hielt Ausschau nach einer Küste, einem Fels, einem Boot, irgendetwas an dem ich mich hätte festhalten können, nur war nichts davon in Sicht. Ich war alleine und orientierungslos. Ich hatte Angst. Je länger der Zustand anhielt, desto panischer wurde ich. Schließlich fühlte ich mich nicht nur in der Welt verloren, sondern auch mir selbst fremd. Ich war ein- und ausgesperrt zugleich. Fast so, als habe meine Geliebte, der es gelungen war, Räume in mir zu erschließen, die ich bis dahin nicht kannte, vor ihrem Auszug aus meinem Leben sämtliche Türen im Haus meines Seins verriegelt und den Schlüssel eingepackt. Manchmal fragte ich mich, ob sie mich womöglich vergiftet habe, denn in etwa so fühlte ich mich. Das Atmen fiel mir schwer, jede Bewegung glich einem Kraftakt, ich fürchtete schon, dieser zunehmenden Lähmung des Körpers und Verhärtung des Herzens ganz zu erliegen, als die Anfrage für die Reportage kam.

Unter normalen Umständen hätte ich sicher abgelehnt. Ich wusste nichts über religiöse Phänomene, das Auftreten von Wundern, Manifestationen des Göttlichen, all das war mir fremd. Nur fand ich das Thema interessant: Ein Bild, das weinte, ein totes Material, das vermochte Tränen zu vergießen, wo es mir selbst so schwer fiel, dem Kummer eine Form zu geben, interessierte mich. Zumal Syrakus mich faszinierte. Vielleicht wegen Henri Salvador, den ich zu dieser Zeit in einem klaren Anfall von Selbstzerstörungswut in Dauerschleife hörte, der sang: «J'aimerai tant voir Syracuse.» Wegen der Geschichte, diesen vielen Zeitebenen, die sich hier übereinander schichteten wie in einem klebrigen Sfogliatelle, der vielen Mythen, Demeter, Persephone, die Unterwelt, Arethusa und ihre misslungene Flucht vor der unerwiderten Begierde eines Mannes. Vielleicht weil ich gehört hatte, Ortigia sei schön, aber auch ein bisschen kaputt, melancholisch, sanft und rau zugleich. Oder, und das war, auch wenn ich es nicht gerne zugab, das Wahrscheinlichste: Weil ich trotz meiner tiefen Skepsis insgeheim hoffte, die Madonna könnte auch mich durch ihre Tränen befreien. Ich hoffte, etwas von dem Zauber von damals würde auf mich herunter rieseln, nur hatte ich davon bisher nichts gespürt. Die

Begegnungen rührten mich, der Glaube dieser Leute, ihre Hoffnung, ihre Zuversicht gingen mir nah, doch sie bewegten nichts. Mein Schmerz blieb stumm und hart, mein Sein verschlossen.

Ich schlenderte durch die Via della Giudecca, vorbei an der San Filippo Apostolo Kirche, an deren Eingang der Kirchenjunge gerade ein paar Touristen unter dem Absperrband in die Krypta hinab führte. Runter zu den einbalsamierten Toten, dem gigantischen antiken Tunnelsystem, das während des Krieges als Luftschutzbunker diente, weiter runter zur Mikvah, dem mittelalterlichen jüdischen Bad. In der Via Roma schwirrten Kindergruppen zwischen den Postkartenständern, den Schuhauslagen, den Tischen und Stühlen der Cafes herum, wie kleine Fischschwärme. Ihr Gewusel machte mich nervös, ich flüchtete ins Café Viola und setzte mich in den hinteren Raum. Um mich herum saßen junge Leute an langen Holztischen vor ihren Computern, ein alter Herr las im Giornale di Sicilia, an der Bar gurgelte die Schaummaschine. Irgendein deutscher Besucher hatte einen Nachmittags-Cappuccino bestellt. Die klar einzuordnenden Klänge waren beruhigend. Ich wollte mich gerade wieder an die Arbeit machen, als Lucio sich zu mir setzte. Er sah aus wie immer, frisch, voller Elan, er kam gerade vom Meer.

– Bereit für Signora Clara?

Signora Clara. Ich hatte sie vollkommen vergessen. Wir waren in einer Stunde mit ihr verabredet. Ein Verkäufer am Markt hatte uns zu Beginn des Aufenthalts eines Morgens über Thunfisch, Pulpo und orange leuchtenden Meerigeln von ihr erzählt.

Die Dame, so sagte er, sei eine jener gewesen, die im Sommer 1953 von den Tränen der Madonna geheilt worden war. Sie sei «una miracolata», eine wundersam Geheilte. Ich war immer wieder in den kleinen, dunklen Laden der Via Vittorio Veneto gepilgert, in dem la Signora zwischen Pelzmänteln, altem Modeschmuck, Tassen, selbstgehäkelten Kinderkleidern und anderem Krimskrams saß und durch ihre dicken Brillengläser nach draußen schaute wie durch eine Lupe. Wir hatten über dies und das geplaudert, nur beim Thema der Madonna und ihrer angeblichen Heilung war sie stets ausgewichen, Fotos wollte sie auf keinen Fall machen. Doch nun war es endlich so weit, sie war bereit, das Wunder zu besprechen und sich abbilden zu lassen, das hatte sie versprochen. Nur interessierten mich die Tränen der Maria gerade recht wenig, was mich beschäftigte, waren die nicht vorhandenen Tränen der Benedetta. Da Lucio sich über meinen schwachen Enthusiasmus zu wundern schien, erzählte ich ihm, was vorgefallen war. Ich sprach von ihren Schreien, davon, dass sie gelitten hatte wie ein Tier, mit viel Lärm, aber ohne sichtbare Spuren. Ich fragte ihn, ob er sich das erklären könne, ob sie Probleme hatte oder ich womöglich dabei war, verrückt zu werden, selbst so zerfressen von meinem Schmerz, dass ich glaubte ihn überall heulen zu hören. Lucio sah mich mit seinem liebevollen Blick an, halb amüsiert, halb in Sorge. Ihn schien die Sache mit Benedetta überhaupt nicht zu wundern.

– Sie ist ein Klageweib, sagte er abwesend, ganz en passant.

Er riss die braune Zuckerpackung auf, schüttete die Hälfte in seinen Espresso und hielt mir wie immer die andere Hälfte hin. Teilen?

Eine Frau, die laut weint, ist ein Klageweib, was für eine dämliche Erklärung.

– Nein, es war keine Klage, kein Gejammer, es klang entsetzlich. Wie ein sehr tiefer und ernster Schmerz, ich habe mir wirklich Sorgen gemacht. Nur ihr Ausdruck war verwirrend. Dass man von dem Gehörten überhaupt nichts sah. Auch, dass sie alles nochmal exakt wiederholte, fast so, als würde sie eine Tonleiter abspulen. Als würde sie proben.

Lucio grinste. Er fand es lustig, wenn ich mich in meinen Gedanken verheddterte. Meine Verwirrung war sein Spass.

– Das sage ich dir doch. Sie ist ein Klageweib. Das ist ihr Beruf.

– Wie meinst du das, das ist ihr Beruf?

– So wie ich es sage: Es ist ihr Beruf. Damit verdient sie ihr Geld.

Ich muss einen bemerkenswert dummen Ausdruck gehabt haben, denn ich verstand wirklich nicht, was er sagte. Klageweiber existierten für mich nur in der Antike, wenn überhaupt noch in einigen Dörfern in Rumänien, Griechenland, bei manchen Stämmen in Afrika oder Ozeanien. Vor kurzem war ich im Zuge der Recherche im Internet irgendwo schief abgebogen und auf eine Dokumentation über Klagefrauen der Elfenbeinküste gestoßen. Es war faszinierend. Diese Frauen simulierten für Geld Leid, so wie andere Lust simulieren. Die Angehörigen konnte sich aussuchen, welche Art der Lamentation ihnen für die Situation angebracht schien: Lautes Weinen für einen geliebten Großvater, Schreien bei einem zu früh verstorbenen Kind, Fluchen nach langer Krankheit, sich auf dem Boden wälzen, androhen, sich ins Grab zu werfen, sich die Haare ausreissen - die Variationen waren endlos. Man bewunderte diese Frauen für ihre Fähigkeit, das kollektive Leid auszudrücken, nur schien mir, als gelten bei uns, in der sogenannten westlichen Welt, ganz andere Regeln. Man war dazu angehalten, die Dinge anzunehmen, sich resilient zu zeigen. Es schickte sich nicht, den anderen mit seinem Schmerz auf die Nerven zu gehen, zu lange oder zu laut zu trauern war für das Umfeld unangenehm, es machte die Leute hilflos und drängte sie fort. Wie konnte es sein, dass jemand damit Geld verdiente, etwas auszudrücken, das wir gelernt hatten zu unterdrücken?

– Erinnerst du dich an die Beerdigung dieses Managers aus Catania, die vor ein paar Tagen in der Kathedrale stattfand? Als der Typ neben uns immer wieder zu seiner Freundin meinte: «Nobody cries. Do you see? Nobody is crying, not even the wife.»

– Ja, das war komisch.

– Dort hätten sie Benedetta gebraucht.

– Warum?

– Weil es schräg wirkt, wenn niemand weint. Als sei es egal oder als nehme man die Realität der Sache nicht an.

– Was soll das denn bedeuten? Als ob Schmerz wie auf Bestellung erscheinen würde. Ist die Crux an Trauer nicht gerade, dass sie unberechenbare Wellen

88

schlägt, kommt, wann es ihr beliebt, geht, wann sie Lust hat, mal nur innerlich brennt, mal nach außen hin wütet? Ist nicht gerade der tiefe Schmerz einer, den man nicht auszudrücken vermag, weil man fürchtet, er könne einen auf dem Weg nach draußen zerfetzen und im Zuge dessen womöglich auch noch andere verletzten?

Lucio sah mich fragend an. Warum echauffierte ich mich so? Ich wusste es selbst nicht. Etwas an dieser Sache störte mich, kitzelte mich unangenehm in der Magengegend. Vielleicht war ich neidisch auf Benedetta. Darauf, dass sie nicht erstickt und leise litt, sondern wusste, wie man das Gift ausspuckt. Darauf, dass sie nicht das Gefühl hatte, in einem reißenden Fluss zu hängen und sich an stetig abbrechenden Ästen festzuhalten. Sie tappte nicht wie ich orientierungslos im Nebel, sie hatte einen festen Fahrplan. Ein Guidebook des Leids, klare Linien, von A nach B.

Lucio dachte nach.

– Ich glaube, es geht weniger darum, mit Tränen zu prahlen als darum, die Angehörigen zu entlasten. Dadurch dass Benedetta lautstark heult, müssen die anderen ihre Gefühle nicht hetzen, sie können sich die Zeit nehmen, die sie brauchen. Zumal es vielen hilft, wenn eine fremde Person ausdrückt, was sie selbst noch nicht auszudrücken, vielleicht noch nicht einmal zu fühlen vermögen. Dadurch, dass sie wild ist, können sie sanfter sein. Sie hat die Großzügigkeit, die der echten Trauer oft fehlt.

Endlich sagte er einen Satz, mit dem ich einverstanden war. Trauer macht tatsächlich geizig und blind.

Blind für das Leben, blind für die Menschen. Blind wie Antonina in der legendären Nacht des August 1953. Die Tränen der Madonna hatten sie aus dieser Blindheit befreit, könnten die Schreie der Benedetta das womöglich auch vollbringen? Lucio stand auf. Es war Zeit zu gehen. Wir zahlten unsere Espressi und machten uns auf den Weg in die Via Vittorio Veneto. Über die Natur Signora Clara's Leid erfuhren wir nichts Neues. Sie blieb ausweichend und vage. Und doch rundete sie unsere Suche nach dem Mysterium der Madonna perfekt ab. Die Tränen waren ihr zufolge weder Tränen des Mitleids noch der Liebe gewesen, sondern schlicht der Ausdruck dessen, was damals, in den Nachkriegsjahren, allen unter der Brust brannte. Angst, Wut, Trauer, Freude, Erleichterung, Scham - Gefühle, die so widersprüchlich waren, dass sie einen emotionalen Stau bildeten. Die Madonna habe diesen Druck durch ihre Tränen gelöst. Die Art und Weise, wie Signora Clara es sagte, sehr sanft, sehr ruhig, mehr dankbar als devot, war schön, glaubwürdig. Auf einmal ergab die ganze Sache auch für uns einen Sinn.

Als ich am nächsten Morgen aufwachte, den Zigarillo-Duft vom Nachbarn roch und den Mann von oben laut schnarchen hörte, schien es mir, als hätten die Erlebnisse des Vortages etwas in mir bewegt. Zum ersten Mal seit Wochen hatte ich den Eindruck, freier atmen zu können. Benedettas Tür blieb fortan verschlossen, ihr Weinen erklang nicht wieder. Wenige Tage später verließ ich Lucio und Syrakus. Mit der Sicherheit, selbst einem kleinen Wunder beigewohnt zu haben. Dem der tränenlosen Matrone der Via Nizza.

Giuliano Bonelli
Siracusa o morte

Und irgendwann spürst du, dass Alleinsein und Einsamsein nicht gleichbedeutend sind und du lernst, dass auch ein Mensch eine Insel sein kann. Der Wein, den du immer im selben Lokal trinkst, ist sehr kalt und das hilft. Am Tisch gegenüber streitet man sich. Es erleichtert dir das Schreiben. Du brauchst das Raue, es gibt dir einen Schliff. Du siehst das Drama, aber es ist nicht deins. Du solltest das aufschreiben, bevor du es vergisst. Bevor du deinem Gedächtnis nicht mehr trauen kannst. Es hantiert mit dünner Tinte und vieles verläuft, bevor du es fassen kannst. Die Leichtigkeit dieses Ortes in Zeilen zu bannen ist ein Kraftakt. Eilig fertigst du deine Notizen und erinnerst dich daran, wie gemächlich die Geschehnisse waren, von denen im Folgenden die Rede ist. Ein Ort, an dem sich das ewige Meer zu schaffen macht, nimmt etwas von dieser Ewigkeit in sich auf. An den Küsten Ortigias, der kleinen Insel Siracusas, drapieren sich die Menschen auf den Felsen, bis ihre Zähne braun werden und die Sonnenstrahlen Furchen in ihre Haut schlagen. Man hat keinen Grund zur Hast, das Leben ist eine verkehrsberuhigte Zone. Man steigt ab, man schiebt.

Ich beginne meinen Morgen auf Ortigia mit Schlafen, meine Nacht war unruhig. Halbstarke Jugendliche veranstalteten in den engen Gassen der Insel auf ihren frisierten Rollern ein Rennen. Sie hupten vor jeder Kreuzung, um sich den anderen Verkehrsteilnehmern anzukündigen und so Zusammenstöße zu vermeiden. Es ist dieses präventive Hupen, das jede italienische Stadt beherrscht, das zu einem Grundton wird, der sich jedoch üblicherweise auf die Tageszeit beschränkt. Noch im Halbschlaf stelle ich mir vor, wie einer der Rollerfahrer mit hoher Geschwindigkeit an einer Hausecke zerschellt. Direkt über der Stelle des Aufpralls befindet sich ein Wandschrein mit der heiligen Maria, die ein Jesuskind in den Armen hält. Eine elektrische Kerze im Schrein beleuchtet die Szene. Sie konnte ihm nicht mehr helfen. Sein Roller zerfetzt, der Aufprall ist so heftig, dass sein Körper zweigeteilt wird. Die beiden Hälften schleudern mit noch hoher Geschwindigkeit in verschiedene Richtungen durch die Gasse. Eine findet man wenig später auf der Hafenmauer, wo sie von der Mittagssonne erhitzt wird und Fliegen über sie herfallen. Ihm konnte niemand mehr helfen. Ich muss an den Begriff malacarne denken, den ich bei einem Freund aus Siracusa aufgeschnappt habe. Die Einheimischen bezeichnen damit einen bösen Menschen oder minderwertiges Fleisch. Er beschreibt präzise den Rollerfahrer vor und nach dem Unfall.

Ich sonne mich auf den Felsen zu Füßen der Diana nel Forte, einer alten Festungsanlage an der Ostküste der Insel, die man über eine Stahltreppe erreichen kann. Die Hauptsaison, in der die Insel überfüllt von Touristen ist, hat noch nicht begonnen, die Badeplattform und die Brücke zwischen den Felsmassiven ist noch nicht errichtet. Nicht weit von mir entfernt, auf dem nächsten Felsvorsprung sitzt ein Mann, oben ohne und in einer ausgeblichenen hellblauen Badehose. Er spielt Gitarre. Seine Haut ist über jedes Ziel hinaus gebräunt, er trägt Glatze, wirkt wie ein Aussteiger und hat vermutlich vergessen, durch welche Tür er sein altes Leben damals verlassen hat. Jedes Mal, wenn sich neue Besucher auf den Felsen legen, stellt er seine Gitarre beiseite, klettert auf den höchsten Felsvorsprung und springt unter größtmöglicher Aufmerksamkeit elegant mit dem Kopf zuerst in die Bucht. Wie motorisiert krault er dann zügig hinaus ins offene Meer. Er hat keine Furcht vor der dunklen Tiefe und dem weiten Blau. Sobald er nass genug ist, krault er zurück und verlässt das Wasser, indem er sich an einem versteckten Tau auf den Felsen zieht, das in einer Spalte befestigt ist. Er ist einer von hier, seine gebräunten Hautzellen flüstern es in die Bucht. Immer wieder rennen Kinder zwischen den Handtüchern barfuß über die spitzen Felsen, an unübersichtlichen Stellen springen sie ins Meer. Bei ihrer Verfolgungsjagd spritzen sie die anderen Badegäste auf ihren Handtüchern nass. Niemand stört sich daran, es sind Kinder, sie wissen noch nicht, dass ein Mensch nicht erst dort beginnt, wo man ihn berührt, sondern bereits weit davor. Über unseren Köpfen jagen Mauersegler durch die Lüfte, sie stoßen Schreie aus, als stünden sie in Flammen. Weiter hinten, wo die Festungsanlage auf dem Felsen beginnt, stehen zwei junge Frauen in sehr knappen, grell farbigen Bikinis. Beide haben an der gleichen Stelle auf dem linken Rippenbogen einen Textabsatz tätowiert. Aus der Entfernung kann ich es nicht entziffern, aber ich vermute, es handelt sich um den Text eines Musikstücks oder einen Absatz aus ihrem liebsten Buch. Sie haben ein Handy in einen Spalt der Festungsmauer positioniert, mit der Frontkamera filmen sie sich. Ich höre leise das Lied, das auf dem Handy abgespielt wird. Es hat einen zügigen Takt und wird sicherlich in den örtlichen Clubs gespielt. Die beiden Frauen bewegen sich dazu aufreizend, klapsen sich gegenseitig auf ihre Hintern und tanzen eine Choreographie, die an einen Striptease erinnert, ohne sich dabei auszuziehen. Sie nehmen ein Video für TikTok auf, oder besser: sie nehmen ein TikTok auf. Die Plattform, die es zur Nominalisierung geschafft hat. Ihr Stativ ist eine tausendjährige Festung, benannt nach der römischen Göttin Diane, der Göttin der Jagd, des Mondes und der Geburt, der Beschützerin der Frauen und Mädchen. Diane blieb ihr gesamtes Dasein lang Jungfrau, sie war nie vermählt. Einem Mythos zufolge ruhte sich ein Jäger während der Mittagshitze in einem schattigen Tal aus, das Diane geweiht war. In seiner Mitte befand sich eine Grotte, in der die Göttin nackt badete. Als sie bemerkte, dass der Jäger sie beim Baden beobachtete, verwandelte sie ihn in einen Hirsch, damit er niemandem davon erzählen konnte. Der Hirsch wurde von seinen eigenen Jagdhunden zerfleischt. Diane war sehr aggressiv in der Verteidigung ihrer Keuschheit. Vermutlich wissen die beiden Frauen nichts vom Mythos der Diane, oder von ihrer Einstellung zur Freizügigkeit. Wenn doch, bewundere ich sie für ihren Mut.

Während ich mich auf meinem Sonnentuch auf dem Felsen ausbreite und meine Hüfte in einer Furche des Gesteins einrastet, erinnere ich mich an die Sommer meiner Kindheit, die ich größtenteils bei meinen Großeltern in Italien verbrachte. Am letzten

Schultag vor den Sommerferien verabredeten sich meine Freunde für LAN-Partys, später für Hauspartys und irgendwann für Urlaube. Ich verpasste all das, stattdessen lag ich am Strand und blickte auf das Mittelmeer. Ein erschöpfender Anblick, der schlichtweg nicht fassbar war, egal wie sehr ich mich anstrengte. Noch grenzenloser war nur das Meer bei Nacht, wenn es aus der Dunkelheit rauscht. Das Leitbild des uferlosen Gedankens. Neue Freundschaften schloss ich in diesen Sommern keine. Mi scusi, sono tedesco, non parlo italiano. Es tut mir Leid, ich bin deutsch, ich spreche kein italienisch, war mein meistgesagter Satz, wenn ich mich dann doch mal von meiner Familie entfernte und von einheimischen Kindern meines Alters angesprochen wurde. Ich war nicht ehrlich mit ihnen, ich erzählte ihnen nicht, dass ich zur Hälfte Italiener sei, mir war es peinlich, nur diesen einen Satz sagen zu können. Heute weiß ich, was sie meinten, als sie mich fragten, ma da dove sei in germania? Ich antwortete nicht, dass ich aus der Nähe von Frankfurt stamme, ich schüttelte nur den Kopf und ging weiter meines Weges. Es waren stets irritierende Dialoge für alle Beteiligten. Die italienischen Kinder dachten, sie hätten etwas Falsches gesagt und mich damit verärgert oder beleidigt. Sie schauten sich gegenseitig fragend an, qual è il suo problema? Was ist denn sein Problem?

Vor den Felsen der Diana nel Forte brodelt es im Meer, etwa hundert Meter von der Bucht entfernt ist die Gischt weiß, der Verlauf der Wellen verändert sich an dieser Stelle. Dort befindet sich der Scoglio dei Cani, der Fels der Hunde. Seinen Namen soll er von der Angewohnheit der Anwohner haben, die unliebsame Hunde an der Diana nel Forte ins Meer warfen. Auf dem Felsen fanden die Hunde dann kurzzeitige Rettung, bevor der Hunger sie hinraffte. Der Scoglio dei Cani wirkt wie ein ausbrechender Unterwasservulkan, als hätte der Etna seine Anschrift geändert. Auf dem rechten Schulterblatt des Mannes, der sich unmittelbar neben mir sonnt, prangt ein Tattoo, nel mio paese nessuno é straniero, in meinem Land ist niemand ein Fremder. Dieser Satz würde mir nicht mehr aus dem Kopf gehen.

Es ist früher Abend und ich treffe einen Freund auf der Piazza del Duomo. Wir haben eine Reservierung für eine Weinverkostung auf der Dachterrasse des Palazzo Beneventano del Bosco, dem Palast gegenüber dem Eingang des Doms. Wir betreten den Veranstaltungsort über einen Seiteneingang und steigen die Stufen hinauf. Wir sind ein wenig zu früh, obwohl wir dachten, wir wären ein wenig zu spät, also betreten wir über eine weitere schmale Treppe eine auf die Terrasse aufgestockte Ebene. Von hier überblicken wir den gesamten Hafen und unterhalten uns. Wir sprechen darüber, wie das Erwachsenwerden aus der Deutung und dem Verstehenwollen der eigenen Kindheit besteht und sich wie eine Spurensuche anfühlt. Es ist ein Prozess, darin sind wir uns einig. Ich erzähle ihm, dass ich in der letzten Zeit hin und wieder Motive meiner Entscheidungen hinterfrage und manchmal eine Antwort in meiner Kindheit finde. Ich entdecke Schlüsselmomente. Ich sage ihm, das sei sehr zufriedenstellend, als würde man einen dicken Knoten mit einem einfachen Handgriff lösen. Er möchte mit einem Freund ein Stück Land etwas außerhalb von Siracusa kaufen und freut sich darauf, das Stück Land zu bespielen. Wir sind beide verblüfft über die Möglichkeit, Eigentümer eines Teils der Erdoberfläche werden zu können, dass Eigentum dieser Art jedoch auch verpflichtet und einen Menschen an einen Ort bindet. Wenn ihm diese Bindung zu viel wird, dann würde er es eben einfach wieder verkaufen, sagt er, worüber wir beide lachen. Diese Möglichkeit bestünde natürlich immer. Es ist ein schönes Gespräch und als wir uns kurz vor Beginn der Verkostung ein Bier an der Bar bestellen wollen, vertröstet man uns. Heute gäbe es nur Weine der Verkostung und erst wenn diese beginnt. An der Bar werde ich Mauro, einem Freund von ihm, vorgestellt, der an der Organisation des heutigen Abends beteiligt ist.

«Hey, Mezzo – nice to meet you.»

«Ciao Mezzo, Mauro, piacere, I thought you were Italian, you have the name and the looks, haha.»

«My Dad's family actually is from a village not far from Siracusa, but I never really learned Italian. My mother is German, so I am part Italian and part German. Parlo un po di italiano ma preferisco l'inglese. Almeno fino a quando non ho bevuto un po' più di vino.»

Mit sechzehn Jahren begann ich einen «italienischen Dialog» mit mir selbst, ich läutete italienische Aktionswochen in meinem Leben ein. Ich war es leid in Deutschland gefragt zu werden, woher in Italien meine Familie ist und wieviel Zeit im Jahr ich noch dort verbringe. Ob ich noch Verwandte dort hätte und ob ich mir vorstellen könne, vollständig nach Italien zu ziehen. Gleichzeitig hatte ich es satt, in Italien Gespräche zu vermeiden und Konversationen aus dem Weg zu gehen. Ich wollte keine Gesprächsrunden mehr sprengen, in denen die Italiener sich aus Rücksicht zu mir auf Englisch unterhielten. Ich wollte nicht mehr den Fernseher anschalten, um dann kein einziges Wort der Nachrichtensprecherin von Rai Uno zu verstehen. Ich mutete mir irgendwann mehr zu, stotterte wenigstens den ein oder anderen Satz, achtete auf meine Aussprache und wies die Menschen stets an, italienisch zu sprechen. Ich würde es schon in groben Zügen verstehen, schließlich wurde seit meiner frühen Kindheit in meinem Umfeld italienisch gesprochen. Man könnte sagen, ich hätte zumindest ein Ohr für die Sprache. In dieser Zeit lernte ich meine italienische Seite kennen: rau und zart, fließend und stockend.

Die Dachterrasse füllt sich recht zügig, im Hintergrund spielt, gedämpft von den Gesprächen der Gäste, Giorno Libero von Delicatino. Die Gäste sind elegant gekleidet, die Männer tragen locker sitzende pastellfarbene Hemden und weite Leinenhosen, die Frauen Abendkleider und Hosenanzüge in kräftigen Farben. Ein Mann mit vollem, dunkelbraunen Haar fällt aus dem Bild heraus. Er steht ohne Begleitung an der Brüstung, ein wenig gerupft und erinnert mich an den tragischen Kapitän des Kreuzfahrtschiffes, das 2012 vor der italienischen Insel Giglio havarierte. Er trägt eine strahlend weiße Hose und ein blaues T-Shirt mit der Aufschrift BaFins most wanted. Unter einer

Pergola ist eine große Tafel angerichtet, ein Pesto wurde direkt auf die Tischdecke aufgetragen, Olivenöl steht gemeinsam mit gefüllten Brotkörben daneben, es wurde Käse aufgeschnitten und überall auf dem Tisch verteilt. Auf einer Anrichte daneben steht ein Eiskübel mit Weinflaschen, es gibt roten und weißen Naturwein von unterschiedlichen Winzern, die heute Abend auch anwesend sind. Bevor die Tafel eröffnet wird, betritt eine Frau in elegantem schwarzen Abendkleid die Terrasse. In ihren Händen hält sie ein aufgeschlagenes Buch, aus dem sie eine Fabel auf Italienisch vorträgt. Überdimensionale Seifenblasen schweben von einem Straßenkünstler auf der Piazza del Duomo zu uns hinauf. Sie schimmern in verschiedenen Farben, wie Benzinflecken auf Asphalt und bewegen sich über unsere Köpfe hinweg. Worum es in der vorgetragenen Fabel geht, kann ich mir nicht zusammenreimen. Konzeptuell führt sie uns wohl vom Wein zum Essen und wieder zurück.

Der Himmel über Ortigia ist bereits tiefdunkel, als sie mit dem letzten Teil der Fabel ein für die Region typisches Dessert ankündigt und uns so kulinarisch in die Nacht entlässt. Die Terrasse ist geschmackvoll beleuchtet, im Hintergrund ragt der Dom in den Himmel, es ist eine fantastische Kulisse. Ich muss an Paolo Sorrentinos La Grande Bellezza denken. Jep Gambardalla, gefeierter Schriftsteller in seinen Mittsechzigern, steht vor dem Abgrund und gleichzeitig inmitten der High Society Roms. Auf extravaganten Partys und unzähligen Soireen spürt er einen Mangel an Tiefe und Bedeutung. Er ist unglücklich und besinnt sich auf seine Vergangenheit zurück. Er wird konfrontiert mit dem Tod einer geliebten Person. Jep ist ein sensibler Charakter und genau aus diesem Grund, so sagt er, sei er zum Schreiben geboren. Außerdem könne er schlichtweg nichts anderes. Ich verstand den Film als eine Liebeserklärung an die Stadt Rom. Eine unmissverständliche Liebeserklärung, ein Film mit einer wahnsinnigen Bildgewalt. Eine Kamerafahrt zeigt die Reiterstatue des Freiheitskämpfers Giuseppe Garibaldi, der Sockel trägt die Inschrift Roma o Morte. Es war Garibaldis Schlachtruf, den er von einem Balkon in Catania rief, kurz nach der Eroberung Siziliens. Rom oder der Tod. Ich erzähle meinem Freund von dem Gedanken an Sorrentinos Film. Er stimmt mir zu.

«I get your point. Smearing pesto on the tablecloth is also a first for me and I don't quite get her performance. But fuck Rome, it's an old shithole.»

Wir stehen den Großteil des Abends am Eiskübel und schenken uns gegenseitig Wein ein. Rot-Weiß-Weiß-Rot-Weiß-Weiß. An der Brüstung will ich sensibel sein, ich weiß nicht, ob ich ein sensibler Mensch bin, doch irgendwie ist das ein sehr sensibler Moment. Dort oben in der Baumkrone Siracusas, umgeben von fremden Menschen und mit den Gedanken in Rom. Mein Freund verlässt das Event vor mir, er fragt mich mehrmals, ob das in Ordnung sei, er würde mich nur sehr ungern hier allein stehen lassen, aber er hat eine unaufschiebbare Verabredung. Ich winke ab, ich habe nichts dagegen noch einen Moment hier zu bleiben, bevor ich den Heimweg antrete. Ich verabschiede mich nicht lange nachdem mein Freund gegangen ist und winke Mauro zu, der etwas entfernt in einer kleinen Gruppe steht. Ich verlasse den Palazzo über den Seiteneingang und finde mich auf der Piazza del Duomo wieder. Im Vergleich zu meiner Ankunft ist er nun beinahe menschenleer. Ein kleines Mädchen rennt einem Ball hinterher, der mit jeder Erschütterung die Farbe wechselt. Ein zotteliger schwarzer Hund schlendert aus einer Gasse hinter mir auf die Piazza. Er spitzt die Ohren und beobachtet einen Moment lang das Mädchen mit seinem Ball. Dann wendet er sich ab und trinkt aus einer der mit Wasser gefüllten Schüsseln, die die Anwohner nachts für die streunenden Katzen vor ihre Türen stellen. Ich blicke hinüber zum Dom. Ein warmer Wind zieht über die Piazza und ich vermisse das Rauschen der Blätter aus meiner Heimat. In Siracusa rauscht nur das Meer. Hier ist jeden Tag Samstag, die Zeit ist auf der Seite der Menschen. Von irgendwoher ertönt ein tiefer Glockenschlag. Ich gehe die Via Cavour entlang, die nun ebenfalls menschenleer ist. Es ist kurz nach Mitternacht, noch vor ein paar Stunden war sie gefüllt mit Menschen mit grauen Haaren und gebückter Haltung. Mir kommt einer der Straßenverkäufer entgegen, die tagsüber am Strand Powerbanks und Armkettchen verkaufen. Er lächelt mich freundlich an und grüßt mich, ich erwidere seinen Gruß. Von den Fassaden platzt der Putz, eine Straßenlaterne entblößt die Falten der Gebäude. Ich denke an die Farbe verbranntes Orange. In Die Ermordung des Commendatore I von Haruki Murakami ist es die Farbe der Lebenskraft und die Farbe des Verfalls. Es muss die Farbe Siracusas sein. Es duftet herrlich.

Auf dem Heimweg streife ich die Ponte Santa Lucia, die Ortigia zusammen mit der Ponte Umbertino mit dem Rest von Siracusa verbindet. An der Brücke ist mit Stahlrohren eine Art Fußballtor über dem Wasser befestigt, es ist lediglich etwas kleiner. Es als Eishockeytor zu beschreiben, das über dem Wasser hängt, ist wohl treffender. In dem Becken zwischen den beiden Brücken wurde Italien am 4. September 2016 erstmals Weltmeister im canoa polo. Sie schlugen den amtierenden Weltmeister aus Frankreich mit einem Golden Goal in der Verlängerung. Ein Spektakel im Becken und auf den Tribünen, so nannte es der italienische Kanu-Verband. Um den Ball aus dem Wasser aufzunehmen, schlägt man bei dieser Sportart mit der freien Hand von oben auf den Ball, damit er aus dem Wasser ins Kanu hüpft.

Über die große Einkaufsstraße Corso Giacomo Matteotti bewege ich mich wieder ins Inselinnere, das schwarze Herz Ortigias, wo sich meine Unterkunft befindet. Horacio, der Pächter des Cafés, in dem ich jeden Morgen frühstücke und mit dessen Küche ich mir die Wand meines Schlafzimmers teile, schließt gerade das Mobiliar auf der kleinen Terrasse vor seinem Café ab. Das Geräusch der rasselnden Ketten begleitet er mit seiner Interpretation von Vamos a La Playa von Loona und als sein Nachbar weiß ich, dass er den Ohrwurm von den Gerüstbauern der Baustelle gegenüber hat. Ich grüße ihn auf Italienisch und wünsche ihm eine gute Nacht. Es ist eine Grußformel, deren Aussprache ich in jahrelanger Übung perfektioniert habe, sie klingt wie aus dem Mund eines

Einheimischen. Ich spüre, dass er wie jeden Morgen unsicher ist, ob er mich auf Italienisch oder Englisch grüßen sollte. Welche meiner Hälften sollte er nur ansprechen? Die deutsche? Die italienische? Und plötzlich ist mir das völlig gleich, denn nel mio paese nessuno é straniero, in meinem Land ist niemand ein Fremder – und das scheint mir eine gute Antwort zu sein. Ich stehe vor der Tür meiner Unterkunft. Mit Schlafen beende ich meinen Tag.

Giovanni Fiderio
Il Vecchio n.3

Il Vecchio entra in libreria di buon mattino con una camicia di lino avana a maniche corte e un cappello da baseball blu, ha in mano un libro pieno di appunti e foglietti tra le pagine:

«Buongiorno, c'è Maria Vittoria?»

«Buongiorno a lei, Maria Vittoria è a Palermo, la troverà domani pomeriggio.»

«Dille che devo parlarle di alcune cose importanti che riguardano quella storia del principe di Branciforte. Ho trovato un libro che potrebbe interessarle.»

«Ok glielo dirò appena la sento. Nel frattempo, se le può interessare, oggi pomeriggio ci sarà la presentazione di un libro sul polo petrolchimico di Siracusa.»

«Ancora? Un altro?» alza gli occhi al cielo «Ma cosa vogliono dal polo petrolchimico? Si sono messi tutti a raccontare storielle, creano miti, cercano eroi. Perchè non vanno a parlare con gli americani?» punta con l'indice Siracusa nord «Perchè non parlano con loro della nascita del polo petrolchimico?» poi con più calma aggiunge «Moratti era solo un pupo all'epoca… »

«Mmm, non saprei.» rispondo io evasivo.

«E infatti non sai niente, qui nessuno sa niente o nessuno ricorda niente» ride sarcastico alzando le spalle; poi si ferma a pensare, fa roteare la mano destra col palmo all'insù e sbuffa, non sa quale delle mille storie che gli passano per la testa vorrebbe raccontarmi, poi sorride lievemente e mi dice «Per raffinare una tonnellata di petrolio ci vogliono circa diciotto tonnellate d'acqua dolce. Questi qui hanno raffinato il petrolio con l'acqua minerale, ah ah ahhhhhh, incredibile!

C'è un grosso giacimento sotterraneo d'acqua dolce che va da Sortino fino a sotto Catania e loro hanno scavato centinaia di pozzi, centinaia davvero, per prelevare acqua minerale e raffinare il petrolio; e prima di quei pozzi erano stati già costruiti due acquedotti per portare acqua dolce al petrolchimico e costarono all'epoca un mare di soldi e non sono mai stati usati per quello scopo. Ma le raffinerie queste cose possono permettersele, capisci?»

«Mi sembra fantascienza.»

«Ah ah ahhhhhh» ride forte «Te la do io la fantascienza: qualche settimana fa a un'altra presentazione un ragazzo chiedeva se magari, dopo tutti questi anni, non fosse il caso di pulire il fondo del porto di Augusta e tirare via tutti i rifiuti e soprattutto il dannato mercurio. Eh! Si, certo! Tutti d'accordo! E perchè non si fa? – mi guarda come mi guardava mio nonno da bambino – Perchè nel porto di Augusta c'è anche la base militare dei sommergibili americani e c'è anche la marina militare italiana, quella si vede.»

Lo incalzo sarcastico «Poi magari per le munizioni e i missili possono andare a rifornirsi a Cava Sorciaro, dentro i monti Climiti.»

Lui risponde perentorio «Quella è un'altra cosa. Non so se quel deposito è ancora attivo, ma di sicuro quella grotta arriva giù fino al livello del mare, in pratica è un'enorme grotta sottomarina scavata all'interno dei Monti Climiti. La base militare ha anche un accesso dal mare a quattro chilometri di distanza e da lì i sommergibili raggiungono il deposito di armi chimiche e armi nucleari.»

«Balle. Non ci credo!»

«Meglio per te. Ciao!»

Il vecchio esce dalla libreria e io rimango dentro le storie ancora per un pò di tempo.

Su internet c'è chi dice che «l'enorme grotta sottomarina» non solo esiste ma ci hanno addirittura girato due film di 007 con licenza di uccidere. Chissà se è vero, sarebbe assurdo, già immagino Oddjob lanciare la sua bombetta mortale contro Sean Connery che attivando il suo Jetpack riesce rocambolescamente a fuggire dalla caverna per poi atterrare sulla splendida spiaggia di Funnucu novu dove l'aspetta l'avvenente Ursula Andress in un bikini mozzafiato.

Esco un attimo fuori dalla libreria a godermi i raggi del sole seduto sulla panchina.

Penso che dovrei riordinare i libri di Ian Fleming che raccontano le grandi storie di James Bond riprese nei film. Si avvicina l'estate, gli amanti del thriller gradiranno sicuramente.

Nel frattempo dall'angolo dell'isolato alla mia sinistra, dove Corso Umberto I incrocia viale Regina Margherita, vedo svoltare Il Vecchio con la sua andatura elegante. Capita che ritorni perchè ha pensato qualcos'altro di inerente all'ultimo discorso fatto.

Ad una decina di metri da me tira fuori l'indice con l'idea:

«Altra fantascienza» mi dice, accennando un sorriso – a proposito di quella zona dove ora ci sono i pontili e le industrie, quel tratto di mare della Targia e di Marina di Melilli ha un microclima tropicale, le acque sono leggermente più calde rispetto alla media.

«Direi che sono molto più calde della media.» rispondo «Mi è capitato di farci il bagno un paio di volte e l'acqua era proprio tiepida, quasi non c'era ristoro nel bagnarsi. Ma pensavo che fosse dovuto agli impianti di raffreddamento delle industrie, al fatto che tirano acqua dal mare.»

«Ah ah ahhhhhh» sbuffa a ridere «sicuramente ha influito anche questo di recente. Ma io ti parlo di quando l'industria non c'era. Lì c'era un microclima tropicale e c'erano pure delle specie di pesci che non si vedevano altrove in Sicilia. C'era il pesce serpente sul fondale sabbioso, agli inglesi piaceva molto, lo cercavano. E più in profondità c'era quel pesce che ha come dei residui di polmoni nelle branchie, dannazione come si chiama?» mi fa un cenno con la mano come a dire «dillo tu»

«Non ne ho idea» rispondo «non ne ho mai sentito parlare prima d'ora.»

«Praticamente è un fossile vivente, un pesce rarissimo.»

Provo a cercare su internet digitando «pesce che ha residui di polmoni» e trovo diversi articoli a carattere scientifico.

«Può essere che si tratti del celacanto?» chiedo provando con un nome che suonava bene.

«Sì esatto! Proprio quello! Il celacanto. L'hai trovato.» risponde esaltandosi «Quel pesce è stato sterminato, non si trova più adesso. I pescatori non avevano familiarità con quella specie, in più aveva un brutto aspetto: i denti in fuori, la livrea scura. E' stato eliminato.»

«Detta così sembra un classico della discriminazione.»

«Che vuoi dire?»

«Pesce sconosciuto, di brutto aspetto, viene eliminato.»

«Ma dai, anche la carne non era buona da mangiare.»

«Comunque qui dice che il celacanto è stato avvistato nei mari del Sud Africa e in Indonesia o tra il Canale del Mozambico e l'Oceano Indiano. Non c'è traccia del celacanto nel mar Mediterraneo.» dico indicando il monitor del computer.

«Ti sto dicendo che c'era anche qui da noi ed è stato eliminato. Non ti fidi di quello che ti dico?»

Mario Fillioley
Villette

Sono di Siracusa, città sulla cui costa nord, quella immediatamente accessibile per la balneazione, a un certo punto venne impiantato un polo petrolchimico. La prima conseguenza fu un improvviso arricchimento della popolazione: posto fisso, stipendio sicuro, tutti i mesi, e dunque possibilità concreta di indebitarsi. La seconda conseguenza furono i debiti e la villetta.

La villetta siracusana è un po' anomala: seconda casa al mare, dista pochissimi chilometri dalla prima abitazione, anch'essa sul mare. Potendo scegliere, la villetta sarebbe stato il caso di costruirsela in montagna, sugli Iblei. Però il mare cittadino era diventato impraticabile: scarichi fognari a parte, sulla costa nord si accanirono anche i moli di attracco per le petroliere, con i relativi sversamenti, e soprattutto durante i primi anni le ciminiere poco regolamentate ci andavano giù pesante coi miasmi. Così a un certo punto non ci fidammo più di fare il bagno ai Piliceddi o a Fondaco Nuovo, e iniziò una specie di transumanza verso le acque cristalline di Fontane Bianche, costa sud.

Doppiato Capo Murro di Porco, ecco la Fanusa e poi l'Arenella: un primo tratto di mare vergine e di comode spiagge sabbiose (in città solo scogli) che da lì, superando Ognina, si estendono per tutta Fontane Bianche fino al gelsomineto della Marchesa di Cassibile. Distanza dall'abitato: circa sedici chilometri. Sedici chilometri si coprono in neanche un quarto d'ora di macchina. Perché spendere tanti soldi per costruirsi una villetta a un quarto d'ora da casa? Probabilmente intervenne il fattore status symbol: non sono più un contadino, adesso faccio l'operaio specializzato, l'impiegato di concetto, il bancario, posso permetter-mi i figli all'università e pure la casa al mare.

A dire il vero, le case di villeggiatura dei nobili, quelle ottocentesche o liberty, erano tutte in contrada Isola, di fronte al porto, e si chiamavano ville. Quelle di Fontane Bianche, Ognina, Arenella, Fanusa invece no: da subito (e per sempre) si chiamarono villette, anche quando superarono in numero e dimensioni quelle nobiliari dell'isola. Un sintomo linguistico, quindi, nel senso che sì, col petrolchimico avevamo più soldi, però in fondo nemmeno tanti. Meglio costruire a due passi da casa, allora. Perché magari così i muri li tiro su io stesso quando finisco di lavorare, la domenica mio fratello e mio cognato mi vengono a dare una mano con gli spioventi del tetto: piano terra, veran-da coperta e primo piano; e poi, se la seconda casa è vicina, controllarla, gestirla, manutenerla sarà meno costoso e più pratico.

Villeggiare dietro casa, a pensarci bene, non è un'idea cretina: conviene. Qua fa caldo fino a novem-bre, e visto che la villetta è così vicina possiamo usarla per la scampagnata del giorno di Pasquetta, la grigliata del Primo Maggio e anche per il ponte di Ognissanti. Quando si chiudevano le scuole, le mogli casalinghe degli operai, insieme ai figli, si godevano mare e giardi-no per ben tre mesi, e il marito poteva rincasare la sera, a fine turno, giusto qualche chilometro di macchina in più, nell'attesa che arrivassero le ferie d'agosto.

Il piano regolatore non esisteva. La Regione siciliana ci metteva un bel po' ad approvare norme e deroghe sul demanio marino, la distanza dall'arenile, la tutela del paesaggio, e intanto nel vuoto normativo io mi tiro su la villetta direttamente sulla spiaggia. Oppure mi recinto questo tratto di scogli qua e ci faccio una scala in cemento che mi porta direttamente a mollo. La discesa a mare privata. Lo scivolo per il gommone. Un cancello sulla sabbia. Poi, a un certo punto, la normativa regionale sulla distanza dalla costa arriva: centocinquanta metri, la metà di quella prevista in Continente. E a ruota arrivano anche le prime sanatorie: Hai visto? Te l'avevo detto io: costruisci, che niente ci fa.

Risultato: Fontane Bianche non ha un lungomare, una piazza, un marciapiede. Solo villette, da un lato e dall'altro della statale 115, l'unica strada che la attraversa (al punto che in quel tratto la chiamiamo Viale dei Lidi).

L'idillio ci mise però un attimo a trasformarsi in nevrosi, e la vicinanza della seconda casa giocò un ruolo fondamentale: se la villetta è a dieci minuti di macchina, non c'è nessuna cesura tra lavoro e ferie estive, e finisce che continui a fare la spola tra il mare e la città, in continuazione e per i motivi più futili. E così eccoli là i siracusani, motorizzatisi da poco, in coda sulla via Elorina per andare a comprare il pesce al mercato di Ortigia e poi ritornare a grigliarselo nel giardino di Fontane Bianche. Su e giù, anche più volte al giorno.

Gli anni in cui io sono stato bambino e poi giovane, a ricordarseli adesso, furono pura schizofrenia. I divertimenti notturni, per esempio. Se ci trasferivamo in villetta, facevo sedici chilometri in motorino ad andare e altri sedici a tornare per una semplice passeggiata al Duomo. Allora i miei genitori, per evitare che io ogni notte rischiassi l'osso del collo su strade extraurbane poco illuminate e peggio asfaltate, decidevano che l'estate prossima basta, si rimaneva in città. Ma in un anno la moda cambiava, e la stagione successiva il posto in cui bisognava assolutamente essere ogni sera era il centro commerciale Frisio di Fontane Bianche. Motorino, trentadue chilometri, su e giù. Mettiti il casco altrimenti ti scippo la testa, diceva mio padre.

Vabbè, poi si cresce. Vai a fare l'università fuori, e quando torni per l'estate decidi che quest'anno invece no, te ne starai in villetta e non ti muoverai da là: sdraiato sull'amaca tesa tra i due pini (com'è rasserenante l'ombra dei pini, pensano i tuoi guardandoti leggere beato). La villetta, però, mentre tu fai l'università, invecchia. Non è tanto che mostri segni di cedimenti strutturali (un po' sì: nel frattempo ha già i suoi vent'anni, e oltretutto l'ha tirata su tuo padre, nei ritagli di tempo, col fratello e il cognato) quanto che è un po' trascurata. I tuoi ci vanno di meno, perché tanto voi figli tornate giusto un paio di settimane in agosto: e allora per due settimane che fai? Non vale neanche la pena di mettersi a ridipingere le tapparelle. E se all'angolo del soffitto si forma un poco di muffa, pazienza, ci pensiamo l'anno venturo.

Finisci l'università e la villetta adesso è proprio malandata. Pure i tossici si sono accorti che ci andate poco. Subite qualche furto. L'arredamento, già poco ricco di suo, ora è diventato spartano. Il forno in pietra ha la canna fumaria otturata dagli aghi di pino (che alberi infestanti, i pini, pensa tua madre mentre la pizza si brucia). La stufa a legna ha lo sportellino rotto. Anche la pavimentazione del vialetto d'ingresso è saltata per via delle radici (mai piantare pini in una villetta, spiega il piastrellista – sfregandosi le mani – a tuo padre che gli sta firmando il preventivo). Tutto sommato però, ogni tanto riesci a portarci una ragazza: l'umidità che qui, d'inverno, fa tanto bohème, il rumore delle onde, niente tv perché se la sono rubata i ladri, giusto un plaid per avvolgervi stretti e non morire di tisi, insomma: se non volevi combinare niente me lo spieghi che ci siamo venuti a fare tu e io qua in pieno gennaio?

La villetta assolveva così la funzione demografica di contrasto alla nascita zero. E ne assolveva pure un'altra: fare da sfogo per il nervoso di tuo padre. Perché in tutto quello stato d'abbandono una sola cosa era in perfetto ordine: il giardino. Tuo padre usava la villetta per scaricare le tensioni su piante e alberi, gli esseri viventi più inermi del creato. Non appena aveva un minuto libero, via in villetta a decespugliare, tosare erba, usare la sega a scoppio per tagliare rami (mai della dimensione giusta per la stufa: fu tentando di introdurvi uno di questi tronchi che si ruppe lo sportellino) e potare.

Grazie a lui, almeno il giardino è curato, sì, ma come lo è la testa di un bambino quando si teme possa prendere i pidocchi. La macchia mediterranea, un tempo lussureggiante su aiuole e vialetti, adesso è il monte di Venere glabro di una pornostar. Le siepi di oleandro, che seppero essere potenti schermature per gli sguardi del vicino, tuo padre, questo estroso coiffeur del verde, ha deciso che quest'anno si portano corte, a spazzola: più moderno, ti dice.

Ma in questo eccessivo nitore del giardino la decadenza della costruzione risalta ancora di più. Bisogna correre ai ripari. Un piccolo investimento iniziale, allora, giusto una rimessa in sesto, e poi via, darsi subito alle locazioni stagionali. Affittasi, anche per brevi periodi. Funziona. Coi soldi si riescono ad ammortizzare le spese di restauro e quelle di manutenzione. La villetta rinasce a un certo splendore (mitigato dal fatto che tuo padre continua a occuparsi del giardino). Solo che non è più casa tua. L'hai prima svuotata e poi riempita di suppellettili che non ti sono mai appartenute. Hai dipinto le pareti di un colore diverso. Sotto ai pini, al posto dell'amaca, c'è un salottino in teak scuro coi cuscini bianco écru che hai visto su Case e giardini e comprato in offerta. E se nei periodi in cui è sfitta ti sogni di portarci quella che nel frattempo è diventata tua moglie, l'ansia di sporcare, rovinare o rompere qualcosa condanna il bambino concepito in quel famoso gennaio a rimanere figlio unico.

La vita è andata avanti, la villetta ha cambiato funzione, ma per fortuna è ancora lì, solida: il mattone che mai tradì la famiglia italiana. Però tuo padre s'è fatto un po' anziano, si stanca. Il sabato ti obbliga ad andare lì insieme a lui, si siede sul muro a secco e inizia a impartirti ordini, affinché sia tu, il suo diretto discendente, a martoriare piante e siepi in sua vece.

Prima di piantare la sega su un ramo d'acacia, esiti. Guardi tuo padre, assiso su quel trono di pietra, e speri che si intenerisca. Invece lo vedi febbrile ed eccitato: un sovrano che comanda al boia l'esecuzione. Però che ci puoi fare? È tuo padre, gli devi ubbidienza. Che la pianta soffra il meno possibile, allora.

Perciò, mentre compio questa specie di deforestazione autunnale azzerando qualsiasi forma di vita vegetale a colpi di decespugliatore, mentre abbasso di altri quattro centimetri la siepe di oleandro e mi ritrovo faccia a faccia col figlio del vicino, obbligato come me dal padre a potare la stessa siepe dal lato opposto; mentre ci guardiamo l'uno negli occhi dell'altro e ci indichiamo vicendevolmente col mento il nostro rispettivo genitore, seduto sul muretto a secco, che ci rimprovera perché non stiamo tagliando bene, non stiamo tagliando abbastanza, non ci stiamo mettendo la giusta dose di ebbro furore; mentre ci sorridiamo complici portandoci l'indice all'orecchio come a significare: possono dire quello che vogliono, perché tanto col rumore che fa 'sto coso non sentiamo niente; mentre il mio terreno, il mio giardino, la mia casa sfumano nei suoi e i suoi nei miei fino a confondersi in un tutto indistinto, sento una specie di afflato, un senso di appartenenza alla comunità siracusana con cui da sempre fatico a venire a patti, e inizio a farmi domande che, se potessi, mi poterei via dalla testa a colpi di cesoia.

Noi, cittadini di questa poco civica città, nel fregarcene di piani regolatori e di distanze dalla costa, nel costruirci a nostro uso e consumo villette sul mare cui abbiamo freudianamente affidato il compito di risarcirci dalla perdita di un altro mare (quello della costa nord), siamo stati veramente nel torto? Abbiamo davvero perpetrato abusi edilizi? Abbiamo peccato contro le nostre stesse risorse?

Prima che le villette mutassero destinazione d'uso, da seconde case a foresterie, io avrei risposto subito di sì, senza esitazione. Anzi avrei aggredito chi mi avesse posto una domanda tanto stupida e gli avrei sventolato sotto al naso l'eccezione, la piantina catastale della mia villetta, comprata da un vecchio e ligio professore di matematica, individuo dalla moralità specchiata, in regola con le cubature, le concessioni, le distanze. Avrei tacciato tutti gli abusivisti di scempio, li avrei presi per miopi e ignoranti, gretti, incapaci di comprendere come, devastando la costa con le loro costruzioni, avessero privato se stessi e la città intera dell'unica vocazione economica in possesso del nostro territorio: il turismo.

Invece qui, avvolto in una nuvola di fogliame che si stacca da queste piante che mio padre, pieno di un odio di cui non riesco a comprendere l'origine, mi incita a massacrare, penso che non lo so più se è così. Da quando anch'io, come un sacco di siracusani, affitto la mia villetta ho dovuto farci i conti. Siti, portali, agenzie, tour operator: tutti richiedono case sul mare. La mia viene spesso scartata perché il mare dista, a piedi, circa trecento metri. Una passeggiata di meno di cinque minuti.

«Quali sono le case che affittate di più?», ho chiesto alle agenzie con cui lavoro di solito.

«Quelle sul mare».

«Ma la mia è sul mare. Le verande si affacciano sul faro, le terrazze guardano il golfo».

«Non hai capito: »sul mare» significa che apri la porta e cadi in acqua».

«E qual è la zona più richiesta?»

«Fontane Bianche».

Siracusa negli ultimi anni ha avuto un'esplosione turistica: calo di presenze sul Continente, controtendenza assoluta nella mia città, e, per quel poco che la mia (assai circoscritta e nient'affatto scientifica) indagine via mail ha svelato, l'esplosione di Siracusa come località balneare per famiglie e piccole comitive sembra legata a questa capacità capillare di offrire alloggi direttamente su scogliere e arenili.

Francesi, tedeschi, russi, belgi, danesi, svizzeri, inglesi, e poi veneti, friulani, lombardi, emiliani: tutti cercano su internet villette sulla spiaggia o con la discesa a mare privata. Come funziona allora questo abusivismo edilizio che deprechiamo e condanniamo da decenni? Sento il ronzio del decespugliatore che mi fracassa i pensieri e me li fa tutti ispidi: vuoi vedere che quando l'abusivismo serviva a risarcire noi stessi dai veleni del petrolchimico era una cosa da terroni incivili, malandrini in ogni molecola del loro DNA, e ora, invece, che serve a rendere più comode le ferie dello scandinavo non è poi così male? Spengo il decespugliatore e chiedo al figlio del vicino se anche loro affittano.

«Sì», mi dice, «ma purtroppo solo nei picchi di stagione».

A suggerirci di affittare, sia a me che a lui, è stato un altro vicino, con la casa sugli scogli. Anni fa, la villetta di questo vicino doveva addirittura essere demolita, c'erano le palle di ferro pronte, poi non se ne fece più niente. Lui, nelle more tra una sanatoria e l'altra, prese ad affittarla, e adesso è sempre piena, anche ad autunno inoltrato. Piena di gente molto alta e molto bionda: padri, madri, bimbi tutti bellissimi e tutti di un fototipo catarifrangente, delle specie di Obelix che da piccoli devono essere caduti dentro la pentola della protezione solare cinquanta. Tutti discendenti di una stirpe vichinga residente in nazioni dove case costruite in una posizione come quella che hanno affittato qui non sono concepibili neanche in sogno.

Di questo nostro obbrobrioso paesaggio costiero balneare, dunque, non è cambiato nulla, se non i suoi fruitori.

«Anzi no, non è vero», dico pieno di un entusiasmo da eureka al figlio del vicino, «è cambiato pure lo Zeitgeist».

«E che è?», s'informa quello, «un diserbante? Pure tuo padre è fissato coi diserbanti, allora?»

«No. Cioè sì, pure mio padre è fissato, ma io intendevo dire che, anche se tutto è rimasto identico, adesso ci ritroviamo in un contesto turistico globale talmente mutato da avere invertito i fattori decisivi per risultare vincenti nell'offerta turistica: fai schifo, mia cara costa siracusana, sei devastata, ma quanto sei comoda, con queste tue villette che saltano direttamente in acqua».

«Senti, fermiamoci, che mi fa male la spalla», risponde il figlio del vicino.

Il giardinaggio è così: stanca il corpo e non appaga la mente. Pure io mi fermo. Ma non provo sollievo. Penso che se funziona in questo modo, allora significa che l'obbrobrio è obbrobrio finché lo guardi da fuori, e se invece lo guardi da dentro casa tua diventa bellezza. Ecco che allora tutti vogliono diventare proprietari, fosse anche solo per una settimana, di una bella casa abusiva.

«Secondo te perché?», chiedo al vicino mentre i nostri genitori si lamentano tra loro di quanto siamo sfaticati, della nostra evidente inettitudine alla deforestazione.

«E che ne so?», mi risponde lui.

«Te lo dico io perché», gli faccio. «È la linea della palma che è salita, che sale ancora, che salirà all'infinito».

«La palma?», dice lui guardando il giardino. «La palma mica è salita: sono tre anni che il punteruolo rosso ce le ha distrutte tutte quante, guarda qua». E mi indica una serie di tronchi senza più foglie. Poi riaccende il decespugliatore.

Mio padre è sempre seduto sul muro a secco. Mi sta guardando con la faccia delusa di uno che aveva pagato per vedere Tyson che stacca a morsi le orecchie e si è ritrovato al Bol'šoj tra piroette in tutù: Finiscilo! Abbattilo!, mi sta gridando con gli occhi. Quando finalmente mi autorizza a spegnere il decespugliatore, io e il figlio del vicino ci stringiamo la mano quasi sotto alle ex palme. Alzare di nuovo lo sguardo verso i due totem è inevitabile.

«Certo che però questo punteruolo rosso sarebbe proprio il giardiniere ideale dei nostri genitori», ci diciamo all'unisono prima di separarci.

Dana von Suffrin
Work

Das einzige, was den herrlichen Vormittag auf der Terrasse störte, war der Geruch nach Katzenurin. Eine kleine Kolonie rotweißer Katzen hatte sich – wie im Süden üblich – von Menschen erdachte Infrastruktur, genauer: diese Dächer hier, als Lebensraum ausgesucht, und Gabi hatte die Nachbarin schon ein paarmal dabei beobachtet, wie sie den Kätzchen Futter auf das Fensterbrett gestellt hatte. Keine Frage, die Katzen störten, aber sie hatte trotzdem gelächelt und kurz gewunken, Siracusa war nicht der Ort, an dem man sich über Dinge aufregte, die man nicht ändern konnte.

Trotzdem war nicht alles unabänderlich. Gabi akzeptierte nicht einfach alles, sie war anders als ihre Mutter und die Frauen vor ihr, sie hatte schon zuviel gelesen und erfahren. Sie war außerdem alles andere als eine Fatalistin, sie war, ganz wie die meisten Menschen, die man ihrer Generation zuschlug, gewillt, jede Gelegenheit, die sich ihr bot, wahrzunehmen. Sie war auch gewillt, zu geben und sich anzustrengen, und obwohl man Jahre später über jene Generation, die ihrer schließlich folgen sollte, behauptete, sie sei faul und nicht arbeitsam, war sie nur gewillt, sich alles zu nehmen, was das Leben noch zu bieten hatte, und diesen Anspruch hatten Menschen wie Gabi schon formuliert, als die meisten sich zwischen Lohnarbeit und Familie aufrieben. Zumindest sagte Michael soetwas, oder soetwas ähnliches. Gabi meinte übrigens nicht materielle Dinge. Sie war jetzt zweiunddreißig und fast sicher, dass sie in zwei oder drei Jahren den Job wechseln würde. Gerade lief es einfach zu gut, und sie hatte noch für das nächste und das übernächste Jahr Event- und Messenauftritte zugesagt. Für den Auftritt auf einer größeren Messe in Tirol hatte sie zweiundzwanzig Tausend Euro verlangt, und die Veranstalter waren sofort einverstanden gewesen. Mit ihrem Kanal verdiente sie monatlich ein paar Tausend Euro, aber das meiste gab sie wieder für Equipment, Kleidung und Reisen aus, und natürlich musste sie auch Spikey Mike bezahlen. Mike stellte ihr am Ende des Monats immer Rechnungen, das war ein bisschen lächerlich, aber auf eine Weise war er ja nur ein Statist. Und ihr Freund, aber das war ja ungefähr das gleiche. Gabi legte das meiste auf einem Festgeldkonto an, außerdem hatte sie ein paar Depots, aber solche der sicheren Sorte. Sie wusste, jeder Dreh, jeder Auftritt würde ihr ein paar Monate Lohnarbeit ersparen.

Alles in allem verdiente sie jetzt ungefähr so viel wie die ärgsten Streber aus der Schule, die keine Minute Freizeit hatten und mit dreißig aussahen wie fünfzig. Gabi sah ungefähr aus wie achtundzwanzig. Sie haushaltete auch wie eine viel jüngere Frau. Das Gute war, dass Gabi überhaupt nicht verschwenderisch war, sie hatte sich einen gebrauchten Opel gekauft und hier auf Sizilien zwang sie Michael dazu, abends Pizza zu essen, das war viel günstiger. Mike blieb manchmal an den schönen, romantischen Restaurants stehen, aber sie zog ihn wie ein Kind einfach weg. Nur wenn andere Leute dabei waren, gaben sie sich verschwendungssüchtig, denn das gehörte zur Show. Gabi war in echt ganz anders. Gemeinsam mit Mike kaufte sie zwei Pizzen, eine vegane für Gabi und eine mit tausend verschiedenen Sorten Fleisch, vor der sich Gabi ekelte. Sie hob den Kassenzettel auf (wenn sie einen bekam). Sie setzten sich mit den Pizzen auf eine Bank nahe des Tempels, und dann rissen sie die Kartons auf. Gabi freute sich jeden Abend wie ein kleines Kind auf diesen Moment. Mike aß abstoßend schnell, er rollte seine Pizzaviertel zusammen und stopfte sie sich in seinen gefräßigen Mund, und gleichzeitig hielt er Gabi noch kurze Vorträge über Politik und Geschichte. Abstoßend. Gabi aß höchstens eine halbe Pizza, und die Hälfte, die sie stehen ließ, verschlang Mike wie ein gefräßiger Köter. Interessanterweise schien es in diesem Teil Siziliens gar keine Straßenhunde zu geben, dachte Gabi. Mike klärte sie auf: In den exklusiveren Regionen, zu denen man Syrakus ohne weiteres zählen konnte, hatte man schon vor Jahren begonnen, wilde und halbwilde Hunde zu fangen und einzuschläfern, nachdem es ein paar unschöne Vorfälle mit Touristen gegeben hatte. Traurig, sagte Gabi, und Mike sagte nichts, und dann drückte er die Getränkedosen zusammen und stopfte die Kartons in den Mülleimer und dann gingen beide Hand in Hand zurück in ihr Airbnb. So war bisher jeder Abend abgelaufen, außer der natürlich, als sie mit Giacomo und Paul gedreht hatten, da hatte es am Set kalte Pasta gegeben.

Außerdem musste sie vorsorgen. Natürlich war es ihr bekannt, dass es für jedes Angebot Nachfrage gab, aber sie spürte, dass langsam die Zeit für einen Wandel kam. Es war schön, alleine auf der Terrasse zu liegen, aber es war nur schön, weil es ein Luxus war, eine kleine Auszeit von der Pause. Zukünftig wollte sie sich die kleinen Auszeiten anders verdienen. Mit Mike hatte sie darüber noch nicht gesprochen, aber was sollte der schon dagegen haben: ein Häuschen im Umland, ein oder zwei Kinder, am besten Jungen, Alltag und Sicherheit. Vielleicht würde Gabi sogar in ihren alten Beruf zurückkehren, sie hatte Soziale Arbeit studiert und sogar zwei Jahre in diesem Beruf gearbeitet. Gabi schloss die Augen, sie versuchte, sich ihre Zukunft ganz genau vorzustellen, sie dachte an die perfekte Einbauküche und an die Blumen im Garten, denn angeblich vergrößerte sich die Wahrscheinlichkeit, dass ein Traum sich verwirklichte, wenn man hinter geschlossenen Augen schon die Versatzstücke dieser Traumwelt zusammenfügte, und so zwang Gabi sich, sich ihr Leben in ein paar Jahren detailgetreu vorzustellen, denn auch wenn diese Methode wahrscheinlich Unsinn war, schaden würde sie nicht. Gabi verbrachte den halben Vormittag so auf der Terrasse, sie lag mit geschlossenen Augen auf einem dieser Plastik-Liegestühle, sie trug ein altes AC/DC-Shirt von Mike und eine seiner Boxershorts, denn in ihrer Freizeit legte sie größten Wert auf bequeme Kleidung, sie trug privat nie Make-Up und am liebsten lief sie einfach in so einem 80er-Jahre-Jogginganzug mit Baseball-Cap und Sonnenbrille herum, dann erkannte sie auch niemand - Mike sagte immer, dass sie ohnehin niemand erkennen würde, denn wer schaute Gabi denn schon ins Gesicht, und je öfter Gabi darüber nachdachte, desto mehr war sie der Meinung, dass diese Aussage einfach eine Unverschämtheit war. Wie um sich zu vergewissern, dass sie ein Gesicht hatte, strich

Gabi mit den Finger über ihre Stirn und strich sich eine Strähne weg. Gabi war kürzlich während einer Yoga-Stunde in ihrem Wiener Fitnessstudio auf einen interessanten Gedanken gestoßen: Unser Körper war gar nicht unser Körper, er war nur ein Körper, den wir uns für eine gewisse Zeit geliehen hatten. Natürlich war auch diese Aussage wieder ein klein wenig esoterisch, aber Gabi war zum Schluss gekommen, dass der Gedanke nicht so falsch war, wir waren aus der rein zufälligen Begegnung von Zellen entstanden, dann gewachsen und gewachsen, und schließlich würden wir nach dem Ende unseres Lebens wieder zu den Elementen zurückkehren, und vielleicht war der einzige Makel des Satzes, dass nicht nur unsere Körper, sondern natürlich auch unsere Seele nur geliehen war. Sie schrieb eine Nachricht an Michael und bemühte sich, nett zu klingen.

Oder, vielleicht würde sie einfach nach Italien gehen? Italien war wunderschön, das war natürlich eine Floskel, aber wie die meisten Floskeln war sie wahr. Obwohl Gabi die üblichen Konzepte von Lebensabschnitten und Aufgaben, die man in diesen Lebensabschnitten angeblich zu bewältigen hatte, in Frage stellte, wusste sie doch, dass etwas daran sie auch anspornte. Früher hatte sie eine Bucket List geführt, darauf standen Orte, die sie sehen wollte, Bücher, die sie noch lesen wollte, inspirierende Menschen, von denen sie noch lernen wollte. Vor ein paar Monaten hatte sie die ganze Liste von ihrem Handy gelöscht. Auf der Terrasse dachte sie wieder daran, und sie war ein bisschen stolz auf sich, denn sie fühlte sich sehr im Moment, und sehr im Moment sein, war etwas, wozu ihre Therapeutin ihr immer geraten hatte. Es gab keinen Grund, an der Situation etwas ändern zu wollen: Sie lag bequem, sie war nicht durstig, sie vermisste nichts, sie konnte einfach liegen und nachdenken, sie musste keine Liste mehr abarbeiten. Gabi belog sich selbst, aber sie wusste das.

Wie spät es wohl war? Gabi versuchte, sich selbst davon zu überzeugen, dass die Uhrzeit ganz egal war, aber es gelang ihr nicht richtig. Immer wieder stellte sie sich die Frage, so als hinge etwas davon ab - dabei hatten Michael und sie an diesem Tag keine Termine mehr, alles war abgedreht, und die Postpoduktion würde in Wien erfolgen. Für sie war die Postproduktionszeit fast die beste, denn Mike verschwand für drei oder vier Tage ganz in seiner Mancave und bediente wie ein Verrückter dutzende blinkende Knöpfe, von denen Gabi nicht einmal wusste, wofür sie da waren. Früher war sie öfter in sein Zimmer gekommen, um wie ein stilles, schüchternes Kind zuzusehen, und das, was sie auf dem Bildschirm sah, hatte erstaunlich wenig mit ihr zu tun gehabt. In der letzten Zeit waren ihr die Produkte fast egal geworden, sie spulte vor, wenn sie das fertige Material sichtete, und mehr aus Gewohnheit denn aus wirklicher Besorgnis achtete sie darauf, dass ihre Brüste einigermaßen vorteilhaft aussahen (was nicht in allen Positionen möglich war) und dass sie ihr Gesicht einigermaßen unter Kontrolle hatte - aber im Grunde war es ihr egal, sie wusste, dass ein Körper, der zufällig ihr Körper war, Dinge taten, die eigentlich nichts mit ihr zu tun hatten, sie litt nicht, aber sie genoss auch nicht, sie verdiente einfach ihr Geld damit.

Heute stand der Tag den beiden also ganz zu ihrer freien Verfügung, Gabi hatte sich vorgenommen, auf dem Weg zum Baden die Ruinen genauer zu betrachten, die in der Stadt waren und zu denen Michael ihr etwas erzählt, was sie sofort wieder vergessen hatte. Sie mochte die Ruinen, sie lief ja mehrmals täglich daran vorbei, und sie versuchte sich, Römer und Griechen in Toga beim Relaxen vorzustellen. Aßen die nicht sogar im Liegen? Gabi hatte nicht viel Ahnung von antiker Geschichte, aber kam es nicht darauf an, sich in die Leute einzufühlen, auch wenn sie schon lange tot waren? Wieso sollte das weniger wichtig sein, als ihre Militärstrategien zu untersuchen? Und das Sicheinfühlen entsprach Gabi sowieso mehr, und sie hatte schon mehrere erbitterte Diskussionen mit Michael geführt, der der Meinung war, ihr Beruf (der ja auch sein Beruf war) war nichts als knallhartes Geschäft und Erzeugung von Illusionen, aber Gabi wusste es ja besser. Sie verstand Michaels Einwand zwar, aber sie wusste trotzdem, dass ihr Job auch eine entschiedene transzendente Komponente hatte, sie hatte in die traurigen, einsamen Augen der Konsumenten geblickt, die sich, als sie Autogrammkarten unterschrieb, kurz weiteten, flatterten, einen Moment glücklich waren.

Die Sonne zerfurchte mit ihren eisernen, gleißenden Strahlen Gabis Stirn. Gabi zog ihre Kappe tiefer ins Gesicht. Syrakus (oder Siracusa, wie Michael sagte), lag außerhalb des italienischen Stiefels, genauer gesagt, kurz vor der Spitze des Stiefels. So viel Sonne, so wenig Land. Was war Sizilien überhaupt? Gabi öffnete Google Maps und zoomte sich heraus, von der Dachterrasse aus Ortigia, und dann aus Syrakus, dann aus der ganzen Insel und schließlich sah sie Europa von oben und stellte fest, dass Sizilien ungefähr dreieckig war. War Sizilien ein Ball, den der Stiefel wegkicken wollte? Oder ein Häufchen, in das der Stiefel gerade trat? Gabi räusperte sich, und dann war ihr plötzlich klar, was beide Bilder über ihre Beziehung zu Michael sagten. Wie die meisten jungen Frauen war Gabi geschult darin, in allen möglichen Belanglosigkeiten, die ihren Alltag durchstreifen, Zeichen und Symbole zu sehen. Ihre Freundinnen und sie rufen sogar gelegentlich bei einer Kartenlegerin in Deutschland an, und ließen sich für 49 Euro die nähere Zukunft voraussagen. Die Kartenleserin hatte immer Recht, aber Gabi hatte sie noch nie zu Mike befragt, meistens hatte sie Fragen zu Geld und Beruf, und natürlich war es Gabi bewusst, dass die Kartenleserin überhaupt nichts wusste, aber trotzdem das hektische, leise Gerede orientierte sie, es erdete sie.

Plötzlich war Gabi gar nicht mehr träge, sie stand auf, ordnete sich das Haar und stieg dann vorsichtig die kurze steile Treppe zum Schlafzimmer herunter. Michael lag noch immer im Bett, er hatte das Laken halb abgestreift. Seine gequälte Haut schälte sich, obwohl Gabi ihm tausendmal gesagt hat, dass er Sonnencreme benutzen soll. Sein ironisches Micky-Maus-Tattoo wirkt auf einmal plastisch, dabei besteht es nur aus hässlichen krummen Linien, aber Michael häutet sich genau dort, wo die Maus ihre Ohren hat. Gabi geht näher hin und macht ein Foto. Gabi ekelt sich, nicht nur vor der Haut, sondern vor allem, es ergeht ihr nicht anders als den Millionen Sündern in den Jahrhunderten vor ihr, die sich aus dem Nachtlager erhoben, wuschen, und dann begannen, Lust und Schuld zu vermischen. Gabi weiß, dass es Männern in dieser Hinsicht noch schlimmer geht, sie hat zwar keinen allzu großen Erfahrungsschatz, zumindest keinen privaten, aber sie kennt den traurigen Blick der Männer, die ein paar Minuten später alles bereuen und sich am liebsten dafür entschuldigen würden, dass sie einen geliebten, der eigenen Mutter verdächtig ähnlich sehenden Körper geschändet haben. Aber: Michael hatte solche Gefühle nie, und das nahm Gabi ihm übel. Hatte er überhaupt Gefühle? Gabi schloss die Tür wieder, sie hatte genug gesehen und genug gefühlt. Es gab ja überhaupt keinen Grund, auf ihn zu warten. Sie packte die große Badetasche, warf ein frisches weißes Handtuch, eine Flasche Wasser und Sonnencreme herein. Sizilien war ganz sicher ein Stiefel, der etwas wegtrat. Trotzdem konnte sie sich nicht ganz entscheiden, das Haus zu verlassen, und so ging sie wieder auf die Terrasse. Sie trank einen Schluck warmes Wasser aus der Plastikflasche, die knisterte und lärmte. Sie rief bei ihrer Mutter an, die, so hoffte sie zumindest, eine nur vage Vorstellung von der Geschäftsreise ihrer Tochter hatte. Sie simulierte ein harmloses Gespräch. So erzählte sie ihr nur Belanglosigkeiten, von den blauen Fischen, die sie unter Wasser gesehen hatte, von den Boutiquen, in die sie nur einen Blick geworfen hatte, von der Pizza. Von Michael erzählte sie überhaupt nichts. Sie hatte gerade aufgelegt und wollte nun wirklich aus der Wohnung gehen, sie schlich sich gerade über die Stiegen und war fast im Erdgeschoss, da stürmte Michael ihr hinterher. Er war nackt und in Panik, aber Gabi befand sich bereits in dem Stadium ihrer Beziehung, in dem der Ekel über sein großes, schlaffes Glied überwog und sie am liebsten gar nicht nach dem Grund seiner Bestürzung gefragt hätte. Mike nahm das nicht wahr, wie auch, und er rief: Du musst sofort Rosa anrufen, wir müssen zurück auf das Boot, und dann erklärte er Gabi alles, und nachdem Gabi sich mit der Geduld jener, die wissen, dass sie einer drastischen Entscheidung den richtigen Boden bereiten müssen, alles angehört hatte, sagte sie nur: Ich gehe jetzt baden.

Sorry Siracusa
English

Sorry Press ®

Sorry Siracusa is the first leg of a nomadic writers residency. Each stop produces a collection of short stories by local and visiting authors. Together, they provide a polyphonic view on the destination through the eyes of literature.

Index
English

Originalle

Index

Giovanni Fiderio
The Old Man n.1

The Old Man enters the bookstore with the index finger of his left hand bent towards the cashier's counter, where the employee sits. So when you turn to see who's coming in, the finger is already pointing directly at you. Once he's crossed the threshold, you notice that his head also leans slightly to the left: it's his way of announcing that the question he's about to ask was already prepared before he left home, and he has held it on the tip of his finger until the moment of delivery.

The rest of his body is relaxed, with a soft, wide stride, in the manner of many tall people.

Then comes an «Eeeeeee, could you please order this book for me, because you definitely don't have it in the store,» he grimaces. «Imagine! No one in this town would know anything about such a book,» he laughs, pleased with the dirty looks he receives. «Nobody reads these books here, and why should they? No one here thinks.«

«What book is it?»

He hands me a handwritten note with the title of the book and the author, twirling his hand as he does so.

«Oh yes, we have this book!» I exclaim after checking the computer. Lucky punch.

«No, that's not right, you're wrong!» he replies, half annoyed.

«No really, it's exactly the book written here, I'll go get it for you.»

«That's impossible. Why do you even have it?»

«We ordered it for the release.»

«So, you're telling me that someone reads this stuff here?»

«It happens.»

«Let me see,» he flips through the book. «Unbelievable! And who in Syracuse would read such a book? I want to meet them.»

Of course, sometimes we don't have the requested book in stock, and in that case, we order it. When the book arrives, it's rare for the Old Man to immediately buy it and take it home to read; that happens only occasionally, with a few books.

Usually, when he comes to collect the book, he holds it in his hand, flips through it, and comments in real-time: «Mmm, impressive» or «Ah! So this author is just a charlatan, there's only nonsense written here.»

Other times, after flipping through it, he realizes that the book wasn't what he imagined, or only certain parts are useful, and then he asks if he can make photocopies of the few pages that interest him. We look at him, baffled and amused by his continuous defiance of normalcy, and we make the photocopies he needs.

It's special treatment, and I must admit we're not always sure why we make exceptions for him. I think it's because he's straightforward and honest, but above all, he has a thirst for great books. He's a passionate scholar with a punk soul, and it's not easy to find people like that at over eighty years old.

Sometimes the book is fine, and he assures us that he'll buy it soon, as soon as he wins a scratch card or the lottery. And he does, to be clear; I must also admit that he wins relatively often. While waiting for the win, he asks us to keep the book in the window or prominently displayed, like bait, just to see if anyone notices it, if anyone flips through it, or even buys it. It must be his way of seeking like-minded people and rejoicing in the fact that out there, someone appreciates a book suggested by him.

Adriano Sack
An Almost Fearless Woman

When Domenico Corsini still hadn't shown up after half an hour, Anette Schwalbinger sighed and ordered another Coco Chanel. She liked the taste of the elder-flower syrup. And even if her old friend did turn up, being slightly tipsy wouldn't be an issue. Together, they had survived many other states of intoxication.

The bar was behind the ruins of the Temple of Apollo in Syracuse. Schwalbinger was the oldest person in the room and there were only two young Americans sipping their drinks at the window. She glanced at the weathered planks of her table, which was made from driftwood. She didn't mind being alone. She loved staring into space and thinking. And she found it amusing that this made other people uncomfortable. The waiter ignored her at first, then addressed her with an exaggerated amount of respect in English. That went too far for her because she was proud of her Italian. She had studied in Florence for four semesters and gained six kilos there. And, even decades later, she sometimes woke up with the taste of fresh, sautéed porcini mushrooms on her tongue. The slight sliminess and the basic freshness—how could she have ever left that city? She had had thirteen lovers there, which had seemed like slim pickings at the time, but which was formidable for a student in religious studies. Now, forty years later, she has kept sporadically in contact with one of these men, namely Domenico Corsini. Maybe because he was the only one who didn't just listen to himself talk. But then he discovered that he liked men a little more than his classmate from Germany. How these two things were connected was something that Schwalbinger—as she liked to be called since it vaguely reminded her of Chekhov—hadn't thought about for ages. Gay Domenico was the most handsome and talented student in her year. And, as his professors would later say, the biggest disappointment.

The two of them had spent many a night wandering through the dimly lit streets of Florence slightly drunk on the austerity and intelligence the city still exuded. Then he fled back to Sicily because his heart had been broken by a German man and his mother had fallen ill. He half-heartedly carried on with his studies in Messina and his messages became fewer and far between and weirder. At first, she had missed him terribly, then the started writing(her dissertation on Savonarola, the preacher of repentance, and his influence on the totalitarian ideologies of the twentieth century. When she was back in gray Stuttgart, weighing her job prospects, she lost interest in religious studies and made her career with the aid of her minor in psychology.

Anette Schwalbinger was a heavyset woman with the firepower of a John Deere lawnmower. Her eyes were the gray of a seagull, and her white hair was pulled back so tightly that it resembled a halo in favorable light. She would have redacted these two sentences from any text: she disliked detours, only relied on humor in emergencies, and refused to be judged by appearances. After her studies, she eventually found herself in the HR department of a large German car manufacturer by a series of twists and turns that will only be hinted at in this story. There, she quickly became indispensable and would eventually go on to claim the title of Chief Officer of Human Resources, a position just below the board of directors. Her hiring was hastily interpreted as a turning point in the newspapers' business sections, which were still in existence at the time. But this was met with immense resistance within the company. One time, during the launch of a compact SUV, she stumbled upon a rowdy group of colleagues with her young employee, Jude Klingendorf, at the center, shrieking and laughing. The moment their boss came within earshot, the group fell silent, and Klingendorf quickly dashed off to grab «top ups.»

Schwalbinger surveyed her male colleagues faces that were reddened by alcohol, some of which were still covered in pimples, and not one of them offered to help Jude with the drinks. They were all looking concertedly at something or other—at their expensive sneakers, at the drinks of their accomplices, and at the other people attending the launch who might come to assist and break the crippling silence. That's when she knew she was pretty much on her own in these parts.

Later, Anette Schwalbinger had gently forced her colleague to reveal the content of the conversation, which revolved around a nickname that made the others smirk. Nervously, with her nose twitching, Jude Klingenhof whispered the words «ball crusher,» but Anette Schwalbinger just shrugged her shoulders. It was clear that she had been a disruptive factor. Because she was a woman, but above all, and this made it much worse, because she was a woman who didn't want to please men. That was even worse than equal pay or the women's quota—and that's why Schwalbinger was seemingly to blame for everything that shook up the world of automotive men. This was a role that, objectively speaking, no human being could be happy about, and yet she was at peace with it. «It's because I can,» she told herself. And she was still convinced that it was so.

She was in Syracuse because her company had made this trip mandatory for «middle management.» It was meant to be for team building—and topics that were vaguely referred to as «Amp Up Corporate Culture!!!» in the schedule. «Another one of those double Anglicisms in German that means both everything and nothing. And then there are those stupid three exclamation marks!!!» she had said to Jude Klingendorf, before taking a bite of the vegetarian burger that had been recently introduced to the cafeteria's menu. Instead of answering, Jude busied herself with the pickle slices that had slipped out of the bun.

Schwalbinger arrived the day before to talk about the Estherians with Domenico after many years of radio silence (she was somewhat persistent in using such old-fashioned terms in her thinking). This early Christian sect had become legendary in religious studies circles. Progressive research had long since agreed that Jesus' friends were not limited to men. It was clear that his «favorite disciple» must have been female or non-binary. The Gospel of John differed in style and, if we're honest, it was better written. That there must have been other women besides Mary Magdalene was something that had been thoroughly erased from history and mythology by men. One of these women was said to be Esther, a widow with four children and owner of a prosperous goat farm. After the community around Jesus dissolved following the crucifixion, she left the farm to her eldest daughter, sparking a dispute among the siblings. Esther, however, boarded a ship that took her from Palestine to Sicily. Although the city of Syracuse paled in comparison to its former glory, it was still a metropolis. There, Esther began preaching and was arrested numerous times. She was only released because a woman couldn't be taken seriously in matters of blasphemy. She went on to establish one of the earliest Christian communities in the Mediterranean. Legend has it, there's a cave, not far from the catacombs of Syracuse, where these pioneers celebrated their rituals.

Schwalbinger was a rationalist. She wasn't sure whether this particular figure had really existed or whether it was a fantasy drummed up by feminist historiography. Nonetheless, Domenico Corsini had written a passionate article about her. The piece had been published in a journal that was considered to be so obscure that, though his former colleagues had in fact noticed it, left their worldview unshaken. After that article, they dismissed him for a provincial eccentric with no future in the academy, if they hadn't already. He earned his living by teaching Italian and writing term papers for students at the University of Catania who were notoriously lazy—all the hard-working ones end up in Bologna or Urbino.

Although Schwalbinger had stopped studying religious history many years ago, her curiosity never faded. Perhaps the man had unexpectedly discovered something interesting. Besides, she was looking forward to seeing him again.

Pretty flabby, was her first thought. Fat arms, a round belly squeezed in a tight t-shirt, and an almost obscenely long and well-manicured pinkie nail that signified prosperity or casual cocaine use, as Anette Schwalbinger well knew. His unsteady gait could be from sore muscles or from day-drinking, she wasn't sure. «More beautiful than ever,» he said with a smile. And there it was again, that flutter in her head. She wasn't in love with him anymore and perhaps she never had been, but this moment made her suddenly remember how it felt when a man or even a woman wanted nothing more than to make her feel good. Maybe the porcini mushrooms weren't the only thing she missed.

«I spoke with the director of Paolo Orsi on the phone. He simply couldn't stop talking. We can head over there first thing tomorrow morning. There's something I want to show you,» Corsini said, excusing his delay. And with that, their shop talk was over. It then turned into an evening of two people who had felt a jumble of emotions for each other and had both come to terms with it. They laughed a little too loudly and disastrously drank one Coco Chanel after another. But when the bartender laid a small envelope on the table in the now empty bar, Anette Schwalbinger stood up, only got lost on her way to the hotel once, and then lay down in the bed that was much too soft.

Corsini's eyes were as red as those in Fra Angelico's famous portrait of the crown of thorns and his sweat had a bitter odor. Still, he was punctual outside Syracuse's Archeological Museum at seven in the morning. Despite his state, he managed to shake off the director after he had called Schwalbinger «most esteemed professor» five times. Corsini led her through the slightly musty building that consisted of hexahedrons and came to a halt in front of a display case of ancient coins. Some of them possessed very fine details and were well preserved, while others had been so eroded by water and time that only profiles were recognizable. The yellowed list with the names of the exhibited objects was barely legible. The coins had probably been rearranged in recent decades, but the list had stayed the same. The museum's chaos made Schwalbinger uneasy, especially since there was no way for her to sort things out with a few resolute moves. Corsini, in contrast, was tapping his foot with excitement—or perhaps it was the amphetamines in his bloodstream. «That's Apollonia, the wife of a high-ranking Roman official. She was one of the first Estherians,» he said, tapping the case so vehemently that Schwalbinger almost intervened. «And this here is Principe Adriano. He had the nicest ass in Syracuse during the High Roman Empire. He was impaled and burned because he had mocked the barbarian gods of the Greeks and Romans in front of the temple of Apollo.»

Schwalbinger asked herself whether High Roman was a technical term since she certainly didn't know it. What was more, her stomach was making unpleasant noises. She shouldn't have skipped breakfast before going to the museum. The sour, rotten smell of her old friend's breath was also beginning to wear her down. «Very fascinating. But we should definitely talk on the phone before your next publication. Maybe we can find it a better home…» She got into the taxi and didn't even bother buckling up because she didn't trust the Italian seatbelts. Corsini waved to her with a burning cigarette.

The car delegation was staying in a luxury hotel next to a giant parking lot close to the fish market. Over-the-top greetings, jokes at the expense of Sicilians, and the standard backslapping: Schwalbinger had programmed her brain to ignore such rituals, tuning them out during events like these while still managing to hear everything so that no unexpected question could take her by surprise. The morning passed without incident, and she had already worked out what the whole trip must have cost after twenty minutes. Which was actually a scandal. But the new SUV had broken sales records again, and business in the Middle East had also recovered. Then Mark Feist took the floor. He was perhaps the most enigmatic figure in the company: a former decathlete whose sports career ended when he broke his left ankle while pole vaulting. His trim tailored shirts revealed that he was still in competitive shape; he worked out four times a week with the CEO in his private gym. His role in the car company was as dubious as it was intimidating. Officially, his title was Agent of Innovation, and it was never clear whether he was parroting the opinions of the head honcho or improvising. More than anything, he loved quoting Peter Thiel and Udo Jürgens.

«We've gathered at this historic location, where the fate of Athens was sealed,» he began with an exaggerated pathos that diverged slightly from fact. «Back then, Athens was the top dog in the Mediterranean. And as the great Austrian singer once said, you learn the most from your mistakes. But I think we can learn even more from the mistakes of others if we take a closer look. We're also the top dog. Not in terms of sales or units sold, but no one can beat us when it comes to innovation and image. ‹Float like a butterfly, sting like a bee.› We're better at that than those Silicon Valley wizards, who to this day have failed to put a decent combustion engine on the road. And even those tricksters in the Far East, who turn our inventions into tin cans at cutthroat prices—even though I might formulate this differently at a meeting in Guangzhou…»

Schwalbinger was just about to switch her selective ignore mode back on when Feist suddenly changed the subject. «To stay at the top, we can't allow ourselves to become complacent. We need to think outside of the box, we need to be disruptive towards ourselves, and slaughter sacred cows. Or at least to put them out to pasture.» Feist's mixture of styles was remarkable; Schwalbinger wondered whether she should jot down the highlights. Overall, the morning was proving to be more entertaining than she could have ever dared to hope.

«And one of those sacred cows is the HR department. It's run by one of my favorite colleagues, who has graciously joined us in Syracuse and got up somewhat earlier than the rest of us, as usual.» Feist bowed in Anette Schwalbinger's direction: «But if we're honest, the HR department is a chop shop where overtime regulations, parental benefits, and diversity are handled with the same care. This has its history and its reasons. But with all due respect, it's no longer state of the art.» Feist had really gotten himself going, which his periodically twitching chest muscles showed. His eyes swept over the audience that was devotedly listening and lingered just a fraction too long on Jude Klingendorf. Meanwhile, among them was Anette Schwalbinger, and her rage had steeled into outward calm. But she felt her hands cramping up. «What I'm about to suggest may come as a shock, but there are numerous case studies from South Korea and Canada, where the most forward-thinking companies have already implemented this exact model. The key words here are decentralization and a radical focus on corporate culture. Terminations, work contracts, overtime regulations, the whole shebang, should all be handled by small units within the respective ones. We don't need a bloated HR department or its endless meetings with the works council for that. The decisive questions, the ones that will determine whether we're still on top of the world in thirty years are diversity, work-life balance, innovation acceleration, flexibility shift. ‹No company HAS a culture, every company IS a culture,› as Peter Thiel writes in his bestseller From

Zero to Hero. We're now going to set up a compact department to this end. The Corporate Culture Cell. Double C.»

That'd have to be Triple C to be accurate, thought Anette Schwalbinger, who hated such sloppiness. But she knew it didn't matter. This was about her head. It was a public execution in the making. But apparently it wouldn't stop there. «And to make this happen, Marius and I agreed,» Feist continued (Marius was, of course, the first name of his gym buddy, the CEO), «that there's no one better for the role than our colleague Jude Klingendorf, who will become our corporate culture superagent.» Feist motioned for her to join him onstage amid the applause.

Jude Klingendorf stood up, gave a slightly ironic bow, and held her hands out flat together in a gesture of modesty and self-congratulation that was reminiscent of Pharrell Williams. Her white dress fit her perfectly and over her left shoulder hung a handbag with a double C on an oblong golden chain. Schwalbinger wondered whether it was a fake, given her employee's previous salary. She was shocked by the disloyal seizure of power. Klingendorf had admired her for years, so much so that it briefly occurred to her that the young woman might be in love with her. «Thank you for your trust,» Klingendorf said, though not a single person present had yet confided any trust in her. «I don't want to make any grand announcements here. In the coming days and weeks, I just want to listen. And I would like to thank my colleague, mentor, and I hope I may say this, friend. I've learned everything from her, and I wouldn't be standing here today without her. Here's to you, Anette Schwalbinger!»

«Did you know about this?» a colleague from the compact car department asked at lunch. Schwalbinger stared at the olive oil stain on his short-sleeved shirt and said, «Of course. It was actually my idea.» This was such a blatant lie that it brought the conversation to a halt, which had been her exact intention. Afterwards, the group went on a boat trip around the island of Ortigia. Despite the glorious May weather, the sea was rough, and the boat kept crashing against the waves, soaking the passengers in the front with sea spray. Jude Klingendorf's dress was so wet that her beautiful breasts were clearly visible. Her sparkling laughter drew even more attention, which was obviously unintentional, until Mark Feist offered her his light summer jacket of a cashmere-silk blend. She smiled and casually turned this offer down. Then she leaned over the edge of the boat and vomited so copiously that it seemed excessive and indecent. For Anette Schwalbinger, it was the only highlight on what had otherwise been an incredibly abysmal day.

Before the aperitivo, a visit to the catacombs was on the program. The tour was optional and came with a trigger warning, as a few real skeletons had only recently been discovered in a previously closed chamber. On this late afternoon, Anette Schwalbinger couldn't stand the tour guide's terrible English and the shuffling pace of her colleagues, so she veered off at the crossroads of the underground paths for a moment of solitude. It wasn't long until she heard the neighing laughter of her colleague from the compact car department from afar. These routes were so outlandish, lined with niches carved into the sandstone, about the same size as the flat beds in a train's sleeping car. Just shorter, of course. When did this growth of humanity begin, actually? With the Industrial Revolution? Like any person who doesn't rely solely on the internet, Schwalbinger became annoyed by details she had once known but couldn't immediately retrieve from her memory. She ducked behind another corner and stopped at the intersection of two corridors. She couldn't hear a thing now. Where were the others? Be that as it may, it was a blessing, this calm in the cool, damp rooms. Then the lights went out.

It was pitch black, in fact. Not even an emergency light was visible. Maybe there weren't any. Anette Schwalbinger sighed. She hadn't forgotten about the shaky Italian power grid and expected the catacomb bulbs to flicker on again in a few seconds. Using the light of her cellphone's flashlight, she felt her way a few steps forward. She just had to find the main axis of the underground passage and then turn right. Then she'd be moving in the direction of the exit. It wasn't all that easy, but she wasn't worried in the slightest. Not even when she saw that her phone's battery was at three percent. Finally, she found the heavy metal door at the exit. It didn't budge and Anette Schwalbinger's knocking resounded soft and dull. She sat down at the threshold and turned off her phone. She didn't have any reception down here anyway, and she wanted to save her battery. So, she waited. And thought.

Her colleagues must have noticed that she had gone missing. They would surely come back soon. But why was it taking so long? Or the power would come back on. Right?

And without realizing it, fear had crept in. In all her conversations and meetings with employees and applicants, Schwalbinger always inconspicuously slipped in two questions: What was their biggest wish? And what was their greatest fear? She understood that people aren't only driven by what they want to achieve. They are also driven by what they desperately want to avoid, by what makes them panic. For a surprising number of people, it was exams. For others, it was crowds. Or a nightmare, a monster, the giant rat in a cage in 1984 that was just waiting to be released to eat someone's face. George Orwell believed that everyone had this one primal fear that could rob people of their humanity if ever triggered. Anette Schwalbinger wanted to find this primal fear. That may sound crude for the personnel manager of a car manufacturer, but it was only a thought experiment, and Anette Schwalbinger didn't have any sadistic tendencies. She always smiled at small children, even though she never regretted her decision to not have any. She even went to the trouble of capturing and releasing wasps that had found their way into her apartment. She found no pleasure in torture, but she did take interest in getting to the bottom of things. That's why she, without any academic expertise, was an expert in phobias. Oddly enough, she had never included herself in this. Spiders, airplanes, barking dogs, crowds of people. None of these frightened her. A lack of fear is a sign of a limited imagination, Martin Suter had once written. Typical Swiss, typical male, Anette Schwalbinger thought. Because fear wasn't something she knew. Except that one, but then she had made her peace with it.

That is until this night in Syracuse, when she was alone in the darkness, cowering before the cold, empty niches and slowly realized that she would have to wait here until the morning. The stone at the threshold of the door was damp, which she had unfortunately only realized once her trousers were clammy and clung to her buttocks and thighs. She stamped her feet to keep warm and to dry the fabric through friction. Then she groped her way through the darkness, but with what goal and to what end? A moment ago, the catacombs seemed to be as quiet as a grave but now she heard the sounds of darkness. Behind her to the left was a nimble scratching; not far from her mincing steps, somewhere it was dripping. She leaned on a wall. In this way, she thought, she wasn't standing defenseless in the dark, and this thought frightened her. Then she noticed that her legs were getting tired. Her left calf was cramping. She was familiar with this sensation. It would get worse with every passing minute.

And since she was a realist, she did what had to be done: with her last bars of power, she shined the light of her phone in the burial niches until she found one at hip height that looked dry and clean. Anette Schwalbinger crawled into the stone recess, where thousands of years earlier some daughter of the great and mighty

161

Syracuse had waited in vain for the afterlife. This is where she was now lying, hoping for the morning. The niche was far from comfortable, and there wasn't much room above her either. When she turned on her side, she nearly touched the stone ceiling. But since she was here, she thought with a touch of irony, then she might as well come up with a strategy to outmaneuver that viper Klingendorf and that ridiculous decathlete. The two of them had a big head start: she was young, looked like Meghan Markle, and was adept at modern power struggles. And he had seen the naked penis of the CEO and knew how many kilos he could lift on a leg press. Classified information. And what was she? An irritable, aging woman with heavy legs and thousand-page biographies of Michelangelo on her bookshelf. A relic of the past. But it was this very thought that cheered Anette Schwalbinger up. She quietly giggled. The whole situation was so absurd, the schemes against her so childish. But more than anything, she giggled because this burial chamber was so uncanny. There it was again, that scratching sound. And this time it sounded like more than four feet making ground. Would they find their way to her chamber? And then what?

She must have drifted off. Her neck was stiff, she was shivering, and a stone was digging into her back, right around her kidneys. Had it been there before? Schwalbinger groped at the stone to throw it out of her niche. How odd, it felt so light! Still slightly dazed from her slumber, she fingered it. It was about the size of an apple, with two indentations and tiny, regular grooves in a row. And as she slowly came back to consciousness, she realized what she was holding in her hand. It was a human skull. So small that it must have belonged to a child. Other people might have thrown it away out of shock, but Anette Schwalbinger gently and firmly held the skull in her hand. In the same way you would hold the head of a child when it needed comfort. She had decided long ago that praying didn't make any sense to her; she didn't like its formulaic nature. But the one fear she acknowledged she had was the nagging feeling that she might be completely alone in the world. And it was here that the undogmatic remnants of religion had stayed with her, guiding her safely through life, and providing assistance: something told her with certainty that she wasn't. So, she held the skull that had once housed a brain and soul and softly said, thank you.

When she woke up again, she saw a pale light and heard two men roaming through the corridors and chatting. They were talking about the soccer player Riccardo Calafiori. «He sits in the team bus in a skirt. And that hair. I'm telling you, he's gay!» one of them said. «So what? He's made millions from the jerseys at FC Bologna. He can screw whoever he wants. Just as long as he stays away from my son.» Schwalbinger knew this kind of banter by heart. And she preferred to elude the two catacomb guards. She slid out of her sleeping niche and quietly made her way towards the exit. Outside, she squinted at the harsh Sicilian morning sunlight. Her Phillip Bree bag was now slightly bulging, since she had taken the skull with her.

«Where were you last night? We missed you,» Mark Feist said as she entered the breakfast room. His smooth forehead furrowed with concern as he flexed the biceps that bulged out of his tight white t-shirt. «You alright, Anette? Can we talk?» Jude Klingendorf asked without removing her sunglasses. «I needed some alone time last night. But tutto a posto,» Schwalbinger said in passing while looking for an empty table. On her way through the room, she could hear stifled giggling. And since Anette Schwalbinger always assumed the best despite her eagle eye for people's intentions, it only now dawned on her that something was up. Maybe her being locked up and forgotten in the catacombs wasn't a mistake. Maybe it had been a spiteful prank.

Anette Schwalbinger sat down at an empty table, removed the child's skull from her ample bag and set it to the right of her table setting. Then she headed to the breakfast buffet. She looked at the dried, pickled plums. Who had come up with those? Schwalbinger knew only a single person who regularly consumed them and that was a colleague with a sluggish bowel. Then she spotted a flat cake with a handwritten sign saying «homemade.» There were only two pieces left and Anette Schwalbinger took both. But since she was a kind, compassionate woman, she felt a pang of guilt for her greediness and inconsideration.

An uncomfortable silence fell over the breakfast room in the luxury hotel. The other guests stared at the child's skull while some tried to keep some conversations going. Mark Feist scraped his chair across the stone floor, then stood up and marched towards the heated egg station. To the left was fried bacon, to the right, eggs that were wet from the aluminum lids' dripping condensation. Feist piled his plate high until it was a mountain of eggs, bacon, and sausages. Then he dropped the lid with a demonstrative clatter and made his way to his table. On the floor in front of him was a large piece of fried bacon in a pool of liquid grease. Feist didn't see it since his eyes, as usual, were fixed on the distance and the future. For a fleeting moment, Schwalbinger thought that life was a slapstick comedy. She could see her adversary slip on the bacon and try to save his plate while the huge mound of congealed egg landed on his white t-shirt and his pectoralis major.

But that didn't happen. Mark Feist, the Agent of Innovation, just stepped on the slice of bacon. And it didn't cause a grotesque accident, it just made a wet, reluctant, smacking sound. Feist was startled. He could have cast his gaze anywhere. At his mountain of eggs with pepper dust sprinkled on top, at the unruly slice of bacon, at the giant parking lot with the broken ticket machines. Maybe even at his table, where his colleagues were trying to ignore the ghostly setting. But he looked at Anette Schwalbinger. Just for a second, but a second too long. And guilt was written in his darting eyes. As if the squeaky bacon had given away his secret.

Schwalbinger ate her almond lemon cake carefully, almost pedantically, and thankfully now without a hint of regret. She enjoyed every bite and decided to visit the Baroque cities in the Southeast on her next trip to Sicily. She hadn't been to Caffè Sicilia in years, but the Cassatina was still supposed to be wonderful. Slowly, she wrapped the child's skull in a napkin, put it in her spacious bag, and got up. She still had to floss and brush her tongue, like she always did before long meetings. Now she knew what needed to be done.

Lucia Moschella
Costa

«Or we could go to the Saline.»

«You need a ticket now.»

«And the Costa Nera?»

«That's closed, too. A piece collapsed.»

«So there are no more free beaches?»

«Kind of,» she says in English.

«Let's go to the reserve.»

«They burned it.»

«But why? Was it really that popular?»

«After the article in the *New York Times,* yes,» she explained. «Come on, amuni'.[1]»

We set off on the scooter without a clear destination, like in high school. I hadn't been back to this city of mine in some time. Here, because of my studies and my work as a marine biologist, there were no pathways or opportunities (most marine biologists I knew here: snorkeling instructors). I left at the age of eighteen. For various reasons—none of which were due to any openly displayed dislike for this place, like those many of my acquaintances displayed—I rarely came back, only at the obligatory times: Christmas, Easter, summer. And not without it causing me a fair amount of discomfort.

When Alice handed me the helmet and invited me to sit on the seat of her Scarabeo, it had been so long since I was here that I could measure it by demolished, rebuilt, and repainted hypermarkets, burned reserves, and beaches eaten away by the sea and by people. This bit had collapsed, that one was incinerated; almost everything had been handed over to private

[1] Let's go

individuals who had turned it into accommodations (they called them «experiences») for tourists.

The day was scorching. I had heard that high temperatures were becoming more invasive around here, and now I felt it on my thighs, where the sun hit directly and the skin gleamed and burned, barely soothed by a breath of wind that wasn't even that cool. From time to time I had to run my palms over my skin to neutralize the heat.

On Alice's Scarabeo, we didn't talk, just like in high school. I remembered her rule: on the scooter, she didn't speak because if she did, she would end up eating her hair, and then she would smell the saliva that had coated it, which gave her the ick, «sette schifi[2].» And besides, talking on the scooter was pointless; you couldn't hear anything.

I didn't know why, at the supermarket, she had invited me to get in touch, but I (and I knew why: I didn't have any other friends here) had written to her in earnest. Changes I was sure of: she had gone back to her signature perfume, Narciso by Narciso Rodriguez, which she first wore at our high school, only to abandon it when half the female population of the school started using it too; she dressed much less casually than before, no more Vans, now she wore Tod's; she had also added some English fillers to her speech, something that even I didn't do after I returned to Italy from my research trips abroad.

As we left the city, the wind whipped up familiar smells—orange blossom, myrtle, scorching asphalt, dry earth, petrol. The landscape by the roadside was

[2] ≙ very disgusting

the same as ever, but now every space seemed secret, unreachable behind signs written in English, aspirational and well-crafted. They looked like puzzles, or random word collages from foreign newspapers.

PITÌTTU – BIODYNAMIC TASTING
MAD – MYSTICAL AGRICULTURE & DESIGN
CAPO BEACH – FASHION SAND RELAIS

Under the signs, sealed entranceways stood triumphant. You could catch glimpses of: fine gravel, olive tree colonnades, geometric hedges, water fountains. Alice turned down a rough, uneven dirt road, swerving around potholes, and braked in front of a large, half-open gate.

«This place is usually doable,» she promised.

We passed through an abandoned building. A sort of former restaurant, former theater, former space for summer Saturday nights. I rummaged through my memory to pull out images of life spent there. A pizza night with a group of my parents' old friends. A contemporary dance recital by one of my cousins. The covers band gig, that band with that scrawny guy you used to sneak off with in the summer of 2009. That place was familiar and unfamiliar: I was sure something significant in my life had happened there, but I wasn't certain what; they were barely sketched, vague episodes. The memories of an abandoned hometown are like this: lucid dreams where you don't know if or how they've repeated themselves.

From the concrete womb, we emerged onto a single rock jutting out over the sea. The water was ultramarine blue, but among the glitter of the waves, a hazy film floated with several hunks of plastic. There were already two couples on the rocks: no room for us.

«Let's sit here and wait for someone to get up,» she said, pointing to a concrete step.

«What was this place?»

«Dunno,» she replied «Ask Alajmo!» she added in English.

We laughed.

Alice had told me shortly before that Alajmo, our former art teacher from high school, had reinvented himself as a critic of the city's «touristification.» During the music festival, he would call the police to have them measure the BPM the castle was being subjected to; when a new kiosk opened by the sea, he would verify any infractions; he was often the only dissenter at City Hall when the mayor handed over Piazza Duomo for the spring summer collection fashion show for Milanese brands labeled MADE IN SICILY. Alajmo, it seemed to me, was the lone «good» and righteous old guard.

«A first-class pain in the ass!» Alice had said. «I work with festivals, with fashion shows. If tourists didn't come to my B&B, what job would I have here? I'd have to leave, like you,» she had said with a smirk. «He has this blog, The Invented Memory, where he points out all the false stories circulating around the city. One day he goes after the tourist Ape Cars, for something illicit or because they tell tourists bullshit, another day he says this miracle didn't happen, or that brochure is wrong—what a drag! Here, drink this,» she said, passing me a plastic bottle with some orange liquid inside. «Nothing *freak*,» she reassured me. «Mineral salts, carnitine, magnesium. Otherwise, you'll faint in this heat,» she said.

I ran a hand over my forehead. I was dripping.

«I'm telling you, people just want little stories to share with their friends at the dinner table once they're back in Connecticut. Who cares if they're true or not,» she said, taking a sip herself. «And with the Madonnina, well, he's gone nuts!»

The liquid left a sour, salty taste in my mouth, with an orange medicinal flavor.

«What Madonnina?» I asked, wiping my mouth.

«The Madonnina hanging on the wall, Alfredo Romano's.»

«Right, I know the one,» I replied.

«He says the Ape Cars tell people it appeared one night, like a miracle.»

I smiled. «I was there when they put it up,» I said. «But really, if it's minchiata³, why do they have to tell it?»

«Listen, once some of my Texan tourists wrote me some private feedback, ‹Hi Alice, just to let you know that we believe there's a ghost in the common room that comes between two and three in the morning and makes a mess of everything, in case you want to call a medium.› They believe in ghosts, get it?»

No, I didn't get it. I didn't follow her reasoning or her ethics. I didn't understand who «her» tourists

³ bullshit

were or why one should or shouldn't believe in ghosts or the Madonna or dietary supplements. I knew that touristification—overtourism, as she would say—was a problem, but I didn't want to argue: I had to get back home on her scooter, and if Alice was still the same as in high school, she was perfectly capable of leaving me stranded in the middle of nowhere.

«These people really aren't budging,» I complained, pointing at the rocks.

«I told you, that's why I usually stay home by the pool. *Te* didn't want to come,» she said.

Te? Why was Alice using Roman dialect now, on top of her English? Anyway, she said there were loads of people, way too many, and tourists in her B&B kept coming one after another; thankfully, they were all foreigners, not stingy like the Italians—demanding discounts, complaining about everything, trashing her place, and still leaving negative reviews. She said that since people started reviewing her as a host, meaning as a person, she had become scared of everything.

Because the reviews weren't just about the house, they were also about her, right? Everyone reviewed everything: B&Bs, second-hand Adidas, concert tickets. And often, they didn't review what they had bought. They reviewed you. The person. Just existing made you subject to being rated. Anyway, she had to say, she had five stars. But she only took foreigners. Italians... Everyone had told her when she first started, and she thought it was just a stereotype. Then she saw it for herself, a hundred percent. There's nothing more to say: Italians ask for discounts, complain about everything, trash your house, and still give you a negative review. No one got up from the rock during the course of our conversation, and Alice would have to head back for a check-in. She ran her hand over her new tattoo, the outline of the island, on her very pale skin. Yes, she knew she was pale, but she didn't have time to go to the beach, and even if she did, well, it was like this, right? There was nowhere to go, and it was too hot. And besides, the sun was impruvulazzato, as if a veil of dust had passed over it. Had I noticed? It wasn't like when we were little—that's how she said it: little. It always had a grayish film over it, even when it was full.

«It's the Scirocco.»

«Mmm,» she replied. «It's been Scirocco for six months now. The last full sunny day I saw, you and I were translating Greek. I don't know. There's a heavy atmosphere. It's like the muddura⁴ has seeped into people's bones. And then there's the slips. Have you heard?»

I looked around as if there was a signal I'd missed or someone who should have filled me in.

«The coast is collapsing,» she explained.

«Oh, yeah, I read about that. Erosion.»

«Yeah,» she seemed uncertain. «It happens constantly now.»

The Red Lighthouse had collapsed one night in January, falling into the sea during a stretch of cold darkness. In the following days, a team of experts—all from the North, for credibility—inspected the seabed and confirmed natural causes.

Things I would discover later:

---

⁴ humidity

1) No sound was heard.

2) During the collapse, the sky went completely dark.

3) Underwater surveys found only a thin blanket of red crystals: the Lighthouse had, in fact, dematerialized.

We were used to coastal slips, but the one at the Lighthouse had broken our hearts—nostalgia for evenings of Tennent's Lager with our high school crushes, the music video shot by two local singers under a full moon, the futile social battle of the citizens who failed to prevent the Lighthouse from becoming yet another exclusive experience for the city. And then, the slip.

«Anyway,» Alice abruptly changed the subject. «Let's go.»

Alice took me back. I thanked her (only then realizing the strangeness of this encounter after such a long absence). I handed back the helmet.

«Listen,» she said to me. «After you left, Matteo and I, for a while, we actually saw each other.»

I froze.

«Matteo Campo,» she clarified, as if I didn't know the surname of my first boyfriend.

Silence fell.

«I thought about telling you so many times,» she said. «Even when you asked me. But I don't know, I was young, I couldn't do it. The words just wouldn't come out.»

I adjusted my skirt.

«Not that it matters now,» she added. «You live abroad, and he has two kids with that chick.»

«Sorry, it's just, I've always wanted to tell you, and lately even more. Then I ran into you at the supermarket, and I thought, it's a sign.»

It didn't matter, now that fifteen years had passed, to tell her that the reason I had left Matteo was an uncontrollable jealousy, not just of anyone, but of her, which I had worked through over many years of therapy—otherwise, I wouldn't have been able to listen to her rambling on pointlessly for hours about problems with her B&B. What could I do with that confession now?

«'Sti cazzi,» I said, who gives a fuck, using her own style of using Roman dialect fillers, and rested a hand on her shoulder.

Two boys sped past us on motorbikes—their skin darkened by the sun, tattoos, no helmets. They noisily sucked their saliva as a sign of «appreciation» towards us.

Towards one, or both of us? I wondered.

«Are you doing anything in the evenings?» Alice asked me.

«I heard about this dinner night at the house of that American chef, Dawn. A Californian friend told me about it,» I said.

«Yeah, I know her,» she quickly replied. Then she made a gesture I knew well from her and others around here: lips down, eyebrows up, meaning: c'ha ffari [5].»

«Do you want to go?»

«I'd like to,» I insisted.

«Do you know how much it costs?»

«No, how much?»

[5] ≙ in the context: not recommendable

«Those dinners start at a hundred euros, if not two hundred,» she said, slamming the scooter's storage pod shut. «I don't know how much you earn, but for me, that's off limits. Those are things for tourists. They place a linen tablecloth in front of you and blanket it with Atlantic oysters and two supermarket anchovies with a bit of herb paste and a fennel sprig that's been pissed on by a cat, they give you some macerated wine and tag you on social media, writing ‹Livin' the Sicilian› dream. If you go, let me know how it is,» she finished abruptly.

«Whose side are you on?» I snapped, even though the dinner had nothing to do with it. «Fake legends are okay, but two-hundred-euro dinners aren't?»

«Stories are one thing. People's money is another.»

At home, I searched for The Invented Memory. It was a clumsy blog, with graphics from the days of 56K connections: plain Calibri text, no bolds or italics, over a pixelated photo of the city, criticized the over-touristification of the historic center and untangled the main points of the tourist discourse, revealing the complexities flattened by slogans. One could agree with the stigma of colonization and the branding of a land, yes. But where did you place Alice, who, if she didn't work in tourism, would have to leave—smirk—like me?

After the section on Hellenic numismatics and the one on the Marine Protected Area, the «GIGIÀN-TI» section stood out in large letters, triumphant. Clicking the button opened a pop-up warning:

WARNING: THE CONTENT OF THIS SECTION MAY DISTURB YOU

Alajmo told of mythological creatures that had always inhabited the stratosphere. According to the legend of an ancient, vanished civilization (how does one trace a legend from a vanished civilization? I wondered)—according to the legend, then, the gigiànti had lived on earth since the Pleistocene, but they had not left at all, Alajmo said: instead, they remained hovering around the earth, unseen, to monitor what we humans were up to. They would take revenge on humans who took too much from nature and rewarded those who honored it. According to Alajmo, this was how the pyramids and ziggurats were built: rewards from the gigiànti for astronomical studies.

Then Alajmo went completely mad: just to give us «a sense» of the size of these creatures, he said that the gigiànti could have used palm trees as cotton swabs, and he attributed the 1990 earthquake, during which the newly built Sanctuary of the Madonna delle Lacrime remained intact, to a dental cleaning attempt by one of the gigiànti: «He tried to use the Sanctuary like we use a Samurai toothpick».

I was about to burst out laughing when I heard an Ape Car stop below my window: the driver was shouting and miming to his passengers, in an English Italian mix, the story of the Fountain of Arethusa. «Alpheus, Greek man, very old, came to Syracuse because here the women are too beautiful! Very, very beautiful. Blue eyes, black hair. And Alpheus from

179

Greece says, Nooo, nooo, I go, too beautiful, I go, I go, I go! And so Alpheus and Arethusa, blue eyes, black hair.»

Ahhh, hmmmm, nice, I could hear the tourists lapping it up, excited.

«OK? Want to take pictures?» asked the driver.

I knew that the legend from Metamorphoses said the opposite: Arethusa, pursued by Alpheus, had begged Zeus to find a way for her to escape him, and the god had agreed to turn the young woman into freshwater. Alpheus, stubborn as ever, transformed himself into salt water and followed her until he could penetrate the Fountain of Arethusa through a small hole at the bottom of the water pool, still visible today.

In the end, I knew the truth: the Fountain was just one of the many outlets of the city's aquifer. As strange as it was to have a freshwater source near the sea, it was still less outlandish than a fountain born from mythical sexual tourism or worse, a romanticized attempt at rape.

I was about to speak when I remembered what Alice had told me that afternoon: it was better not to upset or bother the guys driving the Ape Cars. I shut the balcony window forcefully; the Ape Car, as it started up, belched out an unbearable stink of gasoline.

«Thank you for coming. Enjoy our best life!» said Anne, the American chef, in English.

After passing through the door, the table dazzled me like lanterns mesmerizing a school of sardines: half-lit by antique candelabras, it was set in a ceremonious and decadent manner. From a white lace tablecloth, men and women in flowing linen garments picked at shiny cherries and scattered almonds with a casual precision. The diners popped the pits out of the cherries by squeezing them between their teeth. They chewed, sucked on the pits. Some looked for where to throw them, while others spat them directly on the ground. In their free hand (everyone holding the stem of the glass at the base), they had small amounts of wine, either dirty yellow or pale red. It was a courtyard typical of the island, the kind where people like me would park their sedan or motorbike, hardly ever an electric bike. She had arranged a dinner there. I liked this unexpected change of perspective.

«What a pleasure to meet someone from the city,» Anne said.

«Thanks,» I replied, as if it were somehow my doing. «It's lovely here.»

«Yes, *un* meraviglia,» she responded in slightly-off Italian. «Except for a few things,» she added, gesturing towards the recycling bins.

She pointed out the guests to me:
• a music producer living in Berlin;
• a young Portuguese artist with his agent;
• two Belarusian fashion blogger friends;
• a gay couple who owned an art gallery in the Marche;
• Anne;
• and me.

I quickly picked up on the essential rules: cigarettes were stubbed out inside the oyster shells scattered on the table; it was fine to talk to anyone without first introducing yourself—just being there together was enough of an introduction; if you dared to go refill the water in the jug, Anne would immediately get up and do it for you, so it was better to raise the jug while looking in Anne's direction, and without hesitation, she would run upstairs to the kitchen.

The dinner began with a grand platter of oysters (oysters from where? I asked myself, echoing Alice's question from that morning) and continued with tuna tartare with avocado guacamole from a local producer (do they know how much water that requires? I wondered, thinking about Pergusa Lake, which had shrunk to a puddle) and an overcooked pasta alla siracusana («I don't like chewy chewy pasta,» Anne explained to everyone in English, «I prefer pasta like this,» and she was met with a loud murmur of approval).

I had traveled a lot of the world, but artistic settings still made me feel out of place; I always sifted through my knowledge to say something intelligent, something that could give me, a woman of science, an air of creativity or at least make me seem interesting. People who make art always have a way of doing art, even when spearing a half-boiled potato with a fork.

A few bottles later, the conversations broadened, talking about music, the arts, and the direction of our times. I felt like I was breathing in some of the world's essence—I felt like I was here, at home, but with the «right people». I was fascinated by the kaleidoscope of experiences of my conversation partners, and I was surprised to find so much common ground, to be able to hold my own in so many discussions: LSD microdosing, yet another band by Thom Yorke, Castiglioni's Unghia mirror, Le Creuset cookware. Not unlike some dinners I'd had abroad, I caught myself thinking.

Was it all just a big mix, the world? No, not really. And it wasn't even like Alice had said; with her, I now realized, I had fewer topics to talk about than with these people, who instead seemed sincere, straightforward. These were people like me. With Alice, I never knew what to say, and my afternoon now appeared to me for what it had always been: her monologue.

When the table's conversation shifted to the best beaches near my home, I tried several times to join in, but they were talking about lidos I had never been to, ones I had only seen from the back of Alice's scooter, on Instagram, or at most heard mentioned. They were too expensive, and even if they had been on the cheaper side, they would always have been too costly for us, who grew up having the sea for free.

I then heard Anne suggest to the fashion bloggers that they visit the Marine Protected Area, and I immediately imagined the kind of content they would create for social media: photos of their colorful crochet hats on top of firm shirtless bodies, videos of their «natural» state while eating a peach with juice dripping down their bellies, shots of deeply tanned boys somersaulting off a rock.

They dismissed the beaches quickly when a juicier topic surfaced at the table: the worst restaurants in the city (the tourist traps), which then shifted to the long-term problem of the «locals» and garbage. No one asked for my opinion, and I didn't ask for theirs. In fact, I was more interested in listening. After all, the «local» life I knew was just hearsay. I didn't feel any more local than they did.

«They do this,» Anne said, dramatically gesturing towards the recycling bins. «This crap, in the middle of the temple!» she added.

I remained silent. I wasn't sure if my fellow townspeople were right for using dark, cramped court-yards, with no air and no view, just to store garbage, or if these people were right for setting a grand imperial table a meter away from cockroaches.

By the time we reached the tenth bottle—Anne was slurring her words to the Berlin producer—I went up to the kitchen to refill the water jug. I didn't look for the tap; since I was born, the water in my city had never been drinkable, and some people wouldn't even give it to their dogs.

When I reached the upper floor, I stopped. Was I dizzy, or had this place been turned upside down? The kitchen looked like spilled groceries: clumps of bread dough and whipped butter, supermarket cilantro stems («It's from my neighbor's garden,» she had said), knives smeared with tuna blood, garlic peels, broken plates on the floor, and breakfast dishes in the sink. There were packages for everything scattered everywhere and plastic underfoot. The pasta, a cheap brand, was half on the floor, cooked and stuck to the terrazzo tiles. An oven had been violently shoved into the corner of the room. Two empty packs of almonds were still inside a supermarket bag.

«What a mess,» commented the artist, who had just come out of the bathroom and was making his way through the chaos by kicking stuff aside to get through. I watched him lean over the table, curious, as if scanning it.

«This would make a great painting,» I said.

He smiled.

Then he stopped in front of one of the packages to read the product information. «Ah, local almonds!» he said, laughing, and walked to the door. «I don't know how you do it,» he said, and left.

I was about to run after him when I moved closer —annoyed that I hadn't thought of it first—and read the label.

ORIGIN: CALIFORNIA

Returning from the staircase, I found them all with their noses pointed up. They were looking at a bright, round, and irregular spot in the dark sky, flickering on and off, hidden behind a light nebulous cloud. It had a composite shape: a round top and a sort of basket underneath, like the stylisation of a skull. Must be Musk's Starlink, I heard them say, I think it's one of those floating lanterns. Maybe it's aliens, someone echoed. It was nice to enjoy those speculations and paranormal interpretations, which, I thought, must have been the basic forms of survival for entire communities for centuries. The truth is a privilege of the modern age.

I also considered the possibility of a collective hallucination, like I believed about certain episodes

I'd heard of: the small island where the inhabitants were convinced they had seen real-life mermaids, the miracles of saints and statues. I walked down the stairs with the water jug, placed it on the table, and settled into my seat without saying a word.

«Where were you?» Anne asked me.

«I got some water from the kitchen.»

«Did you see that?»

«Mm-hmm,» I nodded.

«It was strange, wasn't it?»

«Well,» I said. «Maybe, maybe not.»

Anne looked at me, puzzled, and so did the producer.

«Come on, do you know something? Tell us!» the artist said with a smile.

«Okay,» I encouraged myself under his gaze. «You've surely heard,» I began, «of the gigiànti.» I lowered my voice to make sure I had everyone's attention. Only then did I continue. «It's a story we locals believe in,» I said. «If you want, I can tell it to you.»

Lukas Kubina
Workation

Gabi isn't happy with the photos. She dives underwater with her eyes closed and gingerly resurfaces, tilting her head back. Her black hair shimmers freshly over her accentuated collarbones, flowing down her back in a smooth stream. She pulls the wet fine-ribbed tanktop down tightly, straightening it like a second skin. This time she makes sure that you can still see her butt in the black bikini bottoms. She just needs to move a strap to reveal the tan line. After giving her breasts a quick check, she starts striking various poses for the camera lens.

Mike admires how she can tune the world out. It may still be early in the morning, but the bathing platform at Diana rock is already in full swing. Old timers are finishing their morning routine, swimming with powerful strokes towards the horizon. A muscular small man with a bald head is doing exercises. Defying his age, he moves like a young gymnast. A skinny guy camps out next to the three graces. He's making a move and sets down his guitar in their vicinity. But he's about as sexy as a Protestant teacher of religion who firmly believes that hearts can be won over through singing.

Thank you for this lovely morning. Thank you for this new glorious day. Mike hums a song from his school days and like a shadow the lyrics bounce off the walls of his subconscious and dance through his head. Thank you for this lovely morning. Thank you for this new glorious day. He flexes his triceps and stomach muscles to the rhythm of the melody. While Gabi takes pictures, he squeezes his butt cheeks together to make a favorable impression on the young Italian women.

The early risers from the hotels, guest rooms, and private accommodations are mingling with the locals. He hears French, German, Spanish, and Russian. He has already given the Russians dirty looks. Ever since the invasion of Ukraine, they've been automatically suspect to him. A traffic jam forms on the stairs into the water. Behind Gabi's behind, bathers line up, floating in the mellow waves with varying degrees of pleasure, enjoying God's nature, and patiently waiting for her, Gabi, to let go of the swimming ladder. It seems that some people hope for the moment to linger but Mike feels latently uneasy. It doesn't feel right to be so uncivilized on the beach. In Spain and France, women go topless. In Albania, the beaches are deserted. In Italy, it's a totally different deal. How come? The Pope? The Church? Sexual morals? It can't be because of the Ancient Greeks and Romans; they were totally liberal. So it goes. Different strokes for different folks. Different pokes, Ludwig always used to say, «different strokes, different pokes.» Pokes, my ass. Mike wants to bring Gabi's nipple show to a close and puts a lot of effort into making her happy with a flood of images from different angles.

It's a wrap. He's lying on his back and thinking about the Roman Empire. The word «solarium» leads to daydreams. Concepts like these just keep surviving in Italy. Solarium. He thinks about the Romans, who conquered the Greek colony here. About the Roman legionnaire who slaughtered Archimedes. «Do not disturb my circles» were his last words. During his school days, Mike loved to pull this quote out during class breaks. «Do not disturb my circles, Ludwig!» sounds so much better than «Fuck off, Wigs!» His mind drifts aimlessly. He likes getting a tan. Vitamin D. Besides, it suits him better. He's the Mediterranean type. Pale's a no go, he looks like a corpse. So, he submits to the Nordic style solarium in the winter, with its artificial radiation, eye protection, and a loincloth in ten-minute intervals. He enjoys the Sicilian sun much more, of course. He thinks about his friends in Vienna, who are currently struggling with the lousy weather of autumn. He's super happy. He hit the jackpot. Who would have thought that after high school graduation? His friends have turned gray. The better their grade point average, the harder they have it. They fight their way through jobs in law firms, open-plan offices, and creative studios. They've got kids, cars, houses, and not an ounce of exciting sex anymore. They've gotten old. He's stayed young. His undercut is freshly shaven, his ironic tattoos are multiplying, his skin is well oiled and not turning yellow.

Gabi's getting impatient next to him. She starts folding her clothes and packing them in her beach bag. Mike would prefer to go for a long swim, but he knows it's out of the question. He rolls her another cigarette to buy himself some time. Just this one, she says. With her knees drawn up, she chews gum and smokes at the same time. He gazes at the sea full of melancholy. The rising sun makes it shimmer. He feels connected to the passage of time. As nice as the breaks are, Gabi's right. They're here to work. *Workation.*

They head to the market during their lunch break. Quickly they find themselves swept up in a stream of tourists that appear out of nowhere. They had just been at the Temple of Apollo, admiring the ancient stones, and now they're part of a herd that's funneling through the market. Although some of the stalls in the row of shops are closed, the energy of three market criers creates an unbelievable amount of hustle and bustle. Since Gabi and Mike had a productive morning, they take their time. They stop at a merchant who advertises his Atlantic oysters with Diego Maradona and promises a plastic cup of house wine for every order. Gabi and Mike are on the same page: *Work hard, play hard.* After two rounds of oysters, Gabi mentions that she hasn't eaten anything else today. The wine makes Mike care less and less about not mastering Italian grammar and the fact that he barely knows twenty words in the language. In his cheerful mix of Italian and Spanish, he chats with the merchant and the neighboring vendor, a dwarf who peddles medicinal herbs and speaks a dialect so obscure that no one outside of his mountain village could possibly understand it. Gabi excuses herself and throws up just a few steps away in a side street. She wipes her mouth with a napkin, takes a sip of water from a plastic bottle, and returns to her new friends right as Mike is about to order a third round of wine with a symbolic oyster. Just in time she tells him what's just happened to her and that she'd like to end the aperitivo. She adds that now's the time to order a nice bottle of white wine from the restaurant. Now provocatively whispering:

a Grillo. Ice cold. Mike thinks it's a wonderful idea. Gabi may be petite, but she's tough. He likes that. They sit down at a terrace on the market street. To go with the Grillo, they order a fritto misto and a carbonara di mare. They observe the commotion with keen interest: «C'est très touristique,» the French say. «Do you have fish?» the Americans ask the waiter while he lingers between the fish display and the frutti di mare decoration. Among themselves, they talk at length about their «gelato» experience. The Germans keep quiet so no one thinks they're tourists. They pretend to be Italians, the role they've always wanted to play, convinced that no one notices.

Then the sea splits and a cruise ship captain steps on the stage. Mike jokes, Capitano Schettino's on leave. The commander of the sea struts around in his snow-white regalia, trying to catch the eyes of the girls. He even gives Gabi a look and she not only meets his gaze but stares him down, licking her upper lip with the tip of her tongue and crossing her legs so slowly that he could study her panties for several semesters. Flustered, Schettino turns away. Mike and Gabi have a good laugh and order another glass of wine. Because come on, it's so nice out.

The abandoned Bourbonian prison is next to the market on the edge of Graziela, the former fishing neighborhood where small-time crooks have abandoned their careers and people from the north have bought houses and settled, gentrifying the south with their own retirement. The location and dimensions of the empty building are spectacular. The floor plan is rectangular with sides measuring forty by forty-five meters. The three-story ruin reaches a height of twenty-five meters. It was completed in 1845 and, for a time, it was one of the most modern and advanced prisons, that is until the 1990 Santa Lucia earthquake took it out of operation. Locals call it Casa cu n'occhiu («the house with an eye») since it was designed according to the principles of the British philosopher Jeremy Bentham: a polygonal structure with a watch tower in the center that allowed the warden to keep constant vigil without the inmates realizing that they were being observed.

Mike doesn't need any imagination to see the potential. White wine for lunch and a trained eye on the immediate surroundings are enough: it's just a couple of meters from the market. The guest's yachts might be moored in the harbor just behind it. In the distance, the Basilica Santuario Madonna delle Lacrime and Mount Etna are strung along a line on the horizon in front of the bay. The only thing spoiling the flawless view of the sea is the parking garage, but some greenery could provide an aesthetic solution to the problem while also adding an ecological image. Maybe even some tourist attraction could be created and a cactus park built that makes the facilities on Ischia or Lanzarote look ridiculous? With the right means, it should be possible to install a beach club on the dock. Guests could arrive directly in their dinghies and enter the hotel through a tunnel, shielded from the outside world. Hollywood doesn't like being seen.

Hotel Pannottico. A luxury resort. Mike's enthusiasm knows no limits.

Only after Mike and Gabi squeeze through a hole in the rusty steel fence do they spot the two French businessmen who have also entered the plot. They're having an animated discussion, hallucinating about the monetary flows and riches. They're certainly not the first real estate developers to sense the spoils and get swept up in this fever. With their well-heeled suits and beautifully parted, blow-dried hair, they look like messengers from another world.

Mike decisively walks past the two sharks without saying a word and heads towards the main gate. Gabi shakes her hips a little for the Frenchies, then she carefully starts tiptoeing over the debris and the shards of glass to follow Mike. He's unusually agitated.

He actually likes lost spaces and the special kick that comes from being there. But the location check in the empty prison gives him the shudders. What kinds of crimes might the inmates have committed? What did these walls keep locked up for the sake of society? Who else has walked in and out through the gate once its hinges fell off and it was left open? He is able to get ahold of his swooning with deep breaths, and he squeezes through the door's open gap that leads inward. In the dim light, he gropes a few meters into the building before coming to a stop at a point where walls have been broken through, leading into other rooms. He turns on his phone's flashlight and examines the confusing situation. The hallway in front of him probably leads to a stairwell. The left has better vibes. The direct sunlight makes it feel less creepy. He climbs into the first room over trash and debris. There are traces of a campfire on the floor. Empty cans and beer bottles are scattered in a corner. On the wall, he discovers some graffiti: «SEMBRA CHE HO IL CA**O LUNGO 1m.» To the side, a giant cock illustrates the saying. Mike can't help but smile. His Italian's good enough for this note.

A noise startles him. Someone's behind him. He abruptly turns around and sees Gabi groping her way into the room. He breathes a sigh of relief. Oh, it's you. You probably shouldn't wear high heels for location checks. Look at the graffiti, it says, «It looks like I've got a meter-long dick.» The daylight's great here, too. He laughs. You could work with that, couldn't you? Gabi nods passively. She doesn't share his passion for checking out ruins but tags along anyway. After all, they're a team and their success speaks for itself. But where he hopes to make a discovery, she secretly fears it.

And then they hear noises. They can't tell where they're coming from. Somewhat disturbed, they look around in every direction. They're like two deer stuck in the headlights of a car that's about to run over them. If cats fall over one another from the second floor, are they just sighs from the past or is it just the sea breeze making the ruins rattle? Do you even want to know what's making it? Let's get out of here, Gabi whispers. Yeah, that's enough, we're done here, let's go get a coffee. Mike tries to remain casual, but he's scared of his own shadow.

After Work. Mike and Gabi are on a boat trip. Their colleague Rosa recommended an excursion to the coast of Isola di Siracusa on a converted fishing boat. They meet at the harbor. Rosa looks amazing, her thick, brown curls spiral in every which way, her cheerful face and emerald-green eyes in the middle. The low-cut back of her bathing suit exposes a beautiful pattern of birthmarks. She's wearing tight jean shorts over the swimsuit. Mike strongly disagrees with her, no, her twins didn't wreck her body. They board the ship together. Rosa put them on the guest list, so they can pass by without a ticket. They climb a ladder onto the deck and search for somewhere to sit. Gabi lies down in a hammock stretched parallel to the railing. Rosa and Mike take a seat on colorful camping chairs. Together, they form a closed circle. The boat casts off.

Gabi metronomically sways in the hammock from the swell. Her sunglasses are askew and she looks a little disheveled. She's telling Rosa that it kind of feels like she's on the Black Mamba, a ride at the Prater theme park, and suggests that this situation isn't bearable, it'd be better to order a bottle of white wine. Mike goes below the deck to get the wine, three plastic cups, and a cooler. He sizes up the other passengers on the way. Two families have set up a larger camp. The two boys are doodling around on their smartphones. The parents are talking loudly and sadly it's in German. It's the fall vacation in Berlin. Investment talk. To drive the point home, one of the women is even wearing a BITCOIN t-shirt. A strong statement, Mike thinks to himself. And he wonders whether her children are to blame for her body or whether she had always been a hippo. Body shaming. Mike's ashamed of himself. It's not okay. Noisy children are a trigger. Commotion, too. Open cupboard doors, the wrong table in the right restaurant, or the casual genius of the BITCOIN bros. The crypto dudes don't notice his hostility and uninhibitedly shout more buzzwords at each other while drinking bottles of beer.

A guy is sleeping on a hammock next to them. Mike envies his composure and decides to follow his example. As he pours the wine, he snaps back to reality and tries to make sense of the fragments of their conversation. Rosa explains: Everyone who could walk on their own two feet left Sicily. Only those who couldn't escape remained. There are also those who went to the underworld. The nymph Arethusa even had extensive connections down there from the course of her underground river. Gabi laughs a little too loudly. Mike realizes she doesn't know what this has to do with nymphs either. Rosa continues, saying that the only people who come and settle here are unfortunately those who had good reasons to flee their homeland and who, with their dubious backgrounds, can hardly make up for the brain drain. So, as soon as she can escape, as soon as her twelve-year old twins are adults, then she's going to leave too. She's sworn to herself that she will. She'd like to go to New York the most. But Vienna's also interesting to her; she wonders whether it's true that the quality of life is so high there. Every year, she reads the list of the world's most livable cities in the newspapers and wonders what that actually means.

Mike distributes the cups. Rosa only notices him now, her cheeks blushing under her Cubist sunglasses. She remembers to separate work from pleasure and steers the conversation towards the real estate market and the local peculiarities. That's why she points out the Isola's coastline they're sailing along, less than four hundred meters away. You see that, it's actually a nature reserve. But it's being developed, nevertheless. As you can clearly see. From a bird's eye view, from land, and from water. Even better: with no restrictions! No limitations! Illegal? Who gives a shit? You should take a look at the abandoned resort at Punta della Mola. These ruins are waiting for a production. She winks at both of them. Do you see the pool there? Mike and Gabi follow her index finger with their eyes: the end of a swimming pool is hanging from a cliff. The edge has buckled under the load, part of the pool has broken off and plummeted. Behind the wrecked, dried-up basin is the villa clinging to the rock and defending dreams with a sea view. This is what an infinity pool looks like if you know the right fixer. This should be the symbol of Sicily, put it on the flag. Instead of that three-legged figure with a head poking out of her vagina.

They anchor off the coast and lower the boat ladder into the water. The word «vagina» is still ringing in Mike's ears as he steps onto the plank, the way it rolled off Rosa's lips in her English with a thick Italian accent. Vagina. He bobs up and down in the swell. Vagina. At the highest point, he jumps in and does a flawless head dive. Vagina. Back on board, he fetches the second bottle of wine. A DJ's playing Italo-disco and Ibiza House

199

on deck. The BITCOIN bros and girls are keeping to themselves, dancing. As Donatella Milani's «Ci Stai» comes on, Rosa pulls Mike out of the hammock to join her and Gabi. Barefoot and in wet bathing suits, they dance around one another in a circle. Rosa catches Mike looking at her with a gentle sense of desire. She smiles at him then turns around and shouts the chorus across the Ionian Sea, towards the Middle East. Next comes a Rihanna anthem, and Rosa and Gabi explode at the same time. They throw themselves into each other's arms and belt out: *'Cause I didn't mean to hurt him / Coulda been somebody's son / And I took his heart when I pulled out that gun / Rum-pum-pum-pum / Rum-pum-pum-pum / Rum-pum-pum-pum / Man down.*

Mike's soul is aflutter. It started when they returned to Ortigia at dusk. A civilian sea rescue boat under a Spanish flag was at the entrance to the harbor. Two Italian frigates were not far off. The sun set in the west over Isola; a flock of starlings flew in fantastic formations over the Arethusa spring to the east. Couples were standing on the promenade. They gazed at the sunset or took pictures of each other.

A little after that, the boat was moored in the harbor. Rosa left a fleeting goodbye kiss on Gabi's and Mike's cheeks, then took off on her scooter. At this rate, it will take her a good while to arrive in Agusta along the country road, where she'll get dinner and life advice from her parents and then take the twins home and put them to bed. Mike and Gabi are sitting in front of a bar at the Arethusa spring, admiring the play of light from the red sun at dusk. One day on Earth over. He has just received a message that his best friend became a father. The baby's doing well. His wife's doing well. All is well. Mike has missed something monumental again because he's on a work trip. An African street vendor senses his sudden misfortune and does what life has taught him. He takes advantage of the situation and makes a business proposal: This powerbank porta fortuna! Really, the powerbank brings good luck? Of course it does! Laughing, Mike gives him a euro. The African man gives back a broad smile and moves on.

An Ape that's been converted into a rickshaw stops in front of them. Two American senior citizens in uniform are sitting on the back seat: he's wearing his grandaddy Nikes, Bermuda shorts, and a wide polo shirt. She's in short leggings, ON sneakers, a tank top, and a visored cap that would make her driver look like a golf caddy if he weren't so full of sprezzatura. With his sunglasses tucked into his slicked back hair, the driver leans over his phone and speaks in Italian for a long time. When he's done, he turns to his passengers on the back seat and plays the English translation: Arethusa was once a beautiful nymph who loved hunting and sports. One hot, sunny day, she went bathing in the Alpheus River only to be taken off-guard and pestered by the river god of the same name. In flight, Arethusa was able to call on the goddess Artemis for help. Artemis transformed the desperate nymph into a spring whose stream flowed under the Peloponnese and beneath the sea, only to emerge again on the peninsula of Ortygia, which is part of Syracuse. The machine's female voice is interrupted by a call that the tour guide takes on loudspeaker. Pronto! He turns on the ignition and chugs off with his tourists, one hand on the wheel and the other holding the phone he's speaking into. A billboard is mounted on the back of the Ape: Ortigia Ape Experience. Tours in every language!

Gabi was tired and staggered back to the apartment on her own. After drinking in the sun, she was toasted by the Campari Soda and couldn't get the boat trip out of her legs. Unlike Mike, who's now in a good groove, his delight like a boat swing. No one can stop energy like this; they'll have to stabilize or fall off. His procession leads him to the grocer near Cala Rossa, who has set up three tables and sells bottles of cold beer in the evening. The son of the owner greets the hungry wolf like an old friend and sets out a large bottle of Moretti in front of him. Mopeds and pedestrians are out on the Corso. Literally every local greets the merchant and he answers with a hand gesture; it's visibly awkward for him. Village idiot? Mascot? With kind eyes and a shrug, he seems to make a comment on Mike's thoughts. The beer's really refreshing. Mike takes two big slugs and feels recovered.

Sitting next to him is a Spaniard from the sea rescue. The print on the chest of his vest leaves no room to doubt that he's a real anti-fascist. Well, well, an anti-fascist sailor who's currently trying to put the moves on two young American women by explaining to them how the Middle East conflict can be resolved. Mike only has to drink quietly to be able to hear them with one ear. What he overhears doesn't surprise him much: post-colonial struggle for freedom. Israeli genocide. Western oppression. Palestinian victims. Oversimplified and incoherent argumentation. Oh well, Mike thinks to himself, this Monolo's not the brightest bulb. Usually he can't stand stupid anti-Semitic activists. Just the other day, he had to unfollow his dealer in Vienna because she was spreading undignified lies and spiteful agitation on Instagram. With a heavy heart of course, but decency and morality were more important to him than cocaine and ecstasy. It's another story with Manolo. Mike's a little jealous. Saving people from drowning. Humanism against global injustice. That makes sense. Manolo's life has a purpose. His job is his calling. Monolo doesn't need to make indulgences, donations, or distribute alms. Manolo sleeps quite well at night, too.

Mike's got a massive headache. His skull's under high pressure. It takes him a minute to recognize the room he's waking up in and he's struggling to keep his eyes open. How'd he get home? Why is he lying in a wet bed? His body's on fire. He discovers scrapes on his right forearm, a bruise on his thigh, and swollen scratches on his ankle. His skin is salty. With these hints, the shards of memory slowly come to the surface. He was swimming in the moonlight. He was one with the sea. It penetrated him. Its raging penetrated him. Weightless. Carefree. He wanted to stay longer under the water with each dip under. He penetrated the sea. His raging drunkenness penetrated the sea. When he was finally ready to get out of the water, the swell threw him against the breakwater. Or was it because he was drunk? He barely felt the blow.

Message from Gabi: *Where are you, honey bunny? Today's our last day. Get out of bed!* Mike shuffles into the kitchen. He makes some coffee and swallows an 800mg ibuprofen with a glass of hot, boiled water. Yesterday was amazing, but today Mike feels like he's in an empty bathtub where the water's just been drained. Uncomfortable. He starts his morning routine: breakfast—protein shake for the body—push-ups and sit-ups—the cage fighter variety—and then he packs his swimming gear to head to the platform on the rock. Out of nowhere, he remembers the Spaniard. He packs his swimming things to bathe in a sea that people drown in. What a bunch of buzzkills. He throws his bag over his shoulder and opens the door. A vague suspicion holds him back and makes him turn around. Mike hastily opens his laptop. Where are the files? He immediately freezes. The first time in Sicily. Where are the files? The folder is empty. Okay. Mike tries to not panic. He gets the memory card and inserts it into the slot. Cold sweat's on his forehead. Shit, the memory card's empty too. Of course it is, he's the one who erased it yesterday. As he springs up to bang his head on the wall, his swimming bag slips off his arm. He slams his head against the tiles. Once. Twice. Three times. FUCK. Although the pain brings some relief, he stops before his head busts open. Instead, he throws a chair across the room and rips the plastic tablecloth off the table in one go. The laptop flies to the floor. Unde-terred, he tears a small oil painting (a naïve still life) off the wall and hurls it at the wall opposite.

FUCK. What a disaster. Five whole days of work. Five full days of production: gone. Ten thousand euros: pulverized. FUCK FUCK FUCK. Trembling, he takes a bag of ice from the freezer to cool his forehead. He calms down with effort. He forces himself to think ahead. What else is left. He needs to rebook the flight and extend the Airbnb. Unless it's already been rented out. And what he also needs to get back into is eight hours of sex. Does Rosa even have time to shoot the threesome again? She has to take care of her twins dur-ing the week. Okay, if it comes down to it, she can bring them along and they can play in the room next door. More importantly, she has to give them a discount or what would be even better is if she did it for free. The budget isn't big enough. No way. Cazzo. His cock had just recovered. Even the thought of fucking makes his balls contract. Unpaid overtime hurts.

Giovanni Fiderio
The Old Man n.2

The Old Man enters the bookstore with his finger pointed at the postcard stands.

«There's a monolith similar to this one here from Argimusco, and it's located at Monte Lauro,» he tells me, picking up and examining one of our postcards. «It's a rock that dates back long before the formation of Etna.»

«Interesting,» I reply.

«Millions of years before. That's the interesting point, you see?»

«I think so.»

«We aren't able to imagine such a vast amount of time, we're not used to conceiving of something like that.»

«Okay.»

«By the way, there are several formations like that at Argimusco, whereas at Monte Lauro, there's only one.»

«I didn't know that.»

«Of course not, no one knows. That's why I came. I believe that place would be interesting for the photographer.»

«Certainly, we'll have to go find it.»

«So do me the favor of telling her; pass on my message to her.»

«I won't fail to do so. And remember, the photographer would like to take your portrait.»

«Not a chance. I've already told her I don't want to be photographed. And besides, why? There's no reason why I should be photographed. What purpose would it serve?»

«Who could say? I've never understood how or why she decides to photograph someone. I suppose there's something that fascinates her.» His expression hints at a smile.

«And besides, it seems like you've lived a full life; all these stories you tell open up memories and landscapes for us.»

«Well, sooner or later, you are going to have to pay me for all this information.»

We exchange a playful glance, then I change the subject:

«Where have you been lately? It's been a while since you came to see us. Have you been on a trip?»

«No. My wife was ill. I was ill too. But now it's all passed.»

«I'm sorry to hear that.»

We stand in silence for a moment at the book-store's doorway, watching the line of cars on Corso Umberto I. I think it's best not to delve deeper into the subject; he never likes to talk about his ailments.

I decide to shift the conversation to politics with a touch of irony:

«You were ill because of the elections, yeah? We didn't take it well either.»

«What are you saying? It was obvious how it would turn out months before the campaign even started. I could've written it down for you how it would end.»

«A prophet! Did you also know that the right would win in the rest of Italy?»

«Certainly! And I'll also tell you that it's just fine,

after all. Yes, they won,» he twirls his hand dismissively, «but by how much? By hundreds, maybe thousands of votes. Not millions.»

«But it's still not good.»

«Actually, it is. They have to govern, they have to manage, they have to spend all the money, just like they promised. It's good because this is the beginning of their end.»

Annabelle Hirsch
The Tears

It all started with a cautious whimper. Like that of a dog who's been locked out. A lengthy squeal, a held breath, a juddering sigh, a cautiously expelled tone. I sat in my apartment, in the small room looking out to our tiny courtyard, trying to write. About the Weeping Madonna of Syracuse. The image of the Virgin Mary that shed tears in the summer of 1953, turning the city into the epicenter of the faith for a few weeks.

On the morning of August 29 in that year, Antonina Iannuso awoke from a horrific night. At three in the morning, her pregnancy—difficult to begin with—left her blind, but now as she opened her eyes she rejoiced, realizing she could see again. Yet what she saw was unusual: the plaster cast Madonna plaque above her bed was weeping. Her tears dripped down steadily onto the bed, the pillow being quite wet already. News traveled quickly in Syracuse—in the streets around the harbor, the Apollo temple, around the market, among the boatbuilders and fishermen. Within a few hours, hundreds of people had gathered in front of the house on Via Degli Orti, and in the days that followed, sick and suffering people arrived from all over Italy. They prayed to the weeping Madonna and reached out to moisten their handkerchiefs with her tears, hoping they could relieve them of pain and keep calamity at bay. At some point, the church became involved. Then science, too. They sent a sample of the tears to a laboratory, where they compared them to human ones and in astonishment determined they were identical. It was, they said, a miracle.

A French newspaper commissioned me to reinvestigate this story on its seventy-year anniversary. I was to meet with people who'd seen it firsthand. For ten days, I roamed the winding lanes of the former fishing district Graziella, and the streets around Sanctuario della Madonna delle Lacrime, located not far from where the event transpired, searching for witnesses, together with Lucio, my photographer. We spoke to the priest who in the late 60's had commissioned the gigantic cement tear now built above the former Demeter temple in honor of the Virgin; we visited elderly women and men who had experienced the «miracle» when they were children. We sat in dark kitchens and courtyards where children and cats held whining contests; we were given many espressi, fed almond cookies and an arancino or two, and we almost always heard the same story: «The Virgin wept for four days. Her tears were real. They were tears of mercy. Tears of love.» Some told of how they themselves had cried and been embarrassed by it, while others felt inspired by the event to this day. Others yet found the whole thing simply eerie, among them Niccolo, an elderly man whom we visited at his newsstand the day before. He was ten when the Virgin wept, and his mother dragged him along to the spectacle. In his memory, two strong feelings remain: fear and confusion. I was just about to transcribe my notes from our meeting—I was typing *mi ha fatto paura, mi fa sempre paura* on my keyboard—when I heard someone whimpering in my building.

At first I wasn't surprised. I knew most of my neighbors only as a smell or a sound, and as a result I was accustomed to experiencing them in a more intimate way than a face-to-face encounter ever would have allowed for. I sensed that someone lived across from me, for example, because very early in the morning a swath of cigarillo smoke would waft over to me. Aside from that, the apartment appeared dusty and abandoned, day and night, like so many others on Via Nizza. I knew that the neighbors on the ground floor worked late and had a predilection for oriental stews by the cloud of clove, cardamom, and cumin that would rise up at around 1 a.m.; the people overhead I usually experienced only as a sound. The one man, because he had to explain to his daughter every other day anew that he really couldn't stay home, he had to go to the academy, to teach, and the other, because he snored. His snores were so loud that the entire house trembled and the walls shook; Etna erupted daily above our heads. The only person whose face and name I knew was Benedetta. Her apartment was on the ground floor, directly below mine. She was a friendly, if reticent, woman. I often saw her in her kitchen, sitting and smoking, when I left the house in the morning, to meet Lucio for a swim—our appointment on the rock, always at eight o'clock sharp—or in the afternoon, when I arrived back home after interviewing. We occasionally greeted one another, a *buongiorno* or *buonasera,* or if it should rain we murmured *che brutto tempo* and shrugged our shoulders as if to say, What are you going to do about it. Aside from that, I knew nothing about her, nothing about her life. Until now. Now I knew she had sorrows. She was clearly the one crying.

Had it ended there, I wouldn't have gotten involved. We should all be allowed to cry undisturbed, whether loudly or quietly, whether at home, in a café, in the bus, or on a park bench. I consider undisturbed crying to be a fundamental right, but this tone swelled with every passing minute. What began as a cautious whimper and developed into an expressive blubbering with loads of snot and tears, was now something like a primordial anguish. A suffering that seemed to sit so deeply and push its way up through my neighbor's entrails with such force it sounded as if the violent movement would inevitably split her body in two. As if everything inside was turning to the outside and would soon land at her feet with a loud smack, like vomit. Benedetta screamed, yelped, pounded. She emitted dull and shrieking tones, retched, gurgled, and screamed again. I decided to check on her in spite of my belief in discretion. I walked down to the ground floor, wondered why no one else was doing the same, and knocked. One, two, three times. The fourth time she opened her door.

Si? Yes? She looked at me as if nothing could explain my unsolicited appearance. She was confused, as was I. Where I had expected to find her with a wet face, a black veil of mascara below her eyes, features tense and tortured, wrinkles amplified, the overall picture temporarily hardened by pain, as I knew from myself and others, Benedetta looked as always. Calm, middle-aged, bored. Her bleached hair glowed yellow in the neon light of her kitchen, like a field of grain; she wore a lilac terrycloth sweat suit below her apron. *Tutto a posto?* Everything okay? *Si si, tutto a posto.* Discreetly, discreetly as possible, I peeked into her apartment. On the stove was a metal pot of boiling water, on the table were sheets of newspaper, on top of them shelled fava beans and the cadavers of fresh peas. The TV was on in the background. She was cooking. Are you sure everything is okay? Yes, of course. I stood there, somewhat clueless about what to do, and so she slowly closed the synthetic door to her apartment. She gave me a penetrating look, as if I were the crazy one here, not her. I apologized for intruding and returned upstairs, confused.

I made myself tea and sat back down at my desk. Back to the weeping Madonna. The man in my ear, Niccolo, was just describing the Madonna figure's cheeks, unusually pink although otherwise pale, and as I noted *aveva le guance rosse,* the sobbing began anew. Benedetta rattled off the complete scale of suffering once again. From a choked whimper to a loud crying and eventually the wail of sheer despair. When she began her fourth round, growing increasingly wilder and louder, pounding the table more fiercely each time, and it sounded as if she would soon destroy everything around her, the whole affair began to seem eerie to me. I packed my laptop, paused for a moment in front of her door, and left the house. Outside it was horribly warm. The sun crushed the air into a compact mass, a mix of salt and dust; I found it difficult to breathe. I walked ahead to the rock, the *scoglio,* the peninsula's anchor. Up on the balustrade a few men stood looking down onto the glittering dots on the water, watching the waves throw themselves angrily at the cliff, as if it had done something to them. Below on the rock young men tried to flirt with women who were tanning or reading: *Che leggi? Di dove sei? Hai l'ora?* A fisherman pulled an octopus up on his line, the animal dancing with its arms in the air, like the snakes on Medusa's head, the city glowing light beige, almost white, in the background. The Castello Maniace, the crumbling facades, the cupolas that stuck out in the air like small breasts, looked illusive, so real and yet never entirely within grasp. Like a Fata Morgana, a mirage. Could I possibly have dreamed it all? Did I just imagine the crying, the wailing, the pounding? Did I let my research go to my head or did I, too, simply want someone to mourn for me? To find an expression for the overwhelming silence of pain?

Perhaps I should now mention that back then I also had an ailing heart. A few months earlier a woman I loved or thought I loved disappeared abruptly from my life. One day she was simply gone. No message. Not a word. At first I coped with her absence surprisingly well; I was relaxed, almost cheerful. I was surprised and thought I had fooled myself again, confusing an affair with love, until one day my boat capsized and I fell without warning and without a life vest into the sea. All of a sudden, I thought I would drown. I paddled helplessly through the endless expanse, looking out for a coast, a rock, a boat, something to hold on to, but nothing was in sight. I was alone and had no orientation. I was afraid. The longer the condition lasted the more I panicked. I not only felt lost in the world; I was a stranger to myself. It was almost as if my lover, who had managed to open up spaces inside me that I hadn't known existed, had locked every door in the house of my being and taken the keys with her when she moved out of my life. Sometimes I wondered if she might have poisoned me, since that's how I felt. It was difficult to breathe, every movement was a feat; I was afraid I would succumb fully to the increasing paralysis of my body and the hardening of my heart, when the story commission came in.

Under normal circumstances, I am sure I would have turned it down. I knew nothing about religious phenomena, miraculous events, manifestations of the divine—all this was foreign to me. Only the subject interested me, an image that wept; a dead material that could shed tears whereas I had such a hard time giving a shape to my own sorrow. Syracuse in particular fascinated me. Perhaps because of Henri Salvador, whom I listened to on repeat at the time in obvious fits of self-destructive rage: *J'aimerai tant voir Syracuse.* Because of the history, the many tiers of time that layered on top of each other here, like a sticky Sfogliatelle; because of the many myths—of Demeter, Persephone, the underworld, Arethusa and her failed escape from a man's unrequited desire. Perhaps because I had heard that Ortygia is beautiful, but also a bit rundown, melancholic, gentle and rough at the same time. Or—and this is the most likely reason, even if I hesitate to admit it—despite my deep skepticism, I secretly hoped that the Madonna could also liberate me with her tears. I hoped that some of the former magic would trickle down to me, but up until this point I had not felt a drop. The encounters moved me, the people's faith, their hope, their trust affected me deeply, but they didn't stir a thing. My pain remained mute and hard, my being closed.

I strolled through Via della Giudecca, past San Filippo Apostolo church, where at the entrance an altar boy was leading a few tourists under the barrier rope and into the crypt. Down to the embalmed dead, the gigantic ancient tunnel system that served as an air-raid shelter during the war, farther down to the mikvah, the medieval Jewish bath. On Via Roma, groups of children whizzed between the postcard stands, the shoe displays, the tables and chairs of the cafés like small schools of fish. Their commotion made me nervous and I fled to Café Viola and took a seat in the rearmost room. All around me, young people sat at long wooden tables, using their computers; an elderly man read the Giornale di Sicilia; the milk steamer gurgled at the bar. A German tourist ordered an afternoon cappuccino. The easily classified sounds were calming. I wanted to get back to work when Lucio joined me. As ever, he looked fresh, full of vigor; he had just come from the sea.

– Ready for Signora Clara?

Signora Clara. I'd forgotten her completely. We had plans to meet her in an hour. One morning at the beginning of our stay we learned of her from a vendor at the market, who stood behind tuna, *pulpo,*

218

and glowing orange sea urchins. This lady, he said, was among those healed by the Madonna's tears in the summer of 1953. She was *una miracolata,* miraculously cured. Time and again I had made a pilgrimage to the small, dark shops on Via Vittorio Veneto, where *la signora* sat among fur coats, old costume jewelry, cups, self-crocheted children's clothes and other bric-a-brac, looking out from behind thick lenses, as if through a magnifying glass. We chatted about this and that, but she sidestepped the subject of the Madonna and her alleged healing; taking photos was out of the question. But now she was finally ready to discuss the miracle and to be photographed, she had promised. But the tears of the Virgin hardly interested me now, since I was preoccupied by the nonexistent tears of Benedetta. Since Lucio seemed surprised by my lack of enthusiasm, I told him what had happened. I spoke of her wailing, about how she had suffered like an animal, with a lot of noise but no visible traces. I asked if he could explain it. Did she have problems or was I in the process of losing my mind? So eaten up by my pain that I heard it sobbing everywhere. Lucio looked at me with his loving gaze, half-amused, half-concerned. He didn't seem to wonder at all about Benedetta.

– She's a wailer, he said absently, entirely in passing.

He tore open the brown packet of sugar, poured half of it into his espresso, and held the other half up to me. Share?

A woman who cries loudly is a wailer, what an unnecessary explanation.

– No, that's not it. She was wailing, yes, but it was more than that—it sounded horrific. Like a very deep-set, serious pain. I was very worried about her. But her expression was confusing. The fact that I couldn't see a trace of what I'd heard. And she repeated everything precisely, almost as if she were rattling off a musical scale. As if she were practicing.

Lucio grinned. He always found it funny when I became tangled up in my thoughts. My confusion was a joke to him.

– I'm telling you. She's a wailer. It's her profession.

– What do you mean, it's her profession?

– Exactly what I said: it's her profession. That's how she earns a living.

My expression must have been remarkably dumb, because I didn't understand what he was saying at all. For me wailers only existed in antiquity, and if at all today, then in a few villages in Romania, Greece, as well as a few tribes somewhere in Africa or Oceania. In the course of my research I recently had gotten lost and stumbled across a report on professional mourners on the Ivory Coast. It was fascinating. The women simulated suffering for money, just as others simulate pleasure. Family members can decide what kind of a lamentation is appropriate for the situation: loud crying for a beloved grandfather, wailing for a child who has died young, cursing after a long sickness, throwing oneself on the ground, threatening to jump into the grave, ripping out one's hair—the variations were endless. These women were admired for their ability to express collective suffering, but it seemed to me that here, in the so-called Western world, different rules applied. Here we are urged to accept things, to display resilience. It wasn't proper to bother others with your pain, and mourning for too long or too loudly was unpleasant for the people around you, it made them feel helpless and would push them away. How was it possible that someone made money expressing what we had all learned to suppress?

– Do you remember the funeral for that manager from Catania that took place a few days ago in the cathedral? When the guy next to us kept saying to his girlfriend: 'Nobody's crying. Do you see that? Nobody's crying, not even his wife.'

– Yes, that was strange.

– They could have used Benedetta there.

– Why?

– Because it seems odd when no one cries. As if no one cared, or they didn't accept the reality of the situation.

– What's that supposed to mean? As if pain were available on demand. Isn't that precisely the thing about mourning—it strikes in unpredictable waves, coming and going as it pleases, sometimes burning only on the inside, and at other times raging on the outside? Isn't deep pain something we are incapable of expressing out of fear that it could slash everything to shreds on its way out, and in the course of this possibly even hurt others?

Lucio gave me an inquisitive look. Why was I getting all worked up? I couldn't say myself. Something about this bothered me; it tied my stomach into a knot. Maybe I was jealous of Benedetta. Because she didn't suffocate and suffer quietly, but rather knew how to disgorge the poison. Because she didn't feel as if she were in a rushing river, hanging onto branches that were continuously breaking off. Unlike me, she wasn't fumbling in the fog without orientation; she had a solid roadmap, a guidebook of suffering, clear lines from A to B. Lucio contemplated.

– I think it's not so much about showing off with tears as it is about relieving the relatives. With Benedetta wailing loudly, others don't have to rush their feelings; they can take the time they need. In particular, it helps many people to have a stranger express what they are incapable of expressing, or maybe even feeling yet, themselves. Because she is ferocious, they can be gentler. She has the generosity that people who are truly mourning often lack.

Finally, he said something I agreed with. Mourning really does make you stingy and blind. Blind to life all around you, blind to other people. Blind like Antonina, on the legendary night in August 1953. The Virgin's tears freed her of this blindness; could Benedetta's wailing possibly accomplish the same? Lucio stood up. It was time to go. We paid for our espressi and set off for Via Vittorio Veneto. We learned nothing new about the nature of Signora Clara's suffering. She remained evasive and vague. And yet she rounded off our investigation into the mystery of the Virgin perfectly. According to her, they were neither tears of compassion nor of love, but simply were an expression of what was eating everyone up in the post-war years.

Fear, anger, mourning, joy, relief, shame—feelings so contradictory it led to an emotional blockage. The Madonna relieved this pressure with her tears. The manner in which Signora Clara said it—very gently, very calmly, more thankful than devoted—was beautiful, believable. Suddenly the whole thing made sense to us, too.

When I woke up the next morning and caught a whiff of my neighbor's cigarillo and heard the man upstairs snoring loudly, I felt as if yesterday's experiences had moved something in me. For the first time in weeks, I felt I could breathe more freely. Benedetta's door remained closed from now on, and I never heard her crying again. A few days later, I left Lucio and with the certainty that I had witnessed a small miracle myself of the tearless matron from Via Nizza.

Giuliano Bonelli
Siracusa o morte

And eventually you sense that being alone is not the same as being lonely, and you learn that a person can also be an island. The wine you always drink at the same bar is very cold and that helps. At the table across from you they're arguing. This makes it easier for you to write. You need harshness; it refines you. You see the drama but it's not yours. You should write that down, before you forget it. Before you can't trust your memory. It utilizes a thin ink, and so much dissolves before you can grasp it. Capturing the ease of this place in words is a feat. You write your notes hastily and remember how leisurely the following events were. A place meddled with by the immortal sea will absorb some of that immortality. On the coasts of Ortigia, Siracusa's small island, people drape themselves across the rocks until their teeth are brown and the sun's rays carve furrows in their skin. You have no reason to rush; life is a reduced-traffic zone. You hop off, you push.

My morning on Ortigia begins with sleep; the night was restless. Rowdy adolescents organized a race, speeding through the island's narrow lanes on their tweaked scooters. They beeped at every crossing to announce their arrival to other drivers, thus avoiding accidents. Every Italian city has mastered this preventative beeping—it is the underlying sound—but usually it is limited to day. Still half-asleep, I imagine one of the scooter drivers smashing at high speed into the corner of a building. Directly above the site of the collision is a wall shrine to the Madonna, who holds an infant Jesus in her arms. An electric candle illuminates the scene inside the shrine. But he is beyond her help. His scooter shatters; the collision is so severe that his body splits in two. Both halves are launched through the alley in different directions at an even greater speed. One is found shortly thereafter on the harbor wall, where it will cook in the midday sun, flies descending on it. He is beyond all help. I have to think about the word *malacarne,* which I picked up from a friend from Siracusa. The locals use it to refer to a bad person, or meat of inferior quality. It precisely describes the scooter driver, before and after the accident.

I sunbathe on the rocks at the foot of Diana nel Forte, the old fortifications along the island's eastern coast, which are accessed by steel steps. Peak season, when the island overflows with tourists, has not yet begun, and the temporary pier and the bridges between the massifs haven't been erected yet. Not far from me, on the nearest ledge sits a man, shirtless and wearing faded light-blue swim trunks. He's playing guitar. He's greatly overshot the mark with his tan and has a bald head; he looks like a society dropout who has probably forgotten through which door he dropped out. Every time a new visitor lies down on the rocks he puts down his guitar, climbs to the highest ledge, and jumps elegantly into the water. As if propelled by a motor, he then quickly swims front crawl out into the open sea. He's not afraid of the dark depths or the vast blue. Once he's wet enough, he does the crawl back and climbs out of the water by hoisting himself up a hidden rope, fixed in a crevice of the rock. He is from here, his tanned skin cells whisper it into the cove. Again and again, children run barefoot between the towels over the sharp rocks, and at hidden spots jump into the sea. During the chase they splash the other beachgoers lying on their towels. No one is bothered by this; they are only children, who don't know yet that a person begins not only where you can touch them, but already well before. Over our heads swifts hunt in the air, emitting cries as if they were on fire. Farther back, where the promontory fort begins, are two young women in very scanty, brightly colored bikinis. Both have a block of text tattooed on their left ribcage. I can't decipher it from this distance, but I suspect song lyrics or a paragraph of their favorite book. They have positioned a cell phone in the crack of the fortress wall and are filming themselves with the front camera. I can faintly hear the song coming from the cell phone. It has a quick beat and the local clubs undoubtedly play it. Both women move their bodies provocatively, spanking each other's backsides and dancing a choreography that recalls a striptease, yet without undressing. They're making a video for TikTok, or maybe they're even TikTokers—a platform whose name has spawned a common agent noun. Their tripod is a thousand-year-old fortification named after Diana, the Roman goddess of the hunt, the moon, and birth, guardian of women and children. Diana remained a virgin all her life, she never wed. According to the myth, in the midday heat a hunter once rested in the shady valley consecrated to Diana. In its center was a grotto, where the goddess was bathing nude. When she realized the hunter was watching her, she transformed him into a stag so he couldn't tell anyone about it. The stag was then torn to pieces by his own hounds. Diana was very aggressive when it came to defending her chastity. The two women presumably know nothing about the myth of Diana, or her attitude towards promiscuity. But if they do, I admire their bravery.

As I spread out my sunning towel on the rock and settle my hips into a groove of the stone, I remember the summers of my childhood, which I mostly spent at my grandparents' house in Italy. On the last day of school before summer vacation my friends would make plans for LAN parties, later house parties, and eventually vacations. I missed everything and instead lay on the beach, looking out at the Mediterranean. An exhausting view, which simply was incomprehensible, regardless of how great an effort I made. The only thing even more infinite was the sea at night, murmuring in the dark. A role model for boundless thoughts. I never made friends in those summers. *Mi scusi, sono tedesco, non parlo italiano.* I'm sorry, I'm German, I don't speak Italian, was my most-repeated phrase whenever I strayed from my family and was addressed by local children who were my age. I wasn't honest with them, I didn't tell them that I was half-Italian; I was embarrassed that I could only say this one sentence. Now I know what they meant when they asked, *Ma da dove sei in germania?* I didn't answer that I was from the Frankfurt area; instead I just shook my head and went my own way. These were always confusing conversations for everyone involved. The Italian children thought they had said something wrong and angered or offended me. They looked at each other, *Qual è il suo problema?* What's his problem?

In front of the Diana nel Forte cliffs the sea is bubbling, about a hundred meters away from the cove the foam is white; the course of the waves changes there. That's where Scoglio dei Cani is, the rock of the dogs. This name is said to come from a habit of the local people, who threw unpleasant dogs into the sea from the Diana nel Forte. On this rock, the dogs are said to have briefly found salvation, before succumbing to hunger. The Scoglio dei Cani looks like an erupting underwater volcano, as if Etna had changed its address. The man sunning himself directly beside me flaunts a tattoo on his right shoulder blade: *Nel mio paese nessuno è straniero,* in my country no one is a foreigner. I couldn't get this sentence out of my head.

It is early evening and I meet a friend on the Piazza del Duomo. We have a reservation for a wine tasting on the roof terrace of the Palazza Beneventano del Bosco, the palace across from the entrance to the cathedral. We enter the venue using a side entrance and climb up the steps. We are a bit too early, although we thought we would be a bit too late, so we take another narrow stairway up to the raised platform on the terrace. From here we look out onto the entire harbor, and we converse. We talk about how becoming an adult comprises of interpreting and wanting to understand your own childhood, and how it feels like searching for traces. It is a process, we agree on that. I tell him that recently I've questioned my motives behind certain decisions and occasionally found an answer in my childhood. I discover key moments. I tell him that it is very satisfying, as if I were able to loosen a thick knot with a single simple hand movement. He wants to buy a piece of land on the outskirts of Siracusa and is looking forward to equipping it. We are both astounded by the possibility of owning part of the Earth's surface, but this kind of ownership comes with responsibilities and ties people down to a place. If the obligation should become too much, then he will just sell it again, he says, and we both have to laugh. The possibility would naturally always exist. It's a nice conversation and when we try to order a beer at the bar, just before the tasting begins, they send us away. Today they are only serving wines from the tasting, and only once it begins. At the bar I am introduced to Mauro, a friend of his who was involved in organizing the event this evening.

Hey, Mezzo—nice to meet you.

Ciao Mezzo, Mauro, piacere, I thought you were Italian, you have the name and the looks, haha.

My dad's family is actually from a village not far from Siracusa, but I never really learned Italian. My mother is German, so I am part Italian and part German. *Parlo un po di italiano ma preferisco l'inglese. Almeno fino a quando non ho bevuto un po' più di vino.*

At sixteen I began an «Italian dialogue» with myself, initiating my own Italian cram sessions. I was tired of being asked in Germany where my family in Italy lived and how much time of the year I still spent there. Whether I still had relatives there or could imagine living in Italy fulltime. But I was also sick of avoiding conversation in Italy. I didn't want to disrupt anymore group conversations, since the Italians would always switch to English out of consideration for me. I didn't want to turn on the television again and not understand a single word the Rai Uno news anchor said. At some point I got up the courage, stuttered at least a sentence or two, paying attention to my pronunciation, and always insisted other people speak Italian. I already got the idea of most of what was said; people had spoken Italian around me since my early childhood. At the very least, one could say I had an ear for the language. During this time I got to know my Italian sides: rough and gentle, fluent and faltering.

The roof terrace fills up rather quickly. Giorno Libero by Delicatoni plays in the background, muted by the guests' conversations. Everyone is elegantly dressed, the men in loosely fitting pastel shirts and broad linen trousers, the women in evening gowns and pantsuits in bold colors. A man with thick, dark brown hair sticks out of the crowd. He stands by the balustrade, unaccompanied, looking a bit plucked, recalling the tragic captain of the cruise ship that crashed off the Italian island Giglio in 2012. He is wearing blinding white pants and a blue tee-shirt that says «BaFin's most wanted.» A large table is set up beneath a pergola, pesto is spread directly onto the table cloth, olive oil stands beside a full bread basket, cheese is cut and distributed throughout the table. Next to it, on a sideboard, is an ice bucket with bottles of wine; there are red and white natural wines from various winemakers, all of whom are present this evening. Before the buffet is opened, a woman in an elegant black evening gown steps onto the terrace. In her hands she holds an open book, from which she recites an Italian fable. Oversized soap bubbles float over from a street performer on the Piazza del Duomo. They shimmer in various colors, like drops of gasoline on asphalt, and move over our heads. I can't make sense of what the fable is about. Conceptually, she seems to be leading us from wine to food and back.

The sky above Ortigia is already pitch dark when she concludes the fable, thereby announcing a dessert typical of the region, and so releases us, culinarily speaking, into the night. The terrace is tastefully illuminated, the cathedral towering in the sky in the background, a fantastic setting. I have to think about Paolo Sorrentino's La Grande Bellezza. Jep Gambardella, a celebrated author in his mid-sixties, stands in front of the abyss and at the same time is at the center of Rome's high society. At extravagant parties and countless soirees he perceives a lack of depth and significance. He is unhappy and reflects on his past. He is confronted with the death of a loved one. Jep is a sensitive character and that is why, he says, he was born to write. Besides, he simply couldn't do anything else. I understood the film as a declaration of love to the city of Rome, an unambiguous declaration of love; it is a film that is deliriously visually stunning. A dolly shot shows the equestrian statue of the freedom fighter Giuseppe Garibaldi, the plinth bearing the inscription, *Roma o morte.* It was the battle cry

Garibaldi shouted down from a balcony in Catania, shortly after conquering Sicily. Rome or die. I tell my friend my thoughts on Sorrentino's film. He agrees.

I get your point. Smearing pesto on the tablecloth is also a first for me and I don't quite get her performance. But fuck Rome, it's an old shithole.

We spend most of the evening by the ice buckets, filling each other's glasses. Red-white-white-red-white-white. At the balustrade, I want to be sensitive; I'm not sure if I'm a sensitive person, but in some way it is a very sensitive moment. Up there in Siracusa's treetop, surrounded by strangers and thinking about Rome. My friend leaves the event before me, after asking several times if it's okay; he really doesn't want to leave me standing here on my own, but he has an appointment he can't postpone. I wave goodbye, and I have nothing against lingering a moment before making my way home. I leave not long after my friend and wave at Mauro, who stands a short distance away in a small group. I exit the palazzo using the side entrance and find myself once again on the Piazza del Duomo. In contrast to when I arrived, it is now nearly empty of people. A young girl chases a ball that changes color at every concussion. A shaggy black dog wanders onto the piazza from the lane behind me. It perks its ears and for a moment observes the girl with her ball. Then he turns around and drinks from one of the dishes that the residents fill with water and set out in front of their doors at night for the stray cats. I look over at the cathedral. A warm wind blows across the piazza and I miss the whooshing of leaves back home. In Siracusa only the sea whooshes. Here every day is Saturday; time is on the side of the people. Somewhere, a deep bell tolls. I walk down Via Cavour, now also empty of people. It is shortly after midnight, but only a few hours earlier it was full of people with gray hair and buckled posture. Walking in my direction is one of the street vendors, who sell power banks and bracelets on the beach during the day. He smiles at me pleasantly and greets me; I greet him back. The plaster on the facades is cracking, the building's wrinkles exposed by a streetlamp. I think of the color burnt orange. In the first volume of Killing Commendatore by Haruki Murakami it is the color of vitality and the color of decay. It has to be the color of Siracusa. It smells delightful.

On the way home I wander across the Ponte Santa Lucia, which along with the Ponte Umbertino connects Ortigia with the rest of Siracusa. Above the water, attached to the bridge by steel poles is a soccer goal, but it is slightly too small. It is more accurately described as an ice hockey goal hanging over the water. In the pool between the two bridges, on September 4, 2016, Italy became world champion in canoe polo for the first time. They beat France, the incumbent world champion, making a golden goal in overtime. A spectacle in the pool and on the stands, according to the Italian canoe association. In this sport, to get the ball out of the water you hit it from above using your free hand, so it jumps into the canoe. On the large shopping street Corso Giacomo Matteotti, I make my way back to the island's center, the black heart of Ortigia, where my accommodations are.

Horacio, who runs the café where I eat breakfast every morning and whose kitchen shares a wall with my bedroom, is just locking up the furnishings on the small terrace in front of his café. He accompanies the sound of rattling chains with his interpretation of Vamos a La Playa by Loona, and as his neighbor I know that he caught this earworm from the scaffolders at the construction site across the street. I greet him in Italian and wish him a good night. It's an address whose pronunciation I have perfected through years of practice; it sounds as if it came from a local's mouth. I sense that, as with every morning, now he is unsure if he should greet me in Italian or English. Which me should he address? The German one? The Italian one? And suddenly it is completely irrelevant to me, since nel mio paese nessuno è straniero, in my country no one is a foreigner, and to me it seems like a good reply. I'm standing in front of the door to my accommodations. I end my day with sleep.

Giovanni Fiderio
The Old Man n.3

The Old Man enters the bookstore early in the morning, wearing a short-sleeved beige linen shirt and a blue baseball cap, holding a book filled with notes and scraps of paper between the pages.

«Good morning, is Maria Vittoria here?»

«Good morning to you. Maria Vittoria is in Palermo; she'll be here tomorrow afternoon.»

«Tell her I need to talk to her about some important things regarding that story about the Prince of Branciforte. I've found a book she might be interested in.»

«Okay, I'll tell her as soon as I hear from her. In the meantime, if you're interested, this afternoon there's a book presentation about the petrochemical hub in Syracuse.»

«Again? Another one?» He rolls his eyes. «What do they want from the petrochemical hub? They've all started telling stories, creating myths, looking for heroes. Why don't they go and talk to the Americans?» He points north of Syracuse. «Why don't they talk to them about the birth of the petrochemical hub?» Then, more calmly, he adds, «Moratti was just a puppet at the time.»

«Hmmm, I wouldn't know,» I reply evasively.

«Exactly, you don't know anything, no one here knows anything, or no one remembers anything,» he laughs sarcastically, shrugging his shoulders; then he pauses to think, twirling the palm of his right hand, and sighs. He doesn't know which of the thousand stories in his head he wants to tell me. Then he smiles slightly and says to me: «To refine a tonne of oil, it takes about eighteen tonnes of fresh water. These people refined oil with mineral water, ha ha haaa, incredible! There's a huge underground freshwater reservoir that runs from Sortino to under Catania, and they dug hundreds of wells, truly hundreds, to extract mineral water and refine the oil; and before those wells, two aqueducts had already been built to bring fresh water to the oil refinery, costing a fortune at the time, and they never got used for that purpose. But refineries can afford these things, understand?»

«It sounds like science fiction.»

«Ha ha haaa,» he laughs loudly. «I'll give you science fiction: a few weeks ago at another presentation, a guy asked if maybe, after all these years, it might be time to clean up the bottom of Augusta harbor and remove all the waste, especially the damned mercury. Oh! Yes, sure! Everyone agrees! So why isn't it done?» He looks at me like my grandfather did when I was a kid. «Because in Augusta harbor, there's also a base for American submarines, and there's the Italian navy too, you can see that.»

I push back sarcastically: «Then maybe if they need ammunition and missiles, they could go and resupply at Cava Sorciaro, in the Climiti mountains.»

He responds firmly: «That's something else. I don't know if that depot is still active, but for sure that cave goes all the way down to sea level. Essentially, it's a huge underwater cave dug into the Climiti mountains. The military base even has an access point four kilometers away at sea, and from there, submarines can reach the weapons depot, where they store chemical and nuclear weapons.»

«Nonsense. I don't believe it!»
«Better for you. Goodbye!»

The Old Man leaves the bookstore, and I linger on the stories for a while longer.

On the internet, some people say that the «huge underwater cave» not only exists but that they even filmed two movies there: James Bond, with a license to kill. Who knows if it's true? It would be absurd. I can already imagine Oddjob throwing his deadly bowler hat at Sean Connery, who, by activating his jetpack, barely escapes from the cave, landing on the stunning Funnucu Novu beach, where the beautiful Ursula Andress waits for him in a breathtaking bikini.

I step outside the bookstore for a moment to enjoy the sun's rays, sitting on the bench. I think I should reorder the Ian Fleming books that tell the great James Bond stories adapted into films. Summer is approaching, and thriller-lovers will surely appreciate them.

Meanwhile, from the corner of the block to my left, where Corso Umberto I intersects with Viale Regina Margherita, I see the Old Man turning with his elegant stride. He sometimes returns because he's thought of something else related to our last conversation.

About ten meters from me, he raises his finger with an idea: «More science fiction,» he says, hinting at a smile, «about that area where there are now docks and industries; that stretch of sea at Targia and Marina di Melilli has a tropical microclimate,

239

the waters are slightly warmer than average.» I'd say they're much warmer than average. «I've swum there a couple of times, and the water was really warm, there was hardly any relief from it. But I thought it was due to the factories' cooling systems, the fact that they draw water from the sea.»

«Ha ha haaa,» he bursts out laughing. «Surely that has influenced it recently as well. But I'm talking about before the industry was there. There was a tropical microclimate there, and there were also species of fish that couldn't be seen elsewhere in Sicily. There was the sand-dwelling snakefish: the English loved it, they sought it out. And deeper down, there was that fish that has remnants of lungs in its gills, damn it, what's it called?» He gestures with his hand as if to say «You tell me.»

«I have no idea,» I reply. «I've never heard of it before.»

«It's practically a living fossil, a very rare fish.»

I try searching the internet, typing «fish that has remnants of lungs,» and find several scientific articles.

«Could it be the coelacanth?» I ask, trying a name that sounded right.

«Yes, exactly! That's the one! The coelacanth. You found it,» he responds excitedly. «That fish was wiped out, you can't find it anymore now. The fishermen weren't familiar with that species, and on top of that, it was ugly: its teeth stuck out, its skin was dark. It was eliminated.»

«Sounds like a classic case of discrimination.»

«What do you mean?»

«An unknown, ugly fish, and it gets eliminated.»

«Come on, its meat wasn't good to eat either.»

«Anyway, it says here that the coelacanth has been sighted in the waters of South Africa and Indonesia, or between the Mozambique Channel and the Indian Ocean. There's no record of the coelacanth in the Mediterranean,» I say, pointing to the computer screen.

«I'm telling you it was here too, and it was eliminated. Don't you trust what I'm telling you?»

Mario Fillioley
Villettas

I am from Syracuse, a city with a northern coast easily accessible for swimming, where at some point an oil refinery was established. The primary outcome was the sudden enrichment of the population: a permanent job, a secure salary every month, and thus a solid possibility of getting into debt. The secondary outcome was debts and villettas.

The Syracusan villetta is somewhat anomalous: a second home by the sea, just a few kilometers from the first home, also by the sea. Given the choice, you would have built a villa in the mountains, the Hyblaeans. The city's sea had become unusable: on top of sewage discharges, the northern coast was also plagued by the docking piers for oil tankers and their associated spills, and, particularly in the first few years, the poorly regulated chimneys were thick with haze. So, at a certain point, we no longer had the trust to swim at Piliceddi or Fondaco Nuovo, and a sort of migration began towards the crystalline waters of Fontane Bianche on the south coast.

After rounding Capo Murro di Porco, there is Fanusa and then Arenella: the first stretch of virgin sea and comfortable sandy beaches (in the city there are only rocks) which extend from there, passing Ognina, through Fontane Bianche up to the jasmine grove of the Marchesa di Cassibile. Distance from town: about sixteen kilometers. Sixteen kilometers can be covered in less than a quarter of an hour by car. Why spend so much money to build a villa a quarter of an hour from home? Probably the status symbol factor came into play: I am no longer a farmer; now I am a skilled worker, an office worker, a banker, I can afford to have children at university and even a house by the sea.

To be honest, the holiday homes of the nobility, those from the nineteenth century or in the Art Nouveau style, were all located in the Isola district, facing the harbor, and were called «villas.» Those in Fontane Bianche, Ognina, Arenella, and Fanusa were not; from the beginning (and forever after) they were called «villettas,» even when they surpassed the noble ones in Isola, both in number and size. A linguistic symptom, then, in the sense that yes, with the oil industry we had more money, but not that much after all. Better to build just a stone's throw from home, then. Because maybe that way I can build the walls myself when I finish work, on Sundays my brother and brother-in-law can come to help me with the roof pitch: ground floor, covered veranda, and first floor; plus, if the second house is nearby, checking on it, managing it, and maintaining it will be less costly and more practical.

Holidaying close to home, when you think about it, is not a stupid idea; it makes sense. It stays warm here until November, and since the villetta is so close we can use it for the Easter Monday outing, the May Day barbecue, and even the long weekend for All Saints' Day. When schools close, the workers' housewives, along with their children, enjoy the sea and garden for a good three months, and the husband could come home in the evening, after his shift, just a few extra kilometers by car, awaiting the August holidays.

There was no regulatory plan. The region of Sicily took quite a while to approve rules and exemptions for the maritime domain, distance from the shoreline, and landscape protections, and meanwhile, in the regulatory void, I build my villa right on the beach. Rather, I fence off this stretch of rocks here and make a concrete staircase that takes me straight into the water. The private sea access. The slide for the dinghy. A gate on the sand. Then, at some point, the regional regulations on coastal distance arrive: one hundred fifty meters, half of that which is stipulated on the mainland. And following that, the first amnesties come along, you see? I told you: build, nothing will happen.

As a result, Fontane Bianche doesn't have a seafront promenade, a square, or a sidewalk. Only villettas, on both sides of the State Road 115, the only road that traverses it (and as such we call that section Viale dei Lidi—Seashores Boulevard).

The idyll, however, took just a moment to turn into neurosis, and the proximity of the second house played a fundamental role in this. If the villetta is just ten minutes by car, there's no real break between work and summer holidays, and you end up shuttling continuously between the sea and the city for the most trivial reasons. And so there they are, the people of Syracuse, recently motorized, stuck in traffic on Via Elorina to buy fish at the market in Ortygia to then return to grill it in the garden of Fontane Bianche. Up and down, even several times a day.

The years when I was a child and then a young man, to remember them now, were pure schizophrenia. Take nighttime entertainment, for example. If we moved to the villetta, I would ride sixteen kilometers

245

on my scooter and another sixteen to return just for a simple stroll near the Cathedral. So my parents, to avoid me risking my neck every night on poorly lit and worsely paved country roads, decided the following summer, that's it, we'd stay in the city. But in a year the fashion changed, and the next season the place where you absolutely had to be every evening was the Frisio shopping center in Fontane Bianche. Scooter, thirty-two kilometers, back and forth. Wear your helmet or I'll pull your head off, my father would say.

Well, then you grow up. You go to university elsewhere, and when you come back for the summer you decide that this year, no, you'll stay at the villetta and not move from there, lying on the hammock stretched between two pines (the shade of the pines is so calming, your parents think as they watch you blissfully read). The villetta, though, while you attend university, gets older. It's not so much that it shows many signs of structural sagging (a bit, sure. But now it's already twenty years old, and your father built it in his spare time with his brother-in-law and your uncle), rather it is just a bit neglected. Your parents go there less, because the children only come back for a couple of weeks in August: So what do you do for two weeks? It's not even worth repainting the shutters. And if a bit of mold forms in the corner of the ceiling, have patience, we'll consider it next year.

You finish university and the villetta is now really run-down. Even the druggos have noticed that you rarely visit. You suffer some thefts. The furniture, already sparse, is now truly Spartan. The stone oven's chimney is blocked with pine needles (those pesty pine trees, your mother thinks as the pizza burns). The wood stove has a broken door. Even the paving of the entrance driveway has been lifted by roots (never plant pines in a villetta, explains the tiler—rubbing his hands—to your father as he signs the estimate). All in all, though, you occasionally manage to bring a girl there, the humidity that seems so bohemian here in winter, the sound of the waves, no TV because it was stolen by thieves, just a plaid blanket to wrap tightly around yourselves so you don't die of tuberculosis, basically: if you didn't want to do anything, explain to me why we came here, you and I, in the middle of January?

The villetta thus fulfilled a demographic function of offsetting the nil birth rates. And it fulfilled another one: providing an outlet for your father's nerves. Because in all that state of abandonment, one thing was in perfect order: the garden. Your father used the villetta to relieve his tensions on plants and trees, the most defenseless beings in creation. As soon as he had a free minute, he was off to the villetta to clear undergrowth, mow the lawn, use the chainsaw to cut branches (never the right size for the stove: it was while trying to fit one of these logs that the door broke), and prune.

Thanks to him, at least the garden is well-maintained, but like the head of a child at risk of lice. The Mediterranean scrub, once lush on flowerbeds and pathways, is now the bald mons pubis of a porn star. The oleander hedges used to be powerful screens from the neighbor's gaze, but your father, this whimsical green coiffeur, has decided that this year they should be cut short, like a crew cut: more modern, he tells you.

But in this excessive neatness of the garden, the decay of the building stands out even more. It's time to act. A small initial investment, then just a fix-up, and off to seasonal market. For rent, just for short periods. It works. With the money, you manage to cover the costs of restoration and maintenance. The villetta returns to a certain splendor (tempered by the fact that your father continues to take care of the garden). Only it's no longer your home. First you emptied it and then filled it with furnishings that never belonged to you. You painted the walls a different color. Under the pines, instead of the hammock, there's a dark teak sitting area with ecru white cushions that you saw in Homes and Gardens and bought on sale. And if, however, in the periods when it is vacant, you dream of bringing the woman who has in the meantime become your wife, the anxiety of dirtying, damaging, or breaking something condemns the child conceived that famous January to remain an only child.

Life moved on, the villetta changed function, but fortunately it's still there, solid: the brick that never betrayed the Italian family. However, your father has grown a bit old and he gets tired. On Saturdays, insisting you go there with him, he sits on the dry-stone wall, and begins to give you orders, so that you, his direct descendant, might torment the plants and hedges on his behalf. Before setting the saw on an acacia branch, you hesitate. You look at your father, seated on that stone throne, hoping he might soften. Instead, you see him feverish and excited: a monarch commanding the executioner. But what can you do? He's your father, and you owe him obedience. May the plant suffer as little as possible, then.

Therefore, as I carry out this kind of autumnal deforestation, eradicating any form of plant life with strokes of the brush cutter, as I trim another four centimeters off the oleander hedge, I find myself face-to-face with the neighbor's son, forced like me by his father to prune the same hedge from the opposite side. As we look into each other's eyes and point with our chins at our respective parents, sitting on the dry-stone walls, scolding us for not cutting properly, not cutting enough, not putting the right amount of drunken fury into it; as we smile at each other, gesturing to our ears to indicate: they can say what they want, because with the noise this thing makes we can't hear a thing; as my land, my garden, my home blend into his and his into mine until they merge into an indistinct whole, I feel a kind of inspiration, a sense of belonging to the Syracusan community with which I have always struggled to come to terms, and I begin to ask myself questions that, if I could, I would trim from my mind.

Were we, citizens of this uncivic city, really in the wrong by disregarding regulatory plans or coastal distances, and in building villettas by the sea assigning this land the Freudian task of compensating us for the loss of another sea, that of the north coast? Have we really perpetrated building violations? Have we sinned against our own resources?

Before the villettas changed their purpose from second homes to guest houses, I would have immediately answered yes, without hesitation. In fact, I would have confronted anyone who asked such a stupid question, and waved the exception under their nose, the cadastral survey of my villetta, bought from an old and meticulous mathematics professor, an individual of impeccable morality, in compliance with volumes, concessions, and distances. I would have accused all the perpetrators of environmental destruction, calling them short-sighted and ignorant, petty, incapable of understanding how, by devastating the coast with their constructions, they had deprived themselves and the entire city of the only economic vocation our territory possessed: tourism.

Instead, here, wrapped in a cloud of foliage that detaches from these plants that my father, full of a hatred whose origin I cannot understand, urges me to massacre, I think that I no longer know if it is so. Since I, like many from Syracuse, have rented out my villetta, I have had to face the facts. Websites, online portals, agencies, tour operators: they all demand seaside houses. Mine is often rejected because the sea is, by foot, about three hundred meters away. Less than a five minute' walk.

«Which are the houses that you rent out the most?» I asked the agencies I work with.

«Those by the sea.»

«But mine is by the sea. The verandas face the lighthouse, the terraces overlook the gulf.»

«You don't understand: 'by the sea' means you open the door and fall into the water.»

«And what's the most requested area?»

«Fontane Bianche.»

Syracuse has experienced a tourism boom in recent years: a downward trend in visitors on the mainland is completely reversed in my city, and, for what little my (very limited and not at all scientific) email survey has revealed, the explosion of Syracuse as a seaside destination for families and small groups seems linked to this ability to offer accommodations directly on cliffs and beaches.

The French, Germans, Russians, Belgians, Danes, Swiss, English, as well as people from Veneto, Friuli, Lombardy, Emilia: everyone searches online for villettas on the beach or with private sea access. So then, how does this building violation that we've deplored and condemned for decades work? I hear the buzz of the brush cutter that shatters my thoughts, leaving them jagged; could it be that when the building violations served to compensate us for the poisons of the oil industry, it was a case of uncivilized southerners, crooks down to every molecule of their DNA, and now that it serves instead to make the Scandinavian's holiday more comfortable, it's not so bad after all?

I turn off the brush cutter and ask the neighbor's son if they also rent out.

«Yes,» he tells me, «but unfortunately only during the peak season.»

It was another neighbor, the one with the house on the cliffs, who suggested we both rent our places out. Years ago, this neighbor's villetta was supposed to be demolished; the wrecking balls were ready, but it never happened. He, in the meantime between one amnesty and another, started renting it out, and now it's always full, even in late autumn. Full of very tall and very blonde people: fathers, mothers, and children, all beautiful and all with a shining pallor, like little Obelixes who must have fallen into a pot of SPF 50 when they were young. All descendants of a Viking lineage residing in countries where they couldn't even begin to dream of houses built in a location like the one they rented here.

Thus, nothing has changed about this disgraceful coastal seaside landscape, except its users.

«Actually no, that's not true,» I say, filled with eureka-like enthusiasm to the neighbor's son, «the zeitgeist has changed, too.»

«And what's that?» he asks. «A weed killer? Your father is obsessed with weed killers too?»

«No. I mean yes, my father is obsessed, but I mean to say that, even though everything has remained the same, we now find ourselves in a globally changed tourism context that has reversed the deciding factors for being successful in tourism: you're awful, my dear Syracuse coast, you're devastated, but how convenient you are, with your villettas that spill right out onto the water.»

«Listen, let's stop, my shoulder hurts,» replies the neighbor's son.

Gardening is like that: it tires the body and does not satisfy the mind. I stop too. But I find no relief. I think that if it works this way, then it means that the abomination is only an abomination when you look at it from the outside, and if you look at it from inside your own house, it becomes beauty. And that's why everyone wants to become owners, even if just for a week, of a beautiful, unauthorized house.

«Why do you think that is?» I ask the neighbor as our parents complain about how lazy we are, for our evident ineptitude at deforestation.

«How would I know?» he answers me.

«I'll tell you why,» I say. «It's the palm line that has grown, that is still growing, that will grow indefinitely.»

«The palms?» he says, looking at the garden. «The palms haven't grown; it's been three years since the red palm weevil destroyed them all, look here.» He points to a series of trunks with no leaves left. Then he restarts the brush cutter.

My father is still sitting on the dry-stone wall. He's watching me with the disappointed face of someone who paid to see Tyson biting off ears but ended up at the Bolshoi amid pirouettes in tutus: Finish it! Take it down! he's screaming with his eyes. When he finally allows me to turn off the brush cutter, the neighbor's son and I shake hands by the former palms. We can't help but raise our eyes again to the two totems.

«But this red palm weevil really would be the ideal gardener for our parents,» we say in unison before parting.

Dana von Suffrin
Work

The only thing disturbing that gorgeous morning on the terrace was the smell of cat urine. A small colony of orange-and-white cats had chosen a piece of human infrastructure—more specifically, these roofs—for their habitat, as was common in the South, and already a few times Gabi had observed a neighbor setting out kitten food on the windowsill. No question, the cats were a disturbance, but Gabi smiled anyway and waved briefly; Syracuse was not the place to get worked up over things you couldn't change.

Even so, not everything was set in stone. Gabi didn't just accept everything; she wasn't like her mother and the women before her—she had already read and experienced too much for that. Besides, she was far from fatalistic; like most of her generation, she was inclined to take advantage of every opportunity that came her way. She was also inclined to give and to make an effort, and although years later people would claim that the generation after hers was lazy and didn't work hard, she herself was determined to take everything life had to offer her, and people like Gabi had already formulated this aspiration while everyone else was busy wearing themselves out between working nine to five and raising a family. At least Michael once said something to that effect, or similar. Gabi didn't mean material things, by the way. She was thirty-two and nearly positive that she would change jobs in two or three years. For now, things were simply going too well, and she had already agreed to conventions and events next year and the year after. She had requested a fee of twenty-two thousand euros to appear at a largish convention in Tirol, and the organizer agreed immediately. Her channel earned a few thousand euros each month, but she spent most of the money on equipment, clothing, and travel costs, and of course she had to pay Spikey Mike. He would invoice her at the end of every month—it was a bit ridiculous—but in a way, he only had a supporting role. He was also her boyfriend, but in the end it boiled down to approximately the same thing. Gabi put most of her money in a time deposit, and she had a small portfolio of stocks, but only the safe kind. She knew that every shoot, every appearance saved her from a few months of working nine to five.

All told, she earned approximately as much money as the greatest overachievers from highschool, who didn't have a minute of free time and at thirty already looked fifty. Gabi looked approximately twenty-eight. She also budgeted like a much younger woman. The good thing was, Gabi wasn't extravagant at all; she owned a used Opel and here on Sicily she pressured Michael into eating pizza for dinner, it being much cheaper. Mike occasionally stopped in front of one of the beautiful, romantic restaurants, but she just dragged him away like a child. They acted extravagantly only when other people were around, since it was part of the show. In real life, Gabi was very different. Together with Mike she would buy two pizzas, a vegan one for her and one with a thousand different kinds of meat for him, which disgusted her. She would keep the receipt (if given). They sat down with the pizzas on a bench near the temple and tore open the boxes. Like a young child, Gabi looked forward to this moment every evening. Mike ate with repulsive speed; he would fold a quarter of the pizza in half and shove it in his voracious mouth, all while giving Gabi brief lectures on politics and history. Repulsive. Gabi ate half of a pizza at most, and the other half Mike woofed down like a ravenous dog. How interesting, Gabi thought, there seem to be no street dogs at all in this part of Sicily. Mike enlightened her: in the more exclusive regions, Syracuse undoubtedly included, they already began years ago, rounding up the feral and half-feral dogs and euthanizing them, after a few ugly incidents with tourists. Sad, Gabi said, and Mike said nothing at all, and then he crushed his drink can and shoved the boxes in the trash, and they went hand-in-hand back to their Airbnb. So far, every evening had proceeded exactly like this, aside from when they shot with Giacomo and Paul; then there was cold pasta on set.

Besides, she had to take precautions. Of course she knew her work was in demand, but she sensed it was slowly time for a change. It was lovely to lie on the terrace alone, but it was only lovely because it was a luxury, a little downtime from the break. In the future she wanted to earn her «little downtime» differently. She hadn't brought it up yet to Mike, but how could he possibly object? A small house outside the city, a child or two, preferably boys, a daily routine and security. Maybe Gabi would even pick up where she'd left off in her old career; she had studied social work and even spent two years working in the field. Gabi closed her eyes and tried to imagine her future precisely: she thought about her perfect designer kitchen and the flowers in her garden, because a dream is allegedly more likely to come true if you close your eyes and already start to put together the pieces of that dream world, and so Gabi forced herself to imagine in detail her life a few years from now, because even if this method was probably nonsense, it couldn't hurt. Gabi spent half the morning like this on the terrace, lying on a plastic lounge chair, eyes closed, wearing an old AC/DC shirt of Mike's and a pair of his boxer shorts, because in her free time being comfortable was very important to her, and at home she never wore makeup and preferred to walk around in an old 80's sweat suit with a baseball cap and sunglasses, that way no one would recognize her—although Mike always said that no one would recognize her anyway, because who looked at Gabi's face? And the more Gabi thought about this, the more she was convinced of its insolence. As if to convince herself that she had a face, Gabi ran her fingers over her forehead and pushed aside a piece of hair. Recently while doing yoga at the gym in Vienna Gabi had an interesting thought: our bodies are not our bodies; we are each simply lent a body for a certain period of time. Of course this idea, too, was a tad esoteric, but Gabi concluded that it wasn't so off: we all arise from a purely random encounter of cells, then we grow and grow, and finally at the end of our lives we revert to the elements, and perhaps the only flaw in that statement was this: it is not only our bodies, but of course also our souls that are simply lent us. She wrote Michael a message, doing her best to sound nice.

Or maybe she would just go to Italy? Italy was beautiful—of course that was a cliché, but like most clichés it was also true. Although she questioned common beliefs about life's stages and the tasks one was supposed to accomplish in said stages, she also knew that something about it motivated her. She used to keep a bucket list of places she wanted to see, books she wanted to read, inspiring people she wanted to learn about. A few months ago, she deleted the entire list from her cell phone. She thought about it again now, on the terrace, and was a bit proud of herself because it made her feel very in the moment, and very in the moment was something her therapist always encouraged her to be. She had no reason to want to change anything about her situation: she was lying comfortably, she wasn't thirsty, she wanted for nothing, she could just lie there and think, she didn't have to make any more lists. Gabi was being dishonest with herself, but she knew it.

What time was it, anyway? Gabi tried to convince herself of time's utter irrelevance, but she didn't quite succeed. She asked herself the question again and again, as if something hinged on it—and yet she and Michael didn't have any dates today, everything was already wrapped up, and the postproduction would wait until Vienna. For her, postproduction was almost the best time since it meant Mike would disappear for three or four days in his mancave, like a crazy person, adjusting the dozens of blinking buttons, whose functions were an utter mystery to Gabi. She used to frequently enter his room, in order to watch like a silent, shy child, and what she saw on the screen always had startlingly little to do with her. Recently she had become almost indifferent to the end results; she would fast forward when she saw the finished material, and more out of habit than any real concern she would ensure that her breasts looked more or less attractive (which admittedly wasn't possible from every angle) and that she more or less had her face under control—but when it came down to it, she was indifferent; she knew that a body, which just happened to be hers, did things that didn't actually have anything to do with her; she wasn't suffering, but she wasn't having a good time, either—it was just how she earned a living.

So they were free all day, and Gabi wanted to go swimming, and on the way she intended to take a closer look at the city ruins, about which Michael had told her something she immediately forgot. She liked the ruins; she walked past them several times a day and tried to imagine Romans and Greeks taking it easy in togas. Didn't they even eat lying down? Gabi didn't know much about ancient history, but wasn't the point to empathize with people, even if they'd been dead a long time? Why should that be any less important than examining their military strategies? And empathizing was more Gabi's thing, anyway, and she already had several intense arguments with Michael, who was of the opinion that her profession (which, after all, was also his profession) was merely a stone-cold business, the production of illusions—but Gabi knew better. She understood

Michael's argument, of course, but nevertheless she also knew that her job had a decidedly transcendent component to it; she had looked into the sad, lonely eyes of her consumers while signing autographs and seen their pupils briefly dilate, flicker, momentarily happy.

The sun furrowed Gabi's brow with its adamant blazing beams. Gabi pulled her hat down deeper over her face. Syracuse (or Siracusa, as Michael called it) was outside the Italian boot, or to be specific, right in front of the boot's toe. So much sun, so little land. What was Sicily, anyway? Gabi opened Google Maps and zoomed out, away from the roof terrace and out of Ortygia, then away from Syracuse and off the island altogether until she finally saw Europe from above and determined that Sicily was approximately a triangle. Was Sicily a ball that the boot wanted to kick away? Or a dog pile it was stepping into? Gabi cleared her throat and suddenly understood what both images said about her relationship with Michael. Like most young women, Gabi had a talent for recognizing signs and symbols in every last trivial detail she came across in daily life. She and her friends even occasionally called a fortuneteller in Germany, to learn, for forty-nine euros, what tomorrow would bring. The fortuneteller was always right, but Gabi never asked her about Mike—instead she asked questions concerning money and her career, and of course Gabi was aware that the fortuneteller knew absolutely nothing, but the hectic, quiet chatter nevertheless gave her direction; it grounded her.

Suddenly Gabi was no longer lethargic. She got up, fixed her hair and carefully walked down the short, steep stairwell to the bedroom. Michael was still sleeping, the sheets half cast-off. His afflicted skin was peeling, although Gabi had told him thousands of times to apply sunscreen. His ironic Mickey Mouse tattoo suddenly appeared sculptural, and yet it only consisted of ugly crooked lines, but Michael's skin was shedding exactly where the mouse's ears were. Gabi approached and took a photo. Gabi was disgusted— not only because of his skin, but because of everything; she was no different than millions of sinners in centuries past, who arose from their beds, washed themselves, and began complicating desire with guilt. Gabi knew that in this respect men have it even worse; she didn't have a sizeable amount of experience, at least not personally, but she was familiar with the sad looks of men who regret everything minutes later and more than anything else would like to apologize for having disgraced a beloved body, so suspiciously like their own mother's. But Michael never had feelings like this, and Gabi held that against him. Did he even have feelings at all? Gabi shut the door again; she had seen and felt enough. After all, there was absolutely no reason to wait for him. She packed the large beach bag, threw in a fresh white towel, a bottle of water and sunscreen, Sicily was definitely a boot that was kicking something away. Yet she couldn't quite manage to leave the house, and so she went back out onto the terrace. She drank a sip of warm water from the plastic bottle, which crackled and chattered. She called her mother, who—she at least hoped—had only a vague idea about her daughter's business trip. She simulated a harmless conversation. She only told her about trivial things: the blue fish she had seen underwater, the boutiques she noticed in passing, the pizza. She said nothing about Michael. She hung up, and then she really wanted to leave the apartment; she crept down the stairs and was nearly on the ground floor when Michael stormed her from behind. He was naked and all in a panic, but Gabi had already arrived at the stage in their relationship where her disgust at his large, limp member outweighed everything else, and she would have preferred not to even asked why he was distressed. Mike didn't pick up on it, and he yelled: You have to call Rosa right away, we have to go out on the boat again, and then he explain it all to Gabi, and after she had listened with the patience of someone who knows the importance of laying the groundwork before making a drastic decision, she simply said: I'm going to the beach.

That way

This way